Purple Silk in Andromeda

A Cosmic Romance of Life on Earth

Alan Anderson

Old Sultana Press

San Francisco, California

2012

Purple Silk in Andromeda

A Cosmic Romance of Life on Earth

Old Sultana Press
San Francisco, California

www.oldsultanapress.com

Old Sultana Press hardcover edition May 2012

Publisher's note: Incidents, events, locations, and persons living or dead described in this book are based on and inspired by real events, real locations, and real people.

Printed in the United States of America

Library of Congress Control Number: 2010924610

Anderson, Alan K.
Purple Silk in Andromeda: A Cosmic Romance of Life on Earth
ISBN 978-0-578-05253-3

To Mom and Dad

And others, living and dead and here and gone, who inspired the characters and lived the events described in this book

– Contents –

Introduction

I discovered you sitting alone and I knew you were sad. A tear drifted down your sweet face in a private moment and you said nothing. "Are you okay?" I asked. "Do you want me to leave?" You said I should stay and I made you a paper airplane and you smiled. You talked of China and we talked of life, and nothing since has been the same.

My name is Aaron Grey, and you don't know me. I didn't know myself until I began to find out a few years ago outside a train station in San Jose. I'd been drinking and romancing the club car attendant, talking about nothing in particular, but making earnest plans to meet again. The last stop came too soon, as always for a man in his cups, and I waited for my ride in the empty parking lot. It was late night or early morning. I don't exactly remember and I guess it doesn't much matter. The air was damp and cold and the sky was as dark as it could get on a moonless night. I noticed around me and fancied myself a character in a Hopper painting—some lone soul under the dim, yellow light that hung high off the station's weathered brick façade. My head was bowed, reading, when I saw from the corner of my eye someone coming my way from out of the darkness. It was a woman, by the swing of her hips, and she was walking straight towards me. I shut the book with a snap and stood up straight. She was thin and plain and worn at the edges—a shapely, straw-haired blonde in frayed jeans and a wrinkled, white blouse too inadequate for the cool night air. She looked me straight in the eye and spoke like she'd known me for years. "Where're you going?"

Surprised, I stammered. "Uh...downtown...waiting for a friend to pick me up...he's late, though." Studying her while I waited to see if she was going to say more, I felt sorry for her. Her face was pretty, but tired. And though I was tired, too, and almost didn't care if she said anything or not, the cheerless girl hiding behind clear blue eyes spoke.

"You're a writer, aren't you?"

I was stunned. No one ever called me a writer, and I'd certainly never presumed myself to be one. But when she said it, for the first time, I believed it. "How'd you know?" I asked.

She shrugged her shoulders and smiled, and nothing more was said. I wondered what a girl like her was doing out late on a night like this, but I said nothing of that, either. I told her my name was Aaron, and I thought she was an angel. "My friend—I don't know when he's going to show—but do you need a lift?" I asked.

"Can you take me downtown?"

She'd no sooner asked, when an open jeep came up over the coarse, stony gravel, skidding, the tires spitting stones, and stopped precisely in front of us. I introduced the girl as "Angel" and told her to jump in the back. We dropped her off outside a restaurant on south First. I watched her walk down a side street and into the darkness and she never looked back. I never saw her again, but I never forgot her, either, and I began my story about Pei Ling.

Book One

Chapter One

Into The World

Chengdu Plain in China is a vast, fertile alluvial fan cradled by great mountains. In the spring when the air is still, the plain is heavy with the scent of cherry blossoms and freshly turned earth. The Minjiang River flows here, and along its banks, giant bamboo towers over a flat, endless landscape and offers the only shade for as far as the eye can see. It seems lush, and old and young women sit in the shade of the bamboo and embroider clothes and crafts to be sold in the West.

The men work in the fields, where water flows at the mercy of the Minjiang. In good years, the river is kind. In wet years, the river goes mad. It devastates the land and its people in a hell fury of floods and ravenous water. Indeed. Here on the Chengdu, life and death circle about one another like characters in a Chinese opera. Happiness is tempered by fate, for this piece of earth has not been kind to the people who work it. Floods and earthquakes have erased five million souls in little more than two generations, yet the people continue to have a passion for their land. It is the crucible of their existence, and the people work hard, at once reverent and wary of the Minjiang. The horrors of nature exacted by water and quaking earth are kept in the deep and silent places of their hearts, and life on the Chengdu is lived as routinely as anywhere on earth.

Fai Sheng was a laborer for the Sichuan irrigation district, a maze of locks and levies built before Christ by Li Bing. Though the man-made project is little defense against the great river in very wet years, its genius of design mutes the angry waters, and the people who work the irrigation district are held in high regard.

On this day, Fai Sheng knelt at the edge of a small canal to cool himself with a splash of water. He looked up at the bright China sun, raised his hands to the sky, and prayed. "I do not want to marry the ditch tender's daughter," who happened to be Su Li—a "catch," according to the men of the village. Nonetheless, Fai Sheng longed against all hope that he would awaken from a sleep and find his impending marriage a fleeting dream. The arranged union, however, was as real as the hard sun that bore down on his back.

Fai Sheng saw for now that the water was flowing freely and without consequence, and it would be hours before his labor would be needed to reset the waters' flow. So as he did what he always did at times like this, he trekked up Yulei Mountain, where his world lay before him—the great plain, the tempestuous river, and the village where he lived far below.

On a terrace near the summit, Fai Sheng pondered the scene in silence, and in the stillness, a fluttering butterfly alit on his dense, ebony hair. Nearby, a beehive hung from the thick branch of an ancient China pine. By its size, the hive must have been there for a very long time, and Fai Sheng was puzzled that he hadn't noticed it before. He studied the hive and determined it as a kind of microcosm of life as it is lived on the Chengdu Plain—a world of predetermined activity, laboring deliriously in support of life and its unbroken continuation.

"My family eats, the bees work, the water flows, everything is good," said Fai Sheng looking up to the sky. "Why must I marry the ditch tender's daughter?" He dropped his head toward the ground in near despair and knew in his heart of hearts that this dalliance with the gods was foolishness. So what of his dreams and desires? Longings and aspirations are not realized in this earth-borne episode, and he knew it. He would work in the fields of the Chengdu Plain, and Su Li, like the generations of women before her, would embroider in the shade of the bamboo along the banks of the Minjiang.

So in those days, Fai Sheng and Su Li married and they grew to care for one another as a man and woman should. The family's great happiness was the birth of a son who would make economic contributions to the family. Their disappointment, at least outwardly and underscored by the subtle looks on the faces of the villagers, was the birth of Pei Ling, an economic drain and liability that would require marrying off. Fai Sheng, while accepting well-meant sympathies from his neighbors, was quietly delighted by the birth of his beautiful daughter and offered many silent prayers of thanks.

By the time Pei Ling was in her teens, the political order had placed women, officially, at least, equal with men. Pei Ling could study electrical engineering at the university, a fate that to her was only slightly better than being married off. Pei Ling wanted to go to America.

After the family suffered through the drowning death of their only son, Pei Ling became the sole heir of attention, affection, and love—and concern about her wanderlust and desire to leave the village. While most relatives and friends were at first against Pei Ling going to America, she worked her irrepressible magic and convinced not only her family, but nearly the entire village that it would be good for them to sponsor her to study in the West. Work and study in America would allow her to send money home, and she could serve as a conduit for those who wanted to immigrate to America.

On the morning of the day Pei Ling left, Fai Sheng talked with his only daughter and now his only child to offer a last bit of fatherly advice. "Look around," he said expressively sweeping his hands across the yard and the fields and pointing to the house and the village where the generations of family were born, lived, and died. "There is nothing more to life than this."

"I know, father," she said. And she did.

The bus approached and father and daughter embraced one last time, and Pei Ling arrived in San Jose in January and moved into what was called the golden triangle.

Chapter Two

First Encounter

The escarpments that embrace the Chengdu Plain are craggy, raw peaks, the bastard sons of the Himalayas. The plain itself is a sensuous beauty, a woman of uncontested fertility, whose air glides gently through the body as an ethereal saber, piercing the soul with harmony and tenderness. For those who recognize it, such wounds are received as a special condition of life on earth. When Pei Ling came to America, she brought with her this gift of the Chengdu and the distinctive properties that come with it. As most lose their innocence to know the evil of this world, some, like Pei Ling, retain their innocence forever and know the truth always. Pei Ling was, shall we say, a different kind of girl.

I met her on a crisp, bright morning waiting for the laundromat to open. She stood in the doorway holding a small wicker basket with a few odds and ends of clothing. I thought she looked ordinary, at first glance. Her short-sleeved white blouse was as bright as daylight itself, and her coarse, black hair was pulled into a ponytail. She wore glasses with black frames that looked like they came from the government. Looking past the obvious, I saw the stirring face of exceptional beauty. Her lips were supple and reddish brown like the color of cocoa, her skin tender and smooth like the underside of a fawn. The cool, morning air brushed her silky cheeks the color of saffron. She was tall and muscular, and smoldered with sensuality. I feared she would grow impatient and leave and I stumbled for words.

"Doing your laundry?" We were outside a laundromat. Could I have asked a dumber question? She kindly responded with a pleasant, but distant smile, and I wondered if she understood me. "Maybe the guy will show up soon," I ventured. "Uh, what's your name..." As I finished the lyric in my mind, "...is it Mary or Sue," she turned, meeting my eyes.

"My name is Kati."

"You go to the university?" I asked.

"Yes." Her eyes darted from mine and as quickly, returned.

"What do you study?" I asked.

"Electrical engineering...How 'bout you?" She spoke in a tremulous lilt—deliberate, soft, and pleasing as poetry. I was in heaven.

"Yeah, me too...not electrical engineering, but I go there. I'm a teacher," I said.

"Oh, you are a professor!"

"No, not yet...maybe someday."

"But you teach at the university?"

“Yes,” I said.

“Then you are professor!”

She was insistent. “Okay, I’m a professor if you say...” Time seemed to pass more quickly than one can explain. As I fumbled for words, she picked up her laundry and briskly walked away.

"See you..." I said. My words trailed off as she reached the other side of the street, but I felt saved when she looked back.

"The man is not coming," she said, and she disappeared into the gentrifying neighborhood near the university. I took it to mean she decided the laundromat was not going to open anytime soon—at least not soon enough for her. No matter. I was flush with exhilaration from talking to the girl who said her name was Kati. Surely, I would run into her again, but when? How would I reach her? No phone number. No address. All I knew was that she was an electrical engineering student and that I found her both hopelessly appealing and marvelously mysterious. Her compelling presence left me with no alternative other than to find her again—and soon. In fact, it started to seem like an emergency. My mind raced for ideas, but I didn’t have any. Panic turned to frustration, and frustration to desperation. Wait! I knew what to do. If I hung around the rotunda of the engineering building long enough, I'd surely run into her. The next day, I did just that, from eight in the morning until noon. It was an ugly wait.

Unlike the rich patina and comfortable mustiness of the old campus buildings, the engineering building was a modern structure—the design of a plumber-turned-decorator—a monolithic edifice of white concrete and chrome resembling a giant restroom. As the hours dragged on with no sign of Kati, hope became hopelessness, and the more I thought about what I was doing, the crazier it seemed. Maybe, I thought, I was blowing my impression of Kati out of all proportion. If we met, we met. Why bother with something over which I had no control. I thought about what Ro would advise—forget the schemes and just see what happens next. It was certainly the less stressful thing to do.

Chapter Three

The Telephone Number

I met Ro on New Year's Eve. He had a band that had been called upon to entertain for a local, art gallery fund raiser. "Roamin' Rogan," his friends called him. He adorned his on-stage persona with a burgundy fez and a purple muumuu made of a kind of carpet bag-type fabric. He was a performance artist, and he called his music "anti-music"—a cacophonous medley that, for me, musically reflected life as I knew it. After his first set, I briskly made my way to the bandstand and proclaimed the performance shocking. He thanked me for the compliment, and our friendship was struck.

We were an incongruous pair. Where I was a quiet, plain looking guy who blended in with the crowd—and liked it that way—Ro was a gruffly handsome, rough-around-the-edges, loud mouthed kind of guy—who also liked it that way. If people ever gave a thought about us at all, they didn't know what to make of us. Was Ro an artist? An actor? Was I his agent? People didn't have a clue, of course, though on the occasion when I would step it up a bit with a black turtleneck and sunglasses, Ro would chide me for looking like a Langley, Virginia fag. No. Our connection was based on the invisible and invincible pillars of friendship. That's it. No other explanation needed.

It was a Friday evening when we boarded the multi-billion dollar travesty on tracks called light-rail. “How nice of them to build a system no one uses but us,” I mentioned as we got off and headed for our favorite joint in San Jose's Japan town—the Cuban International. A mild September rain had just blown through, and the streets and sidewalks glistened like glass, reflecting gauzy pastels of colorful neon as people sauntered to their favorite night spots. Couples flirted in trendy noodle shops along Jackson Street, where the food was cheap and talk was trashy. The din of clanging pans, Pidgin English, and mindless chatter filled the air.

On the mean end of the street, lonely drunks slipped into the windowless bar where Miho, seductress of mostly pocketbooks, tended bar. She was a look-but-don't-touch femme fatale who fed men's China girl fantasies, and emptied their wallets as they vied to extend the evening's biggest tip in hope of after-hours action.

As we neared Sixth Street, the aroma of fried plantains and spit-roasted pork collided with the scent of yakitori-fired shoyu, sugar, and garlic beef. Rounding the corner, Ro recognized the faint, tinny sound of carioca music. We were at the Cuban International.

"Yeah, that's what I want,” said Ro. “...a big, fat side of pork with plantains, black beans and rice, smothered in gravy."

The Cuban International was Joe's and Maria's restaurant. They didn't cater to or much care for the prissy tech types who gathered in the newer joints on Jackson. "Lite" meals weren't on the menu, nor were they allowed. Joe even tacked up a "Warning: No Vegetarians" sign. He cooked everything with a kind of blunt force trauma and distinguished his fare with spices known only to him. Maria served it up in huge, steaming portions, fit for anyone who ever had a hangover or who was about to have one. "The Cuban" was known throughout the neighborhood as *thee* place for remedy. You might draw from this that Ro and I are heavy drinkers. We aren't. We're hard drinkers.

We wended our way up the stairs to the second floor dining room. Maria met us with a hug and exclaimed in her charming, broken accent, "My boys, my boys, where have you been?"

"Not here," said Ro. Maria didn't notice the crack, but she always smiled. I imagined that whether she'd won the lottery, or stepped in a pile, Maria smiled. She was a saint and she seated "her boys" at the regular table covered with a plastic floral print tablecloth, and a small bouquet of fake daisies. Ro ordered beer and the regular for both of us. Maria nodded and dashed behind a curtain into the tropically hot kitchen and told Joe to prepare two orders of pork with the works.

"You look troubled, my son," said Ro. "What's got yer goat?"

"Ah, nothin'," I said, my expression betraying my words.

"Oh yes there is...chick trouble?"

I didn't want to admit it, but Ro, as was his way, was relentless. "Okay, yeah. I met this chick this morning and now I don't know how to get a hold of her. She's an engineering student. I tried hanging around her classroom thinking I'd bump into her...what a waste."

"An engineering student!" exclaimed Ro. He was whiny and sarcastic in a light-hearted yet serious way. "You *are* nuts, man! You ain't gonna get along with no engineering student...and why would you? They're nerds. What!" exclaimed Ro emphasizing his point. "So here I am, talkin' to a guy down over some gal he doesn't even know when he has all those student chicks hangin' all over him all the time. I just wanna cry in my beer...that I don't have yet!" Ro motioned Maria over and told her we wanted the beer now, and looked me in the eye. "I'd seriously tell you don't waste your time, but you seem...you seem...actually...you seem desperate."

"Slightly crazy, not desperate."

"Oh yes you are, man..."

I cut him off. "Discouraged a little...not desperate...meet the girl and you'd know what I mean."

"I already have," smiled Ro with a self-satisfied grin. "Turn around." Ro leaned towards me and whispered. "Near the register...take a look. That's her, ain't it?"

"How'd you know?"

"Just knew," said Ro. "I'm a genius."

In truth, I didn't believe Ro knew, and he might be a genius, but he knew the rules of randomity. If you say, "She's right there," it's bound to be correct for someone. Just so happened, "someone" tonight was the girl I'd worried about finding again.

"What's her name?" asked Ro.

"Kati." I said.

"Oh, noooo!" Ro said loud enough for everyone to hear. "They all call themselves Kati...or Susie or Mary or something occidental...or is it accidental? Hah!" Kati glanced ever so briefly at Ro and turned to her friends, who were ascending the stairs.

"Geezus," I said, "Keep it down, would ya?"

"Does she know English?"

"I said, keep it down, will ya?"

Ro persisted. "Does she speak English?"

"Well, of course, she speaks English—she couldn't get into school if she didn't, now could she," I said like I was making a point.

"You don't need to know English to get into college anymore...and maybe she doesn't even go to school."

"You're nuts, you dipshit. Her real name is probably unpronounceable to you and maybe even to me and she's tired of people saying "huh" and "what" every time she tells someone her real name. Engineering students don't have to know English anyway...just, you know, on a rudimentary level. Engineering's all numbers...I spoke with her when I met her," I said like I was proving something. "We can communicate well enough."

"I'm sure you can," agreed Ro with a grin.

"Here you are, boys," said Maria, presenting two heaping plates of steaming, south-of-the-border goo. I thanked Maria and Ro ordered more beer.

The gaggle of girls Kati was waiting for skittered up the stairs, chattering and giggling like a bunch of, well, school girls.

Maria hastily put together two tables behind us to accommodate them.

"Well?" said Ro. "Yer girlfriend's here. Aren't you gonna say something?"

"Like what?" Kati hadn't given any clues that she'd even noticed me, and I thought to finish the beer in front of me for courage, should anything happen.

"Oh, boy," said Ro. "She's been eyein' ya since she sat down...and, uh, I gotta say...you *do* have a problem."

"How's that?" I asked.

"She's lookin' good. Real good. And she ain't talkin' like a magpie, either, like the rest of those girls."

I wanted to turn to Kati, but something was off. I didn't know what to say and if I did, I was sure I didn't want to say it.

"Why don't you just get up and go to the can...if ya get my meaning," said Ro. "At least your eyes can meet." Ro was getting a big kick out of this.

"Yeah. Good idea." I got up and passed near Kati's table, but she was in conversation with one of her friends and didn't look at me. When I returned from the john, Kati and the girls were gone.

"Where'd they go?" I asked in mild panic.

"Uh, gone south...like birds, I suppose," said Ro. "How the hell would I know? Soon as you were out of sight she left some money or something with Maria and took off with the other chicks. Why'd it take you so long, anyway? Constipated? Or gussyin' yerself up?"

"Very funny, asshole. Let's go."

As we started down the stairs, Maria ran breathlessly from the kitchen. "Boys! Boys! Wait!" Maria pulled a small red envelope from her apron and pointed to the table where Kati had been sitting. "One of those girls told me to give you this."

"Which one?" I asked.

"The pretty one," said Maria with a look that told me she wanted to know all about everything.

"Thanks, Maria." I could hardly contain my excitement as Ro and I ran outside under the warm glow of the restaurant's yellow marquee.

"What is it?" asked Ro. "What's it say?"

Ro was as excited as I was and I opened the envelope in a hurry. "Says, 'Pei Ling' and a phone number."

Chapter Four

In Dreams

I guessed Pei Ling was her real name, but I didn't call that night. Still, I wondered why she gave me the note. Maybe she remembered me saying I taught at the university and wanted advice on classes. But why didn't she say anything at the restaurant or the morning when I first met her? I hit the sack thinking about all of this and drifted into a dream:

I wish he could have been another composer...Chopin, Lizt, Debussy...but it was Marvin Hamlisch. Laugh if you must, though I like to think Marvin would feel honored, but it's true. I was an unseen observer and saw a man who was like me running with an angry Hamlisch chasing him. Hamlisch caught him and began shaking the man in a rage because he had stolen an original, unpublished composition.

Almost out of sight, far down a long, dark and narrow hall, paneled richly with expensive wood, stood a lone figure, trembling with fear as he watched the confrontation. It was night, but the figure was lit by a full moon shining through a skylight.

Hamlisch, the other man, and me, the unseen observer, saw the figure and together we felt his anguish as our own. The man who was like me opened a closet door, where he had hidden the stolen score and gave it to Hamlisch, who asked the man who was like me why he stole the work. He explained that he needed to give the composition to a messenger or the messenger would die. We understood at once that the lone figure was a messenger. Hamlisch said to the man, "Oh, you should have told me that in the first place...it's all right."

I, the unseen observer, became the man who was like me. I walked down the hall with the score in hand to the messenger whose anxiety increased with each of my approaching steps. I could discern details and features of the messenger as I got closer. He was like me except that where his forearms should be he had wings of light blue feathers that reached to the floor. As I got nearer, the messenger began to panic. He moved his arms slowly and rose to the skylight as to pass through it, but fell to the floor when he reached the closed dome. I was deeply shocked to the core of my being by his fall, and just as soon delighted to discover that I was able to rise to the skylight to show the messenger how to open it. The messenger looked up at me. He became calm and I became him. I moved my forearms in staccato-like fashion, and as if in slow-motion, rose through the skylight and into the nighttime sky.

The sky above me was deep, vivid blue, strewn with stars, with great brush strokes of purple swashes stretching across the entire heaven. I passed through a diaphanous layer of indigo mist and looked down and saw whitecaps on a dark ocean below. A sense of calm unlike any I had ever known flowed through me and around me. Peace was so total and tangible, it awakened me.

I was amazed in my stupor and looked at the time. It was much earlier in the evening than I thought. I turned on the television and discovered I'd slept through the night, through the following day, and to now—early the next evening.

Thank God it's the weekend, I thought. Groggy and disoriented, I turned off the television, grabbed a glass of cold milk, went back to bed, and drifted into another dream.

I was the messenger and I was talking in the Garden Court of the Palace Hotel at a table with Pei Ling and the man who was like me. It was night. Pei Ling and the man who was like me were asking me about my life as a messenger. I notice the discomfort of others near us who were graciously trying to not be obvious in their eavesdropping or gawking at my winged forearms.

The man who was like me, asked why I needed an original composition. I explained that there are more messengers than people who believe in them. As a result, there are many lost messengers. The man who was like me asked what happens to them. I said that those who are not invited into the being of a believer soon die. To postpone death and have another chance, they must secure an original work of art—a painting, a literary piece, a sculpture, a musical composition. The earthly merit of the work does not affect the value of the piece to the messenger. It must simply be unpublished, unsold, and original. I also told Pei Ling and the man who was like me that messengers have no choice into whom they are invited—they must go into the person who first asks. Pei Ling's eyes welled with tears and asked me. I was elated and overwhelmed with humility and gratitude. Her simple declaration saved me.

It was the middle of the night and now I wanted to make that call to Pei Ling, but I stopped myself. In a way, I'd already been in a kind of intimacy with her. It was disturbing, really. The dreams—so vivid, so realistic, so heavy with unknowable meaning—was Pei Ling somehow aware of my dreams? Perhaps the producer, director, and star? I was having a hard time distinguishing her from reality, and sometimes I thought I was going crazy. Instead of acting on my desire, I lie down and fell into a deep sleep and dreamed of her yet again:

I was anxious, thinking I was going to be late for a meeting, but I arrived on time at the door of a modern, two-story house on a rise of land in the middle of a vast, lonely tract of land. I paused before entering the house to look back at the landscape. It was a bright, sunny day, temperate with a cloudless sky. There were no other buildings or human artifacts in sight—only well-kept vineyards on rolling hills as far as the eye could see. I turned to the house, opened the door and walked in. I lingered for a moment in the foyer, and heard a man and a woman engaged in a tense and spirited discussion upstairs. The man's voice was my voice. I hollered up that I had arrived. The man and the woman came out from one of the upstairs rooms and leaned over the balcony to greet me. The tension from whatever it was they were talking about was gone and they appeared delighted and pleased that I had arrived. I felt at ease, but was shocked at what I saw. The man was me and the woman was Pei Ling. I walked outside, astonished and devastated, and asked myself, "If that man is me, who am I?"

This dream disturbed me, and I tried to steady myself, thinking back to a time when life was less complicated, back to the land of my youth, back to the soil I tilled and, always, back to the vines. There were two tractors and I loved driving them—one modern with the latest options, but always preferring the old Case in-line four-banger. It was a ponderous machine, monstrously heavy, with unparalleled traction, navel orange paint faded with age, and as reliable as mom and dad. It was the choice for pulling the French plow and the tandem disks through the fertile earth of the San Joaquin Valley. When it came time to work the soil, I was eager to climb aboard the behemoth, particularly in the early spring when the vines had been pruned and tied, and the purple vetch that had been planted in the fall to return nitrogen to the soil was in full bloom and covered the vineyard floor like a lush, lavender and green carpet. I sometimes imagined it a vineyard in the Garden of Eden. I captained the beast down the rows, pulling the French plow as it swiveled and spun between each vine and gently turned the earth as a mother turns a sleeping child. The sway of the great machine in the soft earth was like being at sea, and the vines were their own magic, each with a distinctive gnarl and twist of the trunk, each with features that set one apart from the other...the currants with their black wood, dark leaves, and tiny fruit that when ripe with sweetness, were set out to dry in the summer sun for use as ornamental raisins; the Muscats with their gray wood, roan leaves, and, distinctive, lush, full flavor. But, oh, the Sultana! A succulent, golden orb of sweetness, seedless and kissed with the muted flavor of her sister Muscat; she was a primitive fruit with a wild nature. She held volumes of sugar without splitting her skin, and was blessed with an inborn immunity to the parasites that plague many modern vineyards. So far as it is known, the Sultana was first cultivated in a land between the Black Sea and the Mediterranean about 4,000 years ago, and planted into the soil of the San Joaquin Valley in the 1920's. For the next forty years, the Sultana was the king of crops, as surely as the Alberta peach was queen.

In those days, the San Joaquin was farmland, where mere decades before, the Miwok Indians would sail from the Tulare Lake Basin at the southern end of the valley, north through the Sacramento Delta and into San Francisco Bay. The Kings River ebbed and flowed with the Sierra snow pack to the east, and primed the wells in the valley with cold, pristine groundwater. In the heat of summer, when a man laboring the earth thought he almost couldn't take it anymore, the icy water seemed a miracle as it bubbled forth from irrigation pipes like cold, liquid diamonds.

My father, John Grey, had purchased twenty acres along the Kings River in '39. With the help of neighbors, the land was planted with Sultanas, five feet apart in rows ten feet apart. Care was simple. A light dusting with sulfur two or three times during the summer to prevent bunch rot and a few irrigations were all it took for Sultanas to yield two and a half tons of grapes per acre over their hundred-year-or-so productive life.

The 1960's, along with the rapid debasement of the culture, heralded the large-scale introduction of herbicides and pesticides responsible for the indirect demise of the Sultana. The period also oversaw ruination of the soil and the spirit of those who farmed it. During that decade and through today, wholesale war was visited on those with reverence for the land by the political whores, union mobs, mega-farmers, and self-serving sluts of agriculture at the University of California. They know who they are, and have no idea what they've done. Evil never does.

While PR pros and an inept media fed the clueless with stories about how issues were complicated, my father and men like him knew the issues were simple—the sluts at UC suckled on the purse strings of politicians who suckled on the coffers of the mega-farmers who suckled on consumers who, through manipulation of the marketplace, paid exorbitant prices for tasteless, hybrid fruit. It was a dirty little arrangement that made rich those who participated, and drove others from stewarding the land. Men like my father were among the last of the post Depression-era farmers to cultivate spirit from the land instead of inflated dollars; who declined to participate in the fouling of the soil and the waters that nursed it, or participate in heartless, hybrid agriculture and the artificial marketing needed to sustain it. These men were the last to farm the San Joaquin in the manner of their ancient predecessors. Economic squeeze plays drowned the tender hearts of the land in a mindless sea of techno-chemicals and moneyed double talk, and once and for all destroyed the fruits of their labor. In time, the Alberta peach also vanished, and the Sultana grape was replaced by the Thompson.

The Thompson is a grape bursting with sugar and juice, and unless you've tasted the Sultana, you wouldn't know the difference. The Thompson is a big grape, yielding twenty-five to thirty percent more fruit than its primitive sister. When synthetic crop enhancers were introduced, the Thompson made economic sense. A grower of the new strain, even after expenses for pesticides and herbicides, netted hundreds of dollars more per acre than a grower of Sultanas because the Thompson was heavier. Vineyards of Sultanas were in steep decline while increased use of chemicals drove up production costs of the Thompson and agri-chemicals became as addictive as any drug. Dead land and subdivisions became the growth industries of the San Joaquin, and by the end of the seventies, the venerable Sultana was all but gone. So severe was its decimation, that today they can be found only in a few backyards or as occasional aberrant stock in commercial vineyards. Some say there are a few vines remaining along the road to Sultana just east of Dinuba.

The farm life for the Grey's finally ended after crazed, red-eyed farm union mobs roamed the countryside setting fire to farm equipment, tools, and supplies. It would take ten thousand uninsured dollars to replace the losses—more than enough to put the Grey farm out of business. Politicians and their urbanite minions insisted that farmers understand the motives of the hordes. Finally, bitterness turned to futility and John Grey sold the vineyard to a corporate farm owned by a valley politician who later resigned from office in disgrace, though I understand he was honored with another political appointment a few years later.

It was a good life, before then. I was a loner, and farming was good for loners. A perfect isolation, away from the frenetic urban life and the mostly useless activity of others, the solitude of rural California and big skies lent itself to thinking. One of the great pleasures was breaking from the routine of field work, shutting down the tractor on a moonless night in the middle of nowhere and looking at the stars. Except for the occasional bark of a dog in the far distance or the low rumble of a far away train, all was solitude. You could see the sky in its full glory, all the constellations and stars that a naked eye could see. It was an exhilarating, limitless wonder, at once fascinating and humbling. The sense that home was somewhere out there ran through me like a low level ache. At the same time, the vast, nightmare of infinity and isolation from whatever it is that all of us are separated from was so big it was frightening. How do we get back home, I would sometimes ask myself. I was fascinated with astronomy, a discipline that matched my appreciation for the works and writings of men like Einstein, Eddington, Faraday, Newton, and Schweitzer. And while I did all the things that farm kids did, I was also known as the local expert for identifying stars and constellations and sought every chance to reflect and think about space or discuss the larger questions of meaning with anyone who was interested.

I learned from a high school counselor that I could make a living from astronomy if I knew enough about it. I enjoyed picturing myself as a professor instilling young minds with answers to the answerless and an appreciation for what we cannot know. So I received my graduate degree in physics in December and taught my first class in January. I was making a living at what I loved most, and affording a way to pursue a doctorate at the cut-rate faculty price. I was on top of the world, or so I thought.

Nearly twenty years later, I was beginning yet another class with the same lecture I'd used since I could remember—a short discourse on science and mysticism based on the writings of A.S. Eddington. The only change to the presentation was my increasing boredom. My heart for the calling I once loved was turning into disdain for the students and perhaps impatience with my own life. Something was missing, and though I didn't know what it was, perhaps another force did. For this same evening, Pei Ling dreamed a dream of childhood when her mother took her to a calm place along the banks of the Minjiang. Pei Ling entered the water and lay on her back to float with her face to the sky. At a place in the great river where bamboo grows thick and bends gently in the current, Pei Ling drifted lazily along and into a stand of bamboo. She lay there for a time as the sun glinted through the leaves and its warmth rested on her sweet face and a certain pleasure came to her. She awoke and thought of the man she saw at the restaurant the night before.

Chapter Five

Enough Is Enough

"At this point in your studies, you're well-versed in the fundamentals of physics," I began with intentional sarcasm. "Some of you might even be able to explain the differences between General and Special Theories of Relativity. You consider yourself highly analytical and possess a strong scientific understanding of the world around you...right?"

I paused and took a turn from my notes and was as surprised as the students by the words that spilled from my mouth. "Let me ask...how many of you know what love is?" A veil of bewilderment drifted over the class as the students looked at each other curiously. An adventurous hand or two lifted through a cerebral haze, but I ignored them. I looked down at the floor and then I looked up, surveying the class. "Uh-huh...an odd question for this class you're supposing? Well...it's my class." I knew I sounded like a selfish bore, but I didn't care. The *bored* of education would have been chagrined, too, but I didn't care about them, either. "Tell me, who among you has been moved by a sunset, a dramatic performance, a work of writing, a musical score, the thunderous crash of an ocean wave?"

A persistent hand rose. "Glad to see some of you are alive," I said with a tight smile. "So then, for all your scientific understanding, you know there's something more out there...something that can't be truly described by equations, quantification, deduction, induction, algorithms or color television."

"I'm not so sure about that," piped a voice from the rear of the room. It was Todd, always first to answer, letting fly with another irrelevant thought. A young man of spare intellect, like most students in recent years, Todd was the rotting fruit of modern, public education, another politically correct, useful idiot steeped in self esteem classes—a product of social experimentation over reading, writing, arithmetic, obligations, and responsibility. Though I found favor with elements of Darwinism, I never believed intelligence was an evolutionary feature of man, and if ever someone proved my theory that humans began devolving from some point in the past, Todd and his kind were it. They were the contemporary arm of society for whom ignorance, intelligence, truth, justice, and right and wrong were relative. He was a Johnny joke, really—Johnny, the student the teacher never called upon because he'd inevitably find a way to reply with something vulgar or stupid.

"Todd!" I exclaimed. "Okay...you're not sure about that?"

"Well, the ocean wave...hydrodynamics explains it completely." He sat smug and self-satisfied, and I thought that I might enjoy kicking his ass.

"If you'll recall, I said be *truly* described. Truth! What is the truth of the matter? Hydrodynamics defines wave formation, but doesn't describe the poetry of it or our emotional connection with it...I'm talking about the wave in human terms. Does that make sense? Better yet, do you...can you understand?" I slowly paced the front of the room. Wandering in my thoughts, I imagined Todd asking me, "If I saw a man beating a donkey to death and stopped him, what emotion would I be showing," so I could answer, "Brotherly love."

Another voice from the back of the room volunteered. "In the larger picture, then, physical laws really hold little truth for us." I briefly fixed my eyes on the girl, surprised, since she'd never before talked in class.

I encouraged her. "I want to agree with you, but I think you want to say something more?"

As I tried to remember where I'd seen her, she continued. "Let's say we can rely on the truth of pure mathematics, but we must take our scientific view to a place where we can ponder its meaning. On its face, it means little to us, but it can inspire awe and wonder about the nature of the physical world when we look beyond physical laws and harmonize them into ourselves."

"Good!" I was impressed. "I think you're getting it." I grabbed some chalk and took the next few minutes writing equations that explained the hydrodynamics of wave formation. I drew a line, and next to the equations I wrote from a Rupert Brooke sonnet:

There are waters blown by changing winds to laughter
And lit by rich skies, all day. And after,
Frost, with a gesture, stays the waves that dance
And wandering loveliness. He leaves a white
Unbroken glory, a gathered radiance,
A width, a shining peace, under the night.

"There," I said. "You have two ways of describing the same thing. Look. The wave in the poem is tidily defined by hydrodynamics, as Todd said, but the feelings evoked by the poem are evidence that something else is out there. In other words, physics reveals the physical reality that we know and touch, and see, and measure. The emotional and evocative forces of the poem tell us there is another truth...intangible and immeasurable...that allows us to consider the very fundamental questions of meaning, existence and who we are."

In the silence that followed, I thought of what Ro might say if he were in the class and, in a way, he was...just outside, in fact. I caught glimpses of him through the door's small window, darting back and forth, making goofy faces and motioning me to hurry.

"Okay," I said to the class. "We'll pick up where we left off on Monday." The usual small group gathered around me. Some asked about exams and the lecture, and some tried to butter me up in hopes of favorable grades. It was always the same, except for the girl from the back of the room whose face I couldn't place. In a soft, diminutive voice, she introduced herself and said her name was Ann.

"You thought I was getting it?" she asked.

"Yes," I said. "I think you have a good understanding of what I was trying to explain today."

"Seriously?"

"Yes, of course. I wouldn't say it if I didn't mean it. In fact, I'd like to talk to you more about it. Do you have some time?"

"Now?" asked Ann.

"Yeah. I'm on my way to dinner with a friend, and we can all talk about the mystery...and I'd like to figure out where I've seen you before."

"You've seen me before?" asked Ann placing her hand on her chest.

"Yes, I'm sure of it," I said. "Somewhere outside of class, but I can't think of where."

"Well, yes then," said Ann. "We can figure out the mystery of where you saw me, and I want to talk to you, too. By the way, did you mean the class will pick up where we left off last Monday? Or we are going to pick up on Monday where we left off today?"

"Oh, boy, this should be good," I said, anticipating an ice-cold beer.

Ann looked puzzled. "Good? You don't know what I want to talk about, and you think it is already good?"

"It's an expression...that I'm intrigued...anxious to know what you want to tell me," I said.

"Well, when you find out, you may not think it is good."

I was even more intrigued and hurriedly placed some loose papers into my briefcase. I motioned Ann ahead of me, and we were out the door where Ro was waiting.

"This is Ann, Ro," I said. "She's coming with us."

"Oh," said Ro, feigning disinterest. "An interloper."

"Interloper? What's that?" asked Ann.

"Like a person who eats cantaloupe without permission," said Ro.

I looked at him. "What the hell are you talking about...wait, I know. You're talking about nothing." I looked at Ann. "He's just having fun. Pay no attention."

"Oh, okay," said Ann seeming to accept my explanation out of deference. "Where are we going?"

"To the Cuban International," I said. "Wouldn't you know, it's in Japan town?" As we walked the few blocks to the restaurant in light conversation, it struck me. "Aha!" I said. "I saw you at the same restaurant we're going to now."

"Really?" said Ann.

"Yes. But your hair was down and you were with another girl. Well, you were with several girls, but there was one. Pei Ling is her name."

"Oh, yes," said Ann as I arrived once again under the restaurant's garish neon light. "I want to talk to you about her."

Chapter Six

In The Dark

"My boys! My boys!" exclaimed Maria. "Good to see you...you have company tonight, and such a pretty young lady, too! You were here the other night, weren't you?" As the effusive Maria good-naturedly droned on, a familiar, unrelenting darkness began to flow over me like cold glue.

"You guys get a table," I said. "I'll be right back."

"Ah, the exquisite pain!" I said to myself rushing down the scuffed yellow linoleum to the head. I looked in the mirror. "Boys? Hell, Maria, I'm as old as you are!" I bent over the sink to splash some water on my face with some crazy idea that it would wash away my thoughts, too. Everything was wrong and nothing made sense and I dried myself with a cheap paper towel and returned to Ro and Ann.

"Are you okay?" asked Ann.

"Not really. But it'll pass...the good thing about this is that sooner or later you're going to feel better."

"Sounds good to me," said Ro as Maria set down a couple of beers for us and a ginger ale for Ann.

I felt like I should apologize, but what for and to whom? And then I started. "We're alone," I said. "All of us. But, you know? We're too scared to think about it. If we thought about it, we couldn't handle it. We'd go nuts. You'd go nuts if you knew how close you were to falling into the abyss...and right now," I said squeezing my thumb and forefinger together for emphasis, "I'm that close."

"The abyss?" asked Ann.

"Yeah. Like hell...alone, emptiness...I can't enjoy anything until I clear this up...and I don't see how anyone else can go about their business until they know, either."

"Well, I don't want to know," said Ro. "It's just as well, isn't it?" Ro wasn't asking a question. He was stating a position that, thankfully, turned the course of the conversation.

This is great," said Ro glancing at Ann. "Coming from a guy with the greatest job in the world. He doesn't get dirt under his fingernails, he's single with plenty of moola, he's got chicks all over the place..."

Ann excused herself to the restroom, and I looked at Ro with an empty stare and a long pause. Ro looked right back at me. "Eat, drink, and be merry, as they say."

"Sorry ol' buddy," I said. "That lost its appeal long ago. I don't know what to make of it. And as far as the teaching 'bidness' is concerned, I've mouthed the same words in class for so long I'm merely a runner on an endless academic production line."

"Yeah, but the chicks," said Ro. "How many you suppose you done over the years?"

"Huh?" I asked losing whatever train of thought I had. "Oh...uh...one more than I should have...but it's been a while, that's for sure," I said to accommodate my friend's point.

"You an' me both," said Ro. "Oh, we can if we want..."

"Really." I said. "Who cares?"

"Speak for yourself," said Ro, punctuating his words with a smoker's hack and swigging a beer. "That's the beauty of it."

"The beauty of it?"

"Ah, don't be a wet rag," said Ro.

"Knock it off," I said. "Here she comes."

Ann sat down and looked at me as if to discern whether I was in better spirits. "Mr. Grey?"

"Ouch," I said. "Please don't call me 'mister'...we're not at school."

"Oh, sorry," said Ann. "What should I call you?"

"Just don't call him late for dinner," said Ro as I laughed at his corny joke.

"Just call me Aaron," I said, still laughing, and asked Ann just what was it that she wanted to talk to me about.

"What I mentioned earlier," said Ann. "The mystery of out there and...Pei Ling...but it can wait."

"You can talk to me about anything...even in front of him," I said pointing to Ro. "We're friends, good friends...best friends."

Ann took a deep breath and almost seemed on the verge of tears. "I...I really can't."

"Hey," said Ro in his cheesiest Bogart accent. "I ain't gonna stay wit you birds all night, ya know. I'm goin' home to have some reeeeal fun...smoke some cigs, hammer some beers...do some business, dig?"

"Sounds like a plan," I said looking at Ann. I motioned for the bill and Maria slipped it next to my plate. Ann reached for her purse. "Forget it," I said. "You're a student. Ro's an artist."

Chapter Seven

The Earthly Delights

We walked down the stairs and into the night. Ro lit a cigarette and threw down the match. It sizzled on the wet sidewalk as he took me aside. “Hey, that chick has a classy chassis, man.”

“Yeah, I know,” I said in a dry, droll tone. “I'll try to be careful.”

“Try?” asked Ro cracking a smile at me and turning to Ann. “Nice meetin' ya...watch out for this dipshit.” I said I'd see him later, and he disappeared around the corner.

“He's funny,” said Ann. “'Dipshit.' I never heard that word. It is funny.”

“He's a funny guy,” I said, looking at my watch.

“Is it getting late for you?” asked Ann.

“Oh, no, but I have to stop by the store before it closes. You said your place is just a block or two from here?”

“Yes. I'm in the small pink house around the corner on Third.”

"Should be easy to find," I said. "Why don't you go ahead and I'll see you in a few minutes."

"Okay," said Ann. "Please take your time. I have to make a call."

I stopped by the liquor store and picked up some smokes for Ro out of habit for the next time we met, a six-pack and a bottle of whiskey for me, and a shot glass, which I was sure Ann did not have in her inventory. Not knowing exactly what Ann was up to, I figured a boiler maker would help navigate my end of the conversation. As a friend once said, if you're going to drink, why fool around? It didn't take long to get the goods and walk the block and a half to Ann's. I hoped she'd made her call, because the drizzle was getting heavier and I wasn't dressed for rain. I knocked on the door and it opened as far as the chain lock would allow. Ann's face peeked through the opening. "Oh, you're here already."

"I can go to the store again and come back," I said in a humorous dig. I caught a glimpse into the room behind Ann and saw her reflection in the mirror on the back wall. Ann was wearing the prettiest red silk panties and no blouse, and I wanted this moment to last for a long time. "Uh, yeah," I said. "It didn't take me long to get what I needed."

"Let me unlock the chain," said Ann innocently, but please wait until I say it's okay to come in." I did as Ann instructed, and in a minute she beckoned. I took a seat on one of the forties-era vinyl chairs in the kitchen and looked around. All those nice feminine things a man doesn't understand but likes in a woman were set about the apartment. A few stuffed animals, some frilly plants, and some lace things hanging from the ceiling to make two rooms out of one. It smelled good in there, too. Ann emerged from the bedroom a moment later, hair down and wearing a red satin robe that swished along her curves as she walked toward me. Ann, who at dinner a short time ago seemed awkward and unsure in a nerdy sort of way, was now a woman in command. "Can I get you tea?"

"Oh, no thanks," I said. "But look what I got." I set out the beer and whiskey. "You want some?"

"No thank you."

"Well, let me put this beer in the freezer," I said and pulled up a chair. Ann sat across the table from me and I asked what was on her mind. She wilted, and looked like she was going to cry again. I wanted to hold her, but restrained myself and waited for her to say something. Finally, she did.

"I need to get married."

I was speechless for a moment. "What?" Ann didn't say anything and looked down. "Are you pregnant or something?"

"No," said Ann. "It is worse...I will have overstayed if I don't return to China by next month. I'm on a student visa. I have to return to my country and they may not let me come back."

I got up to get the beer out of the freezer, popped the cap and took a swig of brew and a shot of whiskey for good measure. I didn't bother to use the shot glass. I looked at Ann who was still looking at the floor. "Well," I said. "You pays your dime and you takes your chances."

"What?" She asked looking at me like a lost dog.

"You gamble on something and sometimes you win and sometimes you lose. What's the big thing about staying here, anyway? China seems as good a place as any."

"My family wants me to live and stay here," said Ann. "It is their dream and hope for me. I can't let them down."

"Really?" I asked. "Everyone's losing their mind in this country."

Ann ignored my comment and slowly panned the apartment looking at nothing in particular and stopped when she got to me. "I have ten thousand dollars."

"Boy, you're just full of surprises," I exclaimed. "You mean you have ten thousand dollars to give someone who will marry you?"

Ann bowed her head, embarrassed. "I am not a boy, and yes, I have money to give to someone who will marry me."

"That's fraud, you know...if immigration finds out, you and whoever goes for the scam could go to jail. You'll be deported, for sure, and then you'll be worse off than now...and you don't want to know anyone who'd go for something like that anyway...a guy that's decent wouldn't go for it, and a guy who would isn't decent. He'd have complete control over you, too. He could do anything he wanted and you'd have to keep your mouth shut." I took another drink. "And by the way, I know you're not a boy."

"Well, Aaron, the reason I wanted to talk to you is I thought maybe you know someone decent who would accept my offer."

I quaffed the last of my beer and thought for a moment. "Actually, I do...Ro...but he's not decent."

"Your friend? He's not decent?"

"I'm kidding. He could use the money, that's for sure...and he's about as decent a guy as you'd want to meet." I poured another drink that was catching up with me fast when I realized I was buying into the whole crazy idea. "Wait a minute, wait a minute...this is nuts. It's sleazy, sordid. Wrong! What the hell's the problem anyway? You're sweet and pretty. You should have plenty of guys who'd take you seriously. Guys who'd want to care for you and wouldn't even have any interest in the money...They'd marry you for...well...love."

Ann struck the vulnerable smile of a younger girl. "That's nice of you to say, Aaron. I've thought of that, too...I had hopes. Things haven't worked out. All the guys just want to play around. I am serious, and now time is running out." Ann fidgeted with her hands and looked down again. "I don't know how this happened, really."

I reached across the table and put my hand on hers. "Yeah, I know. Sometimes we just get blind-sided in life...we live and learn." I pulled my hand back and asked how she knew English so well.

Ann looked up with a smile. "I live and learn."

I laughed. "I guess that makes sense. Well, like I said, the only guy I know who might be willing is Ro. Let me ask him about it and we'll see what happens." I grabbed the last beer from the freezer, took a slug, looked down at the floor, and then at Ann. "I can't believe this. And we never did get around to talking about that mystery out there."

"Yes we did, Aaron," said Ann. "Just now."

I thought for a moment. "Yes, I guess we sure did."

Ann went to the stove and poured herself some tea. "By the way," said Ann. "Pei Ling wants to see you...you're lucky."

"Hah," I exclaimed with the theatrics of one a bit under the influence. "She needs to get married, too?"

"Oh, that's not a problem for her," said Ann. "She doesn't care about staying here. She's returning to China."

"She's returning to China?" I asked, hiding my panic with bravado. "Well, I'm no chump, you know. What does she want to see me for?"

"Chump?"

"Yeah," I said. "A dumb ass...a gullible dolt."

"Oh, oh, oh...I never think you are a dumb ass, Aaron." I got a chuckle out of hearing her say that one. "But I think you could be getting drunk," she said, smiling.

"Could be? I am...but not too drunk to not know what I'm doing or saying...so what's the deal? I mean, what does she want to see me for?"

Ann took on a more serious tone. "I don't completely understand, but she seems drawn to you for some reason...I have no idea."

"Hey, no need to get nasty," I said. "I mean, it's not impossible...is it?"

"No," said Ann. "There are lots of reasons I can think of. You are easy to talk to..."

"But what makes you think I have an interest in her?" I asked, cutting her off.

"Aaron!" she exclaimed with near disbelief. "I knew it at the restaurant and so did Pei Ling. We remember how you were fumbling around and it didn't take much to guess why. We know those things."

"Yeah, darn it...well...I'll be honest. It's just kind of scary to have someone like her drop into my life out of nowhere without me having to work at it. You know...the chase thing and all that stuff with guys."

"Someone like her?" asked Ann.

"So beautiful...like you," I added diplomatically and truthfully.

"That's the way it should work," said Ann.

"You mean like fate?" I said. "I don't believe that for a minute."

"Suit yourself, Aaron. There are no coincidences."

"Don't get me wrong," I said. "I want to see her. I want to more than see her. But, now, after all this thinking about it...all this build up and you telling me that she wants to see...well...I'm kinda nervous."

"Oh, don't be," said Ann. "It's in her hands. And about not having to work at it? I know Pei Ling. You have no idea how much work you will have to work at it, whatever you mean by that...if you're really interested in her...I can't believe I'm telling this to my teacher," she said, mildly flustered.

"Yeah, well, I'm not very good at these things."

"Oh, don't worry so much," said Ann.

I thought of Ann's predicament. "You either," I joked. "Okay, then, where do I sign up?" I answered Ann's question before it came. "It's a figure of speech...what do I need to do for us to meet...me and Pei Ling?"

Ann got up from her chair and looked at the ceiling and repeated the phrase in soft concentration. "Where do I sign up?" I wasn't sure if she was being playful when she suggested next Friday.

"Next Friday?" I shook my head in supreme disappointment. "I'm leaving for Hawaii on Thursday. I can't."

"Not even for Pei Ling?"

"Can't we postpone for a few days?" I pleaded.

"Maybe."

"Maybe? What do you mean maybe?"

"Well," said Ann. "She's here and there. I know I'll see her Friday, though. We have plans. She said something about being gone for a while after that."

"You mean to China?"

"I don't know," said Ann.

I felt an emergency coming on. My upcoming junket to Hawaii was the rarest of chances to study with my mentor and long time friend, Dr. Emile De Broglie, one of the world's most renowned physicists, and an opportunity that was unlikely to come again. I suggested that we get together before I leave.

"Sorry, Aaron, I can't join you before Friday, but use my phone...call her!"

I had no choice. "Okay, okay," I said, waving my hand. "Do you think you could..."

Ann knew what I was getting at and went to the other room. I retrieved the slip of paper with Pei Ling's phone number, took a deep breath, and dialed. She answered on the first ring in a soft, heart-melting lilt.

"Hello?"

"Uh, hi...this is Aaron...Aaron Grey."

"Oh, hi Aaron. I'm so happy you called." Her familiar and comforting tone put me at ease, and I said I was at Ann's.

"You are?"

"Uh, yeah...Ann said you two were going out on Friday, and that it would be okay if I came along."

"Yes, that would be great."

"The problem is I can't make it Friday. I'm leaving Thursday for a few days and I can't change my schedule..." I swallowed hard and continued. "...but I don't want to miss seeing you."

"You don't want to miss me?"

"Yes, I don't want to miss you, and Ann said that after Friday, you might be leaving."

"Aaron, if you want to see me you can see me."

"You mean I don't have to wait until Friday?"

"Yes."

I tried to clarify. "You mean, no, I don't have to wait until Friday."

"I mean, yes, we don't have to wait until Friday," said Pei Ling.

"So we can get together? Just us?"

"Yes."

"Well...okay, then. Would tomorrow be okay? We can have dinner."

"I would like that...where will we have dinner?"

"I was thinking of Café Metropolitan."

"I think I've heard of it...sounds good," said Pei Ling.

"Well, I have your phone number, but I don't know where you live," I said.

"I'm down the street from Ann's...the big yellow house."

"Oh, you live there?"

"Yes, you know it?" asked Pei Ling.

"I've been to some parties there," I said, trying to forget the unforgettable things I'd done there during my party years.

"Well, you won't have trouble finding me then," said Pei Ling. "How about six o'clock?"

Chapter Eight

No Turning Back

Pei Ling answered on the first knock, aglow, smiling, and gorgeous. "You look great," I said.

"Oh, thank you, Aaron. Please come in." I walked into the foyer and turned to watch Pei Ling close the door. She looked at me and smiled. "You look nice too...I like your shoes."

"Yes, a decent man wears leather shoes, particularly if he's meeting someone like you. I got them in Lima."

"Ohio?"

"No. Peru," I said.

"Oh, I'd like to go there."

"Well, maybe we could go together sometime," I blurted. Before she had a chance to respond, if she was going to respond, I changed the subject. "You're not a vegetarian, are you?"

"No, I understand my relationship with the world." There was something curiously poignant about those words, but they certainly weren't a date breaker, and she wrapped a black and gold silk scarf around her neck and gathered her coat.

"Well," I asked, "what are you in the mood for?"

"Oh, I don't know...seafood?"

"Sure," I said. "Where we're going is right for that, too...and they have great steaks, if you change your mind." I started to feel like I was talking too much, like I was about to talk myself out of a sale, though Pei Ling didn't seem to mind.

"Okay," said Pei Ling, locking the door after us. I couldn't recall a woman ever looking better—a black, figure-clinging dress with spaghetti straps, and black pumps with low, sexy heels that accented her profoundly perfect legs. The scent of her just-washed hair kissed the air, and her black, thick mane framed her tender face. We walked out the door and I couldn't help myself. "You look terrific," I said.

Pei Ling stopped and turned to me. "You are too sweet."

Yes, quite the lucky guy I was to be in the presence of this unaffected beauty. Pei Ling was a head-turner, alright. Approving looks from guys and piercing looks from girls seemed to dart our way as we walked down the street. And then came the questions. Where would this go? Why was this happening? Who is this girl and what's going on with her? As much as I wanted answers, I wasn't going to let anything interfere with what all the signals told me was going to be a once in a lifetime evening.

"Oh, this place?" said Pei Ling. "I never noticed where it was...I needed you to take me here," she said smiling.

The restaurant was one of those neighborhood finds, as the chatter goes. It was located up a short burst of stairs in an unpretentious, white bungalow among a row of non-descript houses. Mark, chef and owner, was a kid who, like me, had a passionate interest in artistically good food and, unlike me, a liking for people in general. His father had fronted the investment, and if anyone was going to make a go of it, Mark was. I respected his determination and drive and gave him my business as often as I could. Being a regular and the attention that goes with it didn't hurt, either.

"Aaron! Good to see you again," said Mark, turning to Pei Ling. I returned the greeting, asked about his family, and made the introduction. "Yes, great to be here again, Mark. This is Pei Ling. Pei Ling, this is Mark, chef and owner of this matchless establishment." Pei Ling offered her hand approvingly.

Mark put his hand on my shoulder and showed us to a more intimate table in the rear of the restaurant near the fireplace. "What can I get you?" Mark asked, and sharply clapping his hands once in a clowning attempt at showmanship.

"Got any canned hams?" I asked.

"No, but I've got some canned yams," countered Mark. Pei Ling watched unfazed. "Seriously, I do have a great dish for you tonight. A pan-roasted wild caught salmon filet on a mattress of sautéed asparagus, fresh grapefruit and lime butter reduction."

"Would that mattress be a single or a twin?" I asked.

"Well, yes," said Mark. "The mattress is, in fact, a twin, served with caramelized onions with ginger cloud or new red potatoes and chives with a light balsamic dressing. May I suggest the mixed baby greens and fennel with wild mushrooms? I also have some terrifically fresh mussels that came in just this morning."

Pei Ling looked at Mark, deadpan. "What about a mattress?"

"Hah!" said Mark. "You *were* paying attention. Actually, the filet comes on a pile, a mound, a bed, if you will, of asparagus. I'll give you a chance to look at the menu and be back." Pei Ling tolerated our juvenile game sportingly.

"Well, here we are," I said.

Pei Ling sipped some water and smiled. "What do you think is good?"

"The salmon sounds good...and maybe we could share some mussels. But I think I'll go for the duck breast for the main course. Mark uses a cherry port wine sauce that's ever so sweetly tart...really wakes you up."

"I'm not tired, Aaron. Do I look tired?"

I knew Pei Ling was playing with me. "You definitely don't look tired. It's a figure of speech...like, uh, if I was tired, the sharpness of the cherries would open my eyes very wide." And I opened my eyes very wide for effect. Pei Ling laughed, and puckered her pretty mouth and kissed the air. "Oh, like a lemon!"

We started with champagne, compliments of Mark, a bottle of Fumé Blanc with dinner, and ended with a velvety glass of twenty-five year old port. I laid money on the table, we said our good-byes to Mark, and got our coats and left. Flush with the glow of wine, food, and each other, Pei Ling said she'd like one more drink.

"A nightcap," I said. "Yes, let's have a nightcap. There's a place just down the block...kind of hoity-toity. The customers are sometimes hard to bear, but it's a nice room."

Pei Ling agreed, clutching my arm and laying her head on my shoulder. "As long as I'm with you." she said. I couldn't believe what seemed to be happening. We grabbed a bar side table for two, and Pei Ling excused herself to the ladies' room. I ordered a couple of warm B&B's and made an assessment of the clientele, finding them in contempt, as usual. Things had changed since I was here last. The place was filled with self-congratulating, biological adults, each with a child-like intellect that manifested itself in attire and accoutrements. Skateboards and backpacks all around. What looked like a guy at the bar, apparently rode a bicycle. His goofy helmet and chin strap looked like a shiny blue turd tied atop his head. People obsessed with self while the world goes to hell, I thought. I looked in the kitchen and wondered the odds on one or more of the staff having aids, hepatitis, or tuberculosis, and recalled eating someplace with Ro, who good-naturedly warned me about touching the bread with my hand. Don't worry about my fingers, I said, you should see whose cooking your food. Yes, the place was abuzz with people who thought very highly of themselves. Full of empty laughter, ignorant of the reality around them. People who shared goals, aspirations, and hopes entirely different, even opposite, from my own. The same people you see, as a matter of course, flip off bus drivers, spit at cabs, who have no compunction about telling you what to eat, how to think, what to drive, what to speak, all the while believing with Nazi-like zeal that they make the world a better place. To make matters more ridiculous, they were apparently gathered for one of those dine in support of the disease or syndrome of the day events, and I wondered why with all the dining, running, cycling, speed walking and other useless activities over the years the diseases and syndromes were as evident as ever, and perhaps getting worse. So, I thought, this is what we've come to after a million years of evolution.

On her return, I saw Pei Ling taking a look at the crowd, too. She took her seat across the table from me. "Something wrong?" I asked. With surrender in her voice and a light-hearted tweak of her pert nose, she said she wanted to leave. We left our drinks and ambled out of the trendy dump, arm-in-arm on our way to her apartment, everything seeming quite satisfactory and feeling right with the world. I played with Pei Ling's hand, alternately holding it firmly and stroking the top and palm with my thumb and fingers. I looked for resistance, but there was none. Throwing fate to the wind, I brought her hand up and softly kissed her fingers. "God, I love being with you."

"I love you, too," said Pei Ling. I was startled, and assumed her directness as a language issue. I'd take it anyway, but with the understanding that she really didn't know the significance of her words. After a few minutes, we arrived at her door.

I felt like a kid and said something dumb again. "Well, here we are....oops. I guess I've already said that...at dinner...when we first got to the restaurant."

Pei Ling paid no attention to my awkward words. "Would you like to come up?" she asked.

Pei Ling unlocked the door to the small entryway and opened another door that led to the rooms above. The winding stairs were too narrow for us to ascend abreast, and Pei Ling took the lead. I followed, gazing with excited anticipation pulling me upward with her every step. She unlocked the door to her apartment. It opened to a large, expansive room, furnished with what appeared to be seriously expensive antique furniture. The feel was plush, rich, and comfortable. Pei Ling saw me looking at the décor. "Oh, it's not mine," she said. "It came with the place...the landlord asked if I minded if he rented with the furniture on the condition that I would care for it as much as his family did. Of course, I agreed."

"Yeah. I'm impressed. This stuff is beautiful."

Pei Ling took my coat and hers and hung them in the closet and she took off her scarf and laid it over a chair. I looked at her black leather pumps, the kind with the strap over the ankle, as she removed them. I slipped off my shoes, too. She walked toward a dark hallway and turned back to look at me. "I'll be a moment."

"Wait," I said. She stopped and I walked to her. I drew her face to mine and kissed her. She smiled and looked down. A strap on her dress fell from her shoulder and I softly kissed her again, barely touching her lips. She unpinned her hair and left to the other room. Bingo! I thought. This is really going to happen. I looked around the room again. It was a small place that seemed big...the top floor of an old Victorian, modest, neat, and cared for. The moon was nearly full and filled the room with romance. Everywhere, her feminine hand was evident. A faint scent of jasmine floated in the air. The clouds unexpectedly cleared outside and turned the cool air to an almost summer breeze that blew the wispy lace curtains aside, casting moonlit shadows across the room. I curiously and covertly wandered past the bathroom and into the bedroom as Pei Ling emerged in a white, silk kimono and came to me in silence. In the evening light I saw her beauty in full and felt her profound presence as she moved closer. She looked willfully into my eyes and I gave her soft kisses on her face and her lips and with my hand found the warm, supple skin of her naked back. A tender sweetness enfolded us as we knelt together on the downy bed and the blizzard of Pei Ling's coarse, black hair fell over my face as we descended. I grasped her arching waist, and brushed aside her kimono. Moonlight and shadows drifted across Pei Ling's face. Soft murmurs. Sweet apprehension. Deep kisses. Warm and wet with a woman's scent, fragrant and most wonderful. We kissed again and again and again and then we were done and we were in love. Calm and spent in the silence, we caressed and kissed and more and then a little more.

Pei Ling's back was to me. She reached her hand over her shoulder and touched my face, and turned to me and stroked my hair. "We are no longer the people we were, Aaron," she said softly. "Do you understand?" And I did. It was magical, but I knew we had both lost something...an exquisite happiness and joy, but also sadness in losing something we, or at least I, did not quite comprehend. But I said I understood, and body to body, we fell into a deep sleep and dreamed a dream together. In the early morning hours, my dream diverged from hers and I awoke in urgent pain.

"My leg," I moaned. "It's unbearable." Pei Ling awoke, startled, and tried to comfort me. I moved my hand closer to the pain and was shocked to feel it wrapped in bandages, and afraid to look for fear of what I might see. I imagined a horror of blood or worse and who knows what, and I was more frightened when the pain peaked to white hot. “God!” I begged. “What’s happening?”

“It’s alright, my love,” said Pei Ling. “Calm, darling, calm. I’m going to unwrap the bandage. It will be alright. You will see.”

“No!” I shouted. “Don’t! I can’t look...the pain.” I was about to pass out, but Pei Ling’s assurances and tenderness calmed me long enough for her to begin. To my comfort and astonishment, the heat of pain cooled by magnitudes with each unraveled layer.

“We’re getting closer, my love,” said Pei Ling. Before removing the last layer, she softly kissed me once more. “Don’t be afraid, darling,” she said. “You can look...please...”

My mind flushed with peace and wonder at what I saw. My knee and my ankle faded from sight into the background and what lay between was a vision of awe and unspeakable beauty—a vista of deep space, intense, cobalt blue, dark and strewn with a million stars—and at the same time, a void, nightmarish in its infinity and solitude. I was unable to speak and a few random tears rolled down my face.

“Still frightened, my love?”

I paused and stammered. “Yes...but, no...not now.” Pei Ling kissed me again, and I said I wasn’t sure what I saw. “...like a little universe or something,” I said.

“It is,” said Pei Ling. “It is your vision, and the beehive of my father on Yulei Mountain, and the village from where I came, and all the people you have known and will know now and forever." She paused and added, "It is where we come from and where we will call home one day."

"Am I going to know this tomorrow?" I asked. "In the daylight? In the real world?"

"You will see, darling."

We fell asleep again, and after a time, I got up, drowsy, and stared out the window. The moon had shifted to a dark part of the sky and the room was black. I looked down to where Pei Ling was sleeping to notice a nearly imperceptible light emanating from her ears and nose, and from between her lips and from the corners of her mouth. I thought I should have been frightened, but I was not, and I lay down next to Pei Ling, her warmth and softness comforting me. Flesh on flesh, Pei Ling yielded in silence for a last time before dawn.

We awoke with the first light of day, and I looked at my leg, which was completely normal. I said to Pei Ling that I was not sure what happened or what was real.

"Everything is real, my love," she said reassuringly. "And what are you thinking now?"

"About you. About when the shoe will drop."

"A shoe will drop?"

I tried to explain. "Like something out of left field is going to end this for us, for me."

"Left field?"

"Like if I think of a reason we won't last, the thing that does end it all will be something I least expect."

"What would end us?"

"I don't know," I said.

Pei Ling looked puzzled. "Me?"

"Yeah, maybe," I said.

"There is nothing that could possibly separate us...ever."

"That's a long time," I said, my voicing rising to tease her. "Be careful of what you are saying. I don't think anyone's ever loved me the way you say you do."

"What's not to love about you, darling? I think you never noticed the others. And it's a good thing," she teased. "No one took you before I got you."

"Hah! That's a good one," I said. "If someone had, I'd be here with you anyway."

The early morning sun began to light the sky in deep hues of red and purple, and I looked at the clock. I turned to Pei Ling and kissed her face like a person starved for love and I guess I was. And now I had to leave this wonderful creature. She stirred and asked where I was going.

"It's Thursday, dear. I have to catch that flight to Hawaii at noon, and I haven't even packed."

She sat up in bed, rubbing her eyes. "Oh, yes. It's Thursday."

"Yep. Gonna look at the stars through the big scope."

"Oh, that will be fascinating. I wish I could go with you."

"Me, too," I said almost heartbroken that she couldn't. "But the doc—the guy I'm going to be studying with—well, he's kind of a weird duck in some respects. He'd be upset if someone showed up with me. He's not into surprises unless they're mathematical."

"Weird duck?" said Pei Ling.

"Okay, now, you're being funny," I said. "You know what I mean...not exactly like normal people...but I'll be thinking of you, darling. I'll be thinking of you day and night. I'll be thinking of you on the airplane. I'll be thinking of you when I land. I'll be thinking of you when I eat, sleep, and breath. I'll be thinking of you when I'm not supposed to think of you...you get what I'm trying to say?"

"I think so," said Pei Ling. "I think you're telling me you love me."

We embraced once more before I walked out the door. Outside on the walk, I looked back at the top floor window. She was standing with one hand clasping a drape to cover herself. She smiled a big smile and waved and I went on my way the happiest man on earth.

Chapter Nine

This Side of Reality

I thought of Pei Ling's curious words. "Where you and I will call home one day." What did that mean? I'd had my own great home in life. I had wonderful parents, brothers, sisters, uncles and aunts, a couple of true friends. Still, I felt always away from home and singularly alone. I wasn't like everyone else, and according to everyone else and the way they lived their lives and how they saw things, I guess that was true. I knew who my father was. I didn't have an alcoholic uncle who abused me or a priest or minister who fondled me and I didn't know anyone who did. I never did drugs. I never even tried them. I thought Woodstock was a festival of dirty people and bad music. I found people hardly ever interesting. I was puzzled from an early age why when people made bad decisions, they were dumfounded by the results or blamed someone else. I wasn't much for styles and trends. No tattoos, no body piercings no symbols of self-aggrandizement. I wasn't much for sitting around and discussing the best band of all time. No. I was and am pretty much of a square and I like it like that. And as far as home goes, I called my small apartment home, too. But home, in any real sense of the word, certainly wasn't here. Home was always a place somewhere else, wherever that was. I was always looking for it, but it had always eluded me, and the places I called home never connected with me. Yes, I thought, whatever Pei Ling's version of home was, it must be a very nice place to be.

With my dreams and Pei Ling coming into my life from nowhere, I entertained the possibility of what she said, but the enormity of it, the thought that what she talked about could be real. Well, it was just too much to be taken seriously...at least for now. And that glow. I thought about these things all the way to Hawaii.

"Go you muther," I said to myself as the lumbering jet sped down the runway and poetically rotated up into the air and away from the hard earth below. It was my kind of silent prayer on "wheels up" against the visions I'd have of the great machine falling back to earth. I saw the faces of other passengers as they turned from the pleasant anticipation of wherever they were going on an uneventful flight turn to a sudden end of frantic horror and impending impact with the ground. Should the worst happen, I knew at the core of my being that there would be no screams or shrieking from me—just silent acceptance of the inevitable. But it wasn't to be this time. The flight was a smooth cloudless voyage through an uninterrupted expanse of ocean and sky that appeared stitched together at the horizon with a thin bright thread.

I stepped off the plane in Honolulu in a batik rayon shirt and denim jeans. I was surprised to find De Broglie at the gate.

The doc was a taller than average fellow with a horseshoe of salty hair around a bald pate. He wore the standard uniform of the high IQ'd—a white, short-sleeved polyester shirt a size too small, tan khakis, and leather-soled, burgundy wingtips. He was a good man, and being childless, we had developed a kind of father-son relationship when I spent time studying with him during a summer program I somehow fell into at Oxford. He was an unforgettable mentor with flawless credentials who had garnered a Nobel Prize when it meant something. More recently, his interest shifted to cosmological origins, and I jumped at De Broglie's invitation to share time at one of the world's great observatories.

"Aaron, Aaron, so good to see you," said the doc in his middle European accent, smiling and full of animation. "It's been a long time...five years, no?"

I grabbed his hand with a firm grasp. "Yes, it's been a long time...too long. Great to see *you* again...Say, I thought I was going to meet you in Hilo."

"Yes, yes," said the doc. "That was the plan. But I know how you enjoy good food. I want to take you to dinner tonight. We don't use the facilities until tomorrow."

"I'm up for that!" I said.

"And guess what," said De Broglie excitedly. "If you don't mind, I'd like to forego time exposures and go direct...the heavens are going to be beautiful this week...I'd like to just do that, if you don't mind...and just talk."

I was surprised. "You mean just peer into the heavens? No investigations, no measurements, no calculations? How are you going to get away with that? I mean, you have to have some accounting."

"The university will pay for the time," said De Broglie. "My secretary is very good at the books, and besides, it seems a courtesy for a Noble laureate, don't you think?"

"Well, I don't want you getting into trouble," I said. "But I guess you know what you're doing. Truth is, I'd love it. I just figured there's no way we could justify real time star gazing." I thought about it for a moment more. "Man, those administrators would shit in their pants, if they found out."

"Let dem shit in der pants," said De Broglie. I hadn't seen this side of the doctor. He hadn't much of a sense of humor or a care for banter in the earlier years I'd known him, but now, closer to retirement, he seemed to enjoy letting things slow down a bit. I looked him in the eye and let out a big laugh. "Let dem shit in der pants! Great!" And off to dinner we went, starting with highballs.

My entrée was a charcoal grilled, boneless and butterflied leg of lamb, marinated in mint, red wine, and garlic. It was accompanied by creamed spinach and a crunchy fennel salad with a side of braised shitake mushrooms dressed with a whisper of olive oil, mirin, and rice vinegar. De Broglie had mahi-mahi and a boiled potato. We shared a bottle of red wine.

"Looks good!" said De Broglie pointing with his knife to my plate.

The couple of pre-dinner drinks put me in a loose and relaxed mood and I good naturedly mimicked the doc's accent and he took it that way. "Ya, ya," I said. "You want a bite?"

"Ya vol!" said De Broglie. "...and have some of mine."

"No, thanks, doc...really...I've had enough fish for a while. I'm a red meat man for now...strength and stamina, you know?"

"You're boffing a student?" His words were hilariously out of character for a man of his education and a vocabulary many times larger than mine.

"No," I said laughing. "Never."

"You mention stamina, so I think you are up to something," said the doc.

"I'm the student, and she's boffing me."

"Really?" said the doc, cutting through the slice of lamb I'd shared with him. "Interesting."

"Uh..." I reconsidered. "Cancel that last pejorative, doc. I don't like to talk like that about someone I...I care for or maybe even more than care for....must be the booze."

"Think nothing of it," said the doc. "What's her name, by the way?"

"Pei Ling."

"Ah! Chinese." He stopped for a moment and looked at me with a serious face. "You almost said it."

"What?" I asked.

"Love," said the doc. I never heard you almost say that before. You must be quite smitten with her."

The drive to the summit climbs from the lush, tropic zone of hotel hula girls and luaus to a place above the clouds where vegetation is sparse and the air is cold. In the years since I'd last been there, I'd forgotten how desolate it was—made more so by us being the only souls on site. As we rounded the last curve, the huge, unearthly domes that housed the great telescopes appeared. I stepped on the gas to reach the parking lot and jumped from the jeep.

"I'll be right back," I told De Broglie, and ran to a nearby outthrust of volcanic rock at the edge of the mountain. The silent, great panorama before me struck with a hard sense of loneliness, the kind I'd not experienced in a long time. I was gazing at everything and nothing, but the sight had an eternity about it. Far away on the distant sea, a squall line of forming thunderheads and puffy white clouds reflected on the water like in a Dutch Masters painting. It was a hundred miles away, but looked like I could touch it with the reach of my hand. Looking straight above me to the sky, without a visual reference point, the cerulean emptiness was open and limitless. The incomprehensible vastness dizzied me and caused me to almost stumble, giving way to anxiety as separation from this world became nearly tangible and that whatever it was that was out there tugged at my being and beckoned me home. My boots crunched in the cinder cones as I stepped back in a subdued, darker mood and walked to the jeep where De Broglie was unloading supplies. "What do you think we'll see? I asked.

"Many things," said the doc. "What do you want to see?"

"I remember when you put up those slides of Andromeda and the Pleiades and I really saw them for the first time. The color, the mystery, your almost poetic lecture...it was fantastic."

"Ha, ha. Have I got something for you!" said the doc. "It is more than Andromeda...a little beauty I discovered some months ago. No one knows of it but me...or if they do, they don't know what they are looking at. And now you will know, too."

"What is it?" I asked with curiosity lifting my spirits.

"Patience!" said the doc playfully. "I'm not going to spoil the surprise."

"Now you've got me going, darn it. Let's get this stuff unloaded...when do we have access?"

"Unlimited! It's ours until 6 a.m. Monday."

"You're something else, doc," I said. "It sure pays to be friends with a prize winner."

"Hah! Don't be too impressed with the prize. My work stands on its own merit. The prize is meaningless, of course, except for the money. It is a political event...to puff up the people on the commission...and keep the paparazzi employed." The doc smiled and shrugged his shoulders. "What good is the praise of other men?"

"Well, can't beat the perks," I said.

"It opens a few doors," he agreed.

We put up the last of the supplies and sat down on the bunk beds in one of the two rooms adjacent to the main observatory. It was cold and functional like the engineering building at the university. The bare cement floors and row of gray steel lockers along one wall in the sleeping quarters made the temperature after dusk seem colder than it was. The other room was a tiny space with little more than a refrigerator and a two-burner hotplate. The doc stared at the floor for a moment and looked up at me. "By the way, we're going to lock on to my little beauty at 2 a.m. We should get some sleep...A couple of beers to help?"

"I didn't bring any," I said.

"What?" asked the doc.

"I didn't think you wanted any, and I've cut down, lately."

The doc looked at me, surprised. "You? The great beer meister of Octoberfest?"

"Yeah, yeah, I know. I got started there...and I have you to blame for that...or thank," I said with a laugh. "I remember how I loved the flavor of those beers. I think that's when I seriously started drinking....Hell, for the last couple of years I've been lecturing with a hangover."

"I am sure your students think you are brilliant," said the doc.

"I doubt that, but I'll tell you, that drinking brought out a mean streak in me sometimes, and I really feel bad about how I'd go off on some of those kids."

"Ah," said De Broglie dismissively waving his hands in the air. "They deserved it."

"Thanks," doc. "I know you're being a good friend." And he was.

In the darkness of early morning, I got up, walked through the morning constitutional, and prepared scrambled eggs with onions and smoked salmon with white toast for me and the doc. The scent of the food apparently woke De Broglie and he walked into the kitchen in thermal long johns.

"Oh my, smells good," he said, rubbing his eyes. "You've always been a good cook..."

"I guess," I said. "Always looked at it more like therapy...something I can do well, feel good about, and when it's done, I can eat it. Can't take credit for the pineapple jelly, though...that's from the hula girls at the airport."

"Better take your parka, Aaron," said De Broglie as we headed to the big telescope. "It's cold in the dome."

"I have my thermals on," I said. "That'll be good enough...and how about some hot cowboy coffee?"

"Good," said De Broglie. "You carry this." He handed me a small, impeccably machined olivewood box. It had important weight to it and a rich, worn patina. I held it up for a closer look.

"What is it?" I asked.

"The center of the universe, of course," said De Broglie.

I gave the doc a blank stare. "Oh, yeah?"

"My invention," said the doc. "With it I discovered the surprise I told you about. You will see...open it."

I reached into the box and withdrew a soft, felt pouch with something hard and oval inside. It had the feel of a metal alloy and the shape of one of those Easter eggs where you peeked into one end and saw a whimsical diorama, only this egg had no place to peek.

De Broglie hit the switch to open the dome's great bay doors. The meshing gears groaned like the awakening gasps of a great and wondrous beast. The roof parted to reveal the maw of space, the heavenly splendor, a sight without limit to vision or imagination.

"It *is* gorgeous tonight," I said peering into the starlit sky and imagining the entire facility hurtling through space to some cosmic destination.

"Ya," said De Broglie. "God is with us here...now...I never get over it." We walked the metal staircase to the scope and De Broglie motioned me into the driver's seat.

"Okay," said De Broglie. "Give me Beula."

"Beula?"

"Ya, Beula...my invention." The doc was impatient with excitement. "Named it after my first wife."

I took Beula from my lap and handed it to De Broglie. It was magnetic and made a confident, solid click when the doc snapped it onto the barrel of the big scope.

"What do you mean, *first* wife?" I was half kidding, vaguely seeming to remember that she had died early on. "Planning on getting married again?" I asked.

"No plan," said De Broglie. "But I am hopeful. I am always hopeful. I am not fond of spending my last years alone...you'd better start thinking about that, too, Aaron."

"Plenty of time for that," I said. "If it happens it happens and it will happen when it's supposed to happen."

"You think that's the way it works? I am sorry for you, my friend," said De Broglie leaning back on the railing with a stern face.

"What? What's the problem?" I said.

"I don't want what has happened to me to happen to you...too many lonely years with only memories to live on. It is sadness, my friend, sadness."

"Ah..." I brushed him off good-naturedly. "Let's look at the stars."

"Yes. Let's look at the stars," said the doc focusing on what was before us. "Now, Aaron, before you look through the scope, I must caution you. You are going to see in a way that no one has ever seen the heavens before—except me, of course. Your eyes may feel they are being tugged from their sockets. Don't worry. That is merely a sympathetic reaction to Beula's rendering of perfect clarity."

"Tugged from the sockets? Are you serious?" I said.

"Don't worry about it. It is nothing. Just don't be surprised."

"I'm already surprised," I said. "...and anxious...so let 'er rip!" I dialed in the coordinates to pi less pi equals no pi...our secret, silly code for the presets of our heavenly destination. De Broglie watched my chin drop. I was as still as a dead man with open eyes, transfixed and speechless.

"And what do you see?" asked De Broglie, knowing exactly what I was seeing.

"Um...well, um...it looks like three spheres revolving around a smaller star." I looked again and paused. "But I shouldn't be able to see..."

"Planets?" said De Broglie.

“Well, yeah, but we’re looking at, what? Two million light years? We’ve never been able to visually distinguish objects that far away.”

“Beula,” said the doc. “Distance does not matter.”

“Amazing,” I said, transfixed. “Wait! I was hoping for a closer look, and I’m getting a closer look!”

“Beula,” said the doc.

“Those spheres. They seem to be wrapped in a kind of silk filament....purple. What do you make of that?”

“I don’t know, Aaron. A mystery, don’t you think? Discoveries, particularly those as impressive as this, just lead to more questions.”

“Well, yeah...I have plenty of questions. To start with, how could those objects in Andromeda possibly look so close? As close as our moon through a kid’s telescope?”

De Broglie looked at me warily. “So you think that you are looking at two million light years away?”

“Well, yes,” I said with measured confidence, but wondering why the question. I sensed that the doc was pulling something, and I feigned a way out. “That’s all I’ve ever learned ...you know, Andromeda...two, two and half million light years away.”

“Then you also think there are galaxies billions of light years away...give or take a few?” asked the doc in a good natured taunt.

“I believe the most distant galaxy...yes...has been measured at eleven billion light years...that’s what the science books say.”

"Your books! Your science!" said the doc with well meaning sarcasm, but sarcasm nevertheless.

"What do you mean?" I asked.

"Think about it, Aaron. How can we measure stars eleven billion light years from an earth that your books and your science say is five billion years old?"

"My books? My science?" I was just this side of furious. "It's your science, too! It's Hubble, it's...it's evolutionary cosmology! Everybody knows that. What are you saying?"

The doc looked me in the eye and held his stare. "I would say that somebody is fucked in der head." He paused a moment and added, "and it ain't me."

"Oh," I said. "Now you're talking like a cowboy. And I know what you're going to say...that light eleven billion light years away hasn't had time to get to an earth five billion years old, right?

"How do you explain it?" asked the doc.

"How do you explain it?"

"You tell me first," said De Broglie. And, yes, it occurred to both of us at the same time that we were acting like two playground brats, and we enjoyed a long hearty laugh together. But I knew the doc was right. I was no genius, but this was about honor and integrity and all and...still...I was no match for De Broglie. It was my own ego. Then he hit me with another blow.

"Perhaps you would do well to follow Boyle's rule," said De Broglie.

"And what would that be?" I asked.

"Conflicts between science and scripture are either due to a mistake in science or an incorrect interpretation of scripture—Do you suppose I could have invented Beula if I used your science?"

"'Scripture?' I thought you were a scientist...What are you talking about?"

"I am talking about I am disappointed with you."

"Really?" I asked, trying to keep my chin up and scrambling for an answer.

De Broglie was downcast and remorseful as soon as the words left his mouth. "Aaron, Aaron. I don't mean it. You are a son to me, and I am like the disappointed father."

"Well, I'm sorry I disappoint you," I answered. I didn't know who felt worse, the doc or me, but it was easier for me to feel worse. I knew I'd more or less skated through my career, offering up the answers of the education machine, never challenging what it taught. What other world view would I assume than the one it gave me and to which I willingly acquiesced. I had no one to blame but myself, and it occurred to me that I was perhaps as dumb as Todd, the student I desired to humiliate in class because of my own inadequacies.

The tension began to dissipate and De Broglie finally lifted his head and looked at me. "It's a time thing."

"Huh?" I said, responding like the dummy I felt De Broglie thought I was.

"Yes, there are a lot of people like that these days," said the doc in an attempt to lighten the mood. "Everyone saying 'huh' and 'what'...like they were the only two words they know. I was just hoping you were not one of them."

"I am *not* one of them." I insisted. "Now, what do you mean, it's a time thing?"

"The light years," said the doc. "They are a measure of time not distance. That is the paradigm of Beula. And then there is the moon enigma."

"Okay, what's your version?" I asked like a kid awaiting further punishment.

"Oh, you had some teaching," said the doc with a dash of left over invective. "What? They just zip you through the learning mill, huh?"

"Huh?" I said again, mocking with some sarcasm of my own. "Watch out what you say...it might come back to bite you in the ass."

De Broglie smiled and, of course, I knew what De Broglie meant. As a younger man, I often delighted in what it would have been like to have experienced the wisdom and virtue of a classical education. Learning Greek, Latin, Hebrew. Reading Virgil, Horace and Plato in their original languages...like the founding fathers of the country I was born in and which modern culture, if you could call it that, was fond of denigrating. But the modern college and university systems were designed and run to support the conventional wisdom of today's retrograde human—everyone was entitled to higher education, whether they had the brains to grasp higher ideas or not. In this way, the educational establishment ensured that no one actually got a higher education. Sure, logic and rhetoric were offered, and I did well. But they were ten-week courses. The sum of my education and teaching experience to this point made me wonder why I ever pursued astronomy. I liked it better when I wasn't earning a living from it.

To De Broglie's point about the moon, I knew the fission, capture, and nebular theories, and that's all I had to know. I never had to study theories critically to earn the degree that allowed me into the world of false academia.

"Okay, what about the moon?" I was good with whatever De Broglie would have to say because, inside, I desired knowledge and I knew he could provide it.

"The theories are vain imaginings," said De Broglie. "None of them work. The Fission, because the moon is too big to pass through the Roche limit without breaking up; the Capture, because the orbit would be elliptical instead of circular; the Nebular, because gas doesn't compress in space...there is, in fact, no science that explains the moon's positioning. And if that wasn't enough, going backwards more than a few thousand years, lunar recession would have the moon and earth touching, colliding."

I realized that what De Broglie said was true. Of course, modern theories on how the moon got where it is made no sense. Yet, there they are...bald faced lies taught as fact, and I was one of the educational accessories to the crime, still teaching the nonsense. The recession problem was inarguable. At the current rate, earth and moon would have to have collided some few thousands of years ago. And how could the same science that says everything came into being at once and which is very sure the earth is five billion years old, continue to tell us that a galaxy at the end of the supposed known universe is eleven billion light years away. Something was wrong. I knew it, but I couldn't put my finger on it.

We walked outside into the crisp morning air, De Broglie in silence, and me pondering what he had said about time and moon theory and what I had observed with Beula. I looked at the sky and I looked at De Broglie. "It will take some time to wrap my head around all this, but I know that what I saw was pretty incredible, doc. I'm at a loss for words, really…but there it was, fascinating…intriguing."

Like the great teacher he was, De Broglie nudged me on. "How so?"

"Well, I know it sounds crazy, but it was somehow familiar…like I'd seen it before…almost like I'd been there before."

The first of the day's sun peeked over the horizon and glinted in our eyes. De Broglie looked away from the sun and turned to me. "Perhaps you have."

Chapter Ten

A Call in the Night

We returned to the observatory and I asked De Broglie if he wanted something to eat.

"I will munch on the trail mix," he said. I shook my head with a disapproving smirk.

"What's wrong?" asked De Broglie.

"Well, *trail mix.* Think about it. How can you eat something that sounds like it's who knows what off a hiking trail? Matted hair? Squirrel nuts? Toad dung? Let me make you something."

De Broglie thought for a moment. "Well, when you put it that way, I guess I am not hungry now."

"Aren't you going to get some sleep?" I asked.

"I will. I must figure some calculations for my secretary."

"Yeah…well…I'm going to hit the sack."

"Sleep tight, don't let the bed bugs bite," said De Broglie, and I left for bed.

I had just drifted off when the loud ring of the phone bounced off every hard, cold surface in the building. I sat up, dazed.

"It's for you," said De Broglie.

"Geez, I think I'm having a heart attack...who the hell's calling me here?"

"I don't know," said the doc. "But she sounds delightful."

I took the phone from the doc and said hello. It was Ann. "How'd you get the number here?"

"Aaron, that's the first you think? How I got the number? No, that's not important...I called to warn you about Pei Ling. She's on her way to China with a layover in Hawaii. I dropped her off at the airport a few hours ago and she's upset."

"Warn me?"

"Yes," said Ann. "Pei Ling mentioned that the professor wouldn't like any uninvited visitors."

"You mean she's coming here? Well...that's great. But what's the problem? What's she upset about?"

Ann paused with the pause of bad news. "Her father passed away."

I took a deep breath, at first in denial, and then gathering myself. "Well...It'll be fine," I said. "Don't worry about De Broglie. He'll understand. And don't worry about me."

"Okay, but, Aaron...understand what a profound loss this is for her. Prepare yourself for the unexpected."

"The unexpected?" I asked. "That sounds kinda creepy. What happened?"

"He drowned."

"Whoa," I said. "I could think of better ways to go." The unexpected? Seemed like odd advice, but given the tragedy and how people react, I thanked Ann, hung up the phone and didn't give it another thought except to tell De Broglie, who was shocked.

"Oh, my...that's terrible," he said. "I am so sorry to hear. I remember when I lost my father. But he was an old man. I am looking forward to meeting her, but wish it was under better circumstances."

"Maybe these are better circumstances." I said. De Broglie looked at me with a question mark. "You know... emotional and everything. You get to see the side of a person you don't often see."

"Ah, yes...true," agreed the doc.

"Well," I said. "I'm not going anywhere...I guess I'll just wait."

De Broglie looked at me with wonder and a blank stare that had an answer in it. "Take the jeep and meet her at the airport. There's only the noon flight. That's the one she'll be on."

"You know, doc...you *are* a genius. How much gas do we have?"

"Enough," said the doc. "You'll be going downhill."

Now I was thinking about De Broglie, and with the strain of these new events, *his* health was on my mind. "How about you...you going to be okay?"

"I'll be fine," said the doc, reassuringly. "I'll get some rest...and be fresh when she arrives."

I grabbed the car keys as a pang of sadness bolted through me...the realization that I would never get to prove to Pei Ling's father...if everything went well to the point of Pei Ling accepting my proposal of marriage...if I had any idea of doing that...that I would be a worthy husband to his daughter. And it occurred to me just how far I'd fallen for Pei Ling. I was getting way ahead of myself.

I filled the jeep with gas at the bottom of the hill and arrived shortly after Pei Ling's flight landed. She was sitting on a bar stool in the lounge in conversation with a guy in a cheesy looking Hawaiian shirt, Bermuda shorts, and white tennis shoes. Pei Ling was wearing a silk blouse as yellow as the morning sun and navy blue silk slacks held up with suspenders that...well...do what suspenders do for a girl like her. She saw me approaching and left the guy talking to her talking to himself as she jumped off the chair to meet me. She smiled and put her arms around me. "I'm so happy you're here, darling," she said. "What a surprise!"

"You, too, babe...who was that guy?"

"Oh, he was talking with me...until his flight, I guess."

"Hah," I said with a tease. "Of course he was talking with you...every guy in the place wants to talk with you. So how are you doing?" Pei Ling put her finger on top her head and uncharacteristically turned a pirouette. "Well, pretty good, from the looks of things...the way Ann described you, I thought you'd be a wreck."

"Ann?"

"Yeah...she called to tell me you were stopping here on your way home."

"Oh, that girl," said Pei Ling. "I'm okay, dear...really."

"I was worried I'd miss you and you'd already be on your way up the mountain," I said.

"If I hadn't had to wait for a taxi, you might have," she teased.

"Are you hungry?"

"A little, but we should talk," said Pei Ling.

"Well, sure...okay then, I could go for some food and a beer. I saw a quiet place just up the road on the way back to the observatory."

The South Pacific sun lay low on the horizon, casting long orange shadows over a lush landscape so green it was blue. We drove, holding hands in silence, and looked at each other when I could take my eyes off the road. We soon approached close enough to read the sign: Barney's Noodles-World Famous Saimen-Pork/Chicken/Seafood Saimen and Bottle of Beer $4.95. It was a small place with a half dozen stools perched on a worn, wooden deck and not a customer in sight. A mat of frayed palm fronds covered the overhang above the bar where a small neon sign buzzed the word "Pabst." The rest of the deck was open to the sky and scattered with a few worn out picnic tables and benches. Rickety poles were strung haphazardly with Christmas lights, adding an uncertain gaiety. An unsettling breeze rustled through the field of sugar cane adjacent to the deck and the plaintive sound of the swaying lights clinking against each other made the place almost eerie. Pei Ling sat at one of the tables away from the bar. I walked up, put my foot on the brass rail, and waited. Through a small, steamy window, I could see movement, and out came a stick of a woman with a face like a shoe. She was blonde and worn as the wood on the deck and I guessed as easily broken.

"Not very busy tonight?" I said.

"Nope. You won't be waiting long," said the woman. I couldn't tell if she was joking or angry.

I looked at the menu board and knew what I wanted. "I'd like the pork saimen and a Pabst...make that two."

"Big noodles or little noodles?"

"Big," I said, and called to Pei Ling. "You want a beer?" Pei Ling gave me her signature smile and a thumbs up and I turned to the woman and said "Make it three beers and no glasses." She placed the order through a slot in the bar back, and told me with a straight face that she didn't need glasses, either...that her sight was pretty good and that it must be the tropical air. I laughed and pointed to the shadow through the window. "Is that Barney?"

"That's Barney, alright...world famous saimen maker, father of eight by a previous wife, and a no good S.O.B." She seemed like the kind of gal who could pop off bottle caps with her teeth, but she used the built-in bottle opener and slammed the bottles down hard on the bar as Barney slipped the bowls of noodles through a hole and onto the counter. The subject of Barney seemed to be a sensitive one.

"No wonder they don't do any business," I said returning to Pei Ling and setting our order on the table. "She sure seems angry. But I guess you can't do much to hurt saimen...except pee in it," I joked.

With a weak smile, Pei Ling used her finger to help a noodle on her chin into her mouth. "She wasn't mad at you, Aaron...she's mad at life."

I didn't say anything for a moment, and with my brain in neutral I suddenly thought. "Your father! That must have been an awful shock." I stopped eating and put my arm around Pei Ling's shoulder. "Are you really okay?"

Pei Ling put her free hand on mine and continued eating her bowl of noodles with the other. "Yes. I'm fine, dear."

"Really?" I asked still doubting as she ate her last bite. "Well, when does your flight leave?" She was subdued and quiet, staring here and there with a vacant look, and finally turning to me. "Tomorrow at two...two in the afternoon...I hope you'll be with me."

She seemed to slip in those last words as though I wouldn't notice. I swigged the last of my first bottle of beer. "Oooh, that's going to be tough," I said. "I promised De Broglie I'd stay for the week."

"I know," said Pei Ling. She touched my face softly with her sensuous hand. "But I need you with me."

It seemed like one of those do or die situations, and her words melted me and I would figure a way to break the news to De Broglie. I put one hand on Pei Ling's thigh and grabbed the back of her hair with the other and kissed her on her mouth. "You sure know how to surrender," I said. "Let's get out of this dump." We walked hand in hand as we left and I looked over at

Barney's wife on the way out. "Tell Barney those noodles were great."

"They should be," she yelled. "He didn't pee in 'em this time."

I shook my head and told Pei Ling we didn't get a chance to talk about whatever it was that she wanted to talk about.

"It can wait, for now," she said. "That place was not the place."

We headed for the summit, stopping a time or two in the tropical zone. I was living dangerously, and I knew it, but I couldn't take my eyes off Pei Ling and swerved over the center line a couple of times. She said I better drive with both hands, and I reluctantly followed orders.

At seven thousand feet, it got cold enough to notice and I switched on the heater and grabbed a parka from the back seat for Pei Ling. When we arrived at the observatory, Pei Ling stayed in the jeep for a few minutes to listen to the last of some radio program she was apparently interested in. I went in to see what De Broglie was up to. The doc had just awakened and was running around in his skivvies, looking for a blanket and trying to fry eggs at the same time. For a moment, he looked like an escapee from a lunatic asylum. I nearly laughed out loud.

"Where's dah damn turner?" asked the doc, in a mild panic. "And dah butter."

"You mean the spatula?"

"Yah," said De Broglie increasingly frustrated.

"Forget it," I said. "I'll take care of the eggs. You get a blanket." We were some pair.

Pei Ling peeked around the door with a smile. I walked over to take her by the hand and introduce her to De Broglie. The doc extended his hand from out of the blanket with a welcoming grin. “So this is Pei Ling!”

Chapter Eleven

Getting To Know You

De Broglie, of course, understood what was happening, invoking the best laid plans rule...In matters of women, the best laid plans of men are put aside. We would all leave early...the doc back to his vacation home in Peru, I think he said, and me with Pei Ling for my first meeting with China.

At the kitchen table the following morning with Pei Ling, I reached for a single peanut that the doc must have missed during one of his middle-of-the-night forays, cracked the shell, and popped it into my mouth. “You know, I’m a little nervous about meeting your family. I don’t speak or understand the language, and where we’re going...well...I’ll be a real foreigner, that’s for sure.” I turned to Pei Ling. “What will they think of me with you?”

“They love me,” said Pei Ling. “They love me like they love my father, and they will love you, too.” A tear welled up in her eyes and fell on her blouse, and I went to her and drew her to me and held her as she shook softly with grief.

De Broglie, who had made himself scarce, walked in. "And how are you two love birds doing?" It was an awkward moment, but we needed to head for the airport, and it didn't matter. "I packed my bags and yours, too, Aaron." The doc looked at Pei Ling. "I would have packed for you, too, but I don't know you well enough for that."

"That's okay, Doctor De Broglie," said Pei Ling. "We don't have time to be embarrassed."

"Oh," said De Broglie. "Please call me doc or Emile."

Pei Ling thought for a moment. "What about 'uncle?'"

"Or uncle will be fine," agreed the doc. "Yes, I rather like that. Yes, uncle is good!"

"Okay, then," said Pei Ling with a smile. "Uncle!"

We made our way to the airport by shuttle. As we passed Barney's place, I pointed it out to De Broglie. "Ever eat there?"

"A couple times over the years." The doc seemed fidgety. "I never liked it...the people seem strange. But I was stuck. It's the last chance to eat before up the hill, right?"

At the airport, Pei Ling and I said our goodbyes to De Broglie. I was happy to see her and the doc embrace. I told the doc that we would see him soon and hoped that was the case. It was like saying goodbye to a father.

I had my window seat, and Pei Ling slept most of the way with her head on my shoulder. I never tired of it, though sometimes she seemed to whimper uncomfortably. I could only imagine what she was dreaming and felt anxious, unable to help. A short while before we landed in Chengdu, Pei Ling awakened, eyes sleepy, but able to manage a smile as she rubbed her eyes and looked out the window. “Oh, here we are in heavenly land.”

I wasn’t convinced, but I was glad we were on the ground. We got our bags and walked outside the terminal. I looked around at the busy crowds, the dirty streets, and the smoggy air. “Heavenly land, huh? How do we get to Guanxian, or however you say it?” Navigating the language was like chewing tough meat.

“We will take a bus,” said Pei Ling. “In Guanxian we will take a taxi to the village.” I expected the bus to be a dilapidated pile of bolts, but it was not. It even had air conditioning, and the road to Guanxian was newly paved and smooth as velvet. Looking at the flat, fertile landscape with the great mountains on the horizon I thought back home. The difference, however, was the activity and hustle of these people had an almost tangible sense of purpose.

“I like this place,” I said. Let’s move here.” Pei Ling stared out the window on the other side of the bus without responding. “I’m serious,” I said. “We could live a quiet, sleepy life in a small village. Money would go a long way here, right? We could by a farm and work the land.”

Pei Ling put her hand on my knee and smiled. “Aaron, sometimes you are so innocent to the world...I like that about you...well, one of the things,” she said coyly. “But China is changing, my love. Materialism is a wandering beast in the south. It will soon arrive here to devour the land and the people and you will hate it just like you hate what is happening at home.”

"Home? I don't have a home," I said in knee-jerk reaction. Still, I supposed she was right. "I don't know why I keep hoping...Anyway, I guess we have some hours to go?"

"Yes. You should take a nap, darling," and I did, laying my head in her lap.

It was the end of my workday at the Times and I was standing at the corner of Third and Broadway. Over Angel's Flight to the west, I could see the sun was setting into a deep, orange sky. A disturbed man in dirty, ragged clothes paced the sidewalk. His soiled bare feet and weeks-old beard confirmed his bumness, but this was not a man strung out on drugs or alcohol. I looked close and into his clear, sad eyes and took a start when I saw he looked exactly like me. I asked, "Is anything wrong?" He said he was trying to decide whether or not to kill himself. I said everyone needs to decide for himself.

"No!" the man demanded. "Everyone needs to be loved!" Tears began to form in my eyes as off to the side I saw a girl rush into the intersection and point skyward. She wore a white blouse and a red gingham skirt. Cars and pedestrians stopped in place. Those in cars got out and joined those along the street to fix their eyes on the girl. She was smiling at us all and we experienced a shared euphoria as we looked up into the sky where she was pointing. A bright pinpoint of starlight, so bright you could hear it as a high pitched searing sound, shown directly above. From it, the sky split into five wedges and peeled back from the star to the horizon to reveal a deep, blue heaven with many, many stars. We gasped in wonder as the sky repeated the movement and again peeled away in the same manner as before to reveal an even deeper midnight blue sky with countless stars. Everyone began to rise toward the star. All of us together and individually looked at

one another with total and complete happiness and an abandonment of what was happening to us. As we ascended from Earth, we were each spun in a kind of gauzy cocoon, white and fluffy like cotton candy. As our distance from Earth increased, my anxiety increased and I wanted to return from where we came from.

I awoke looking up at the creamy yellow ceiling of the bus. "How was your nap?" asked Pei Ling.

"How long did I sleep?"

"About and hour," she said, stroking my hair. "Did you dream?"

I looked into those bottomless, dark eyes of hers. "Yes, I dreamed—again." I took a deep breath, rubbed my eyes, and paused in my grogginess. I started to speak before I knew what to say. "You know dear, my life has taken quite a turn since I met you...lots of...well...weird things have happened." I sat up and took hold of her hand. "Who are you...really, babe? Do you know that I almost don't want to know? It sounds crazy, but I'm...I'm kind of scared." The voice inside my head asked me what I was doing. It wasn't the right place or time, but I had no control over this moment that moved forward of its own volition.

"Now you *are* sounding crazy, dear. Here, let me kiss you." And she did. "There's nothing to be afraid of, see? I am who I am...I am who you know me to be."

"There you go," I said. "...talking like that."

She looked at me in silence and turned up the short sleeves of her blouse with a small but what I thought a perceptible sense of nervousness. I took in her perfect form, her beautiful countenance, and her silken skin and wondered if I was the luckiest man in the world or the most cursed, and looked out the window.

"What do you see, darling?" she asked.

I saw the land rise into the distant foothills, and behind them the blue mist of far away places and the massive western reach of the Himalayas. "Are any of those peaks Mount Everest?"

"No, dear. Everest is farther west."

"Well, they sure are big. I used to think the Sierras were big, but they don't compare to this." I kept looking at the grand mountain range, transfixed. "You know, I wonder how many millions of years those mountains have sat there without a care in the world, the wind and ice and rain forming them into what we see now. How many generations must have lived and worked and died while that mass of rock just sat there, oblivious to the human story that took place in its presence."

My question was rhetorical, but Pei Ling answered me. "Oh, you are a poet, dear, but those mountains have not been there for millions of years."

"Oh, really?" I asked. "How long?"

Pei Ling answered matter-of-factly. "About two hundred generations."

I did a ball park calculation and mentally scratched my head. "Four or five thousand years? You're saying those mountains, those mountains...right there...are a few thousand years old?"

"Yes, about that. Probably a little older, because during the time of the patriarchs people lived longer."

"Patriarchs?" I asked. "What are the patriarchs?

Pei Ling corrected me. "*Who* are the patriarchs. The antediluvian patriarchs...the fathers of the generations before the Deluge. Ancient man."

"You mean the Flood? Like Noah's Flood?" I was curious. "Now, wait a minute. You really think those mountains are only four or five thousand years old?"

"I don't think it, dear," said Pei Ling. "I know it. It is the history of the world."

I turned back to looking out the window and thought for a while and remembered as a kid bits and pieces of what she was saying—the whole God and Bible account of creation and the history of Man's existence—but doubted them in high school and discarded them altogether as myths and legends by the time I got to college. I was sure science had proven them wrong. But I knew I had been no match for De Broglie, and though I had a feeling I was about to find myself no match for Pei Ling, I went down my dead end road anyway. "Oh, dear," I said. "It looks like I have to teach you about evolution."

"Evolution?" Pei Ling took on a nearly stern tone. "You don't have to teach me anything about it, dear. It's the cult of Darwinism. Tyrants use it to justify every ugly thing they do to the people they oppress. If humans believe they came up from primordial slime, you can justify doing anything to them, you know."

"Hmmm...the Flood," I said not realizing I was revealing more of my ignorance. "That's some misty legend from ancient history, isn't it? Where'd you ever hear about it? I mean, you know...in China?"

“It is our history, too.” Pei Ling seemed a bit miffed. “It is the history of the world,” she repeated.

“Sounds pretty important to you,” I said.

“Nothing is *more* important.”

“Well, yeah,” I said, sheepishly. “So tell me about it.”

“I'll give you an easy one,” she assured. “How was your Grand Canyon formed?”

If all the questions are that easy, I thought, I got it made. “By the Colorado River...erosion, erosion over millions of years and, man, is it big! You ever been there? We should go.”

Pei Ling wasn't biting. “Do you know how a river delta is formed?”

“Y-e-e-s,” I said nearly rolling my eyes. “Sediment...by sediment flowing with the water and settling at the mouth of a river. Deltas are formed from river sediment. In fact, the Mississippi River delta is so big New Orleans is built on it. We should go there sometime, too.”

“I think you are pretty sure of yourself, Aaron.”

“Well, I'm sure I know what I'm talking about.”

“You think so?” said Pei Ling. “Where is the Colorado River delta?”

I thought for a moment and then another until I ran out of moments. “That's a tough one...let me think...I know! Boulder Dam, it controls the flow from the Colorado. The reduced water flow prevents the sediment from forming a delta.”

I was asking for a knockout, and Pei Ling obliged with a haymaker. “The dam is recent, Aaron. Over those millions of years you talk about...Where's the eight hundred cubic miles of sediment from the hole that makes the Grand Canyon? Eight hundred cubic miles!" she repeated. "There should be a huge delta at the mouth of the Colorado."

"Well, now, that *is* a good one," I admitted.

"You're not ready," said Pei Ling as we pulled into a rest stop.

I stepped out of the bus, scratching my head over Pei Ling's challenge, and considered for the first time that maybe a lot of things I'd learned were wrong...or worse, lies.

Pei Ling took my hand and led me inside the rest stop. I'd been getting accustomed to surprises, and the rest stop was another one. It was modern with food vendors, knickknacks, gewgaws of all kinds, and a bank of telephones. When I called to see what was happening on the other side of the world, things there were not so mysterious. Ro had called on Ann, and all seemed well...maybe, too well.

"Oh, man," exclaimed Ro. "You should see this chick. What a thing you set me up with!"

"Calm down, you dipshit," I said. "You better be treating her right, you asshole."

"You kiddin'? I ain't leavin' this stuff."

"Oh, she's just a piece of ass to you?"

"You dick," answered Ro. "Whattya think, we're all poets or somethin'?" Of course, this is the kind of go-round conversation we always had. I knew Ro was treating Ann well. In fact, he was probably exceeding all expectations and treating Ann better than anyone I could think of. He was a master. I never knew his secret, but he had it, what ever it was. Women loved him.

"So what you callin' for?" asked Ro in a most delightful tone of disdain.

"Just wanted to see how things were going. She pay you the money?"

"No, you jerk...I wouldn't accept it. We had a big fight about it. I nearly hit her in the kisser."

"Oh, man," I said. "Are you drinking?"

"Of course I'm drinking."

"Oh, yeah, of course...I could go for one myself." Now I was wondering if I did the right thing setting them up. "Well, how is she? I suppose she's scared of you and blaming me for everything."

"I don't know," said Ro. "She seems okay. Here, you can talk to her your own self."

"Hi...Aaron?"

I was relieved to hear Ann's voice. "Yes, hi, how are you doing?" I asked.

"I'm fine...fine...we're having a wonderful time. He is so funny. Do you know what time it is over here? It's eleven. It must be tomorrow at three or four in the afternoon over there."

"Yeah, I think it's around that time." I wasn't exactly in a hurry to see where my next conversation with Pei Ling would lead, and I wanted to keep talking with Ann, but it seemed like they didn't want me on the phone much longer. Ro took over.

"Okay, you freak...that's enough talking with my gal."

"Yeah, yeah, you dick," I said.

Ro got serious. "So how's things over there?"

"Fine," I said.

"You sure?"

"Yeah...We'll talk about it later."

"Okay, man," said Ro. "Take care of that girl!"

"I will, and you do the same." I hung up the phone and looked for Pei Ling, but I didn't see her and returned to the bus. I was first on board, and noticed in Pei Ling's seat a small, leather-bound book. I opened it and figured maybe it was a diary. The pages were filled with tiny, handwritten Chinese characters, and I hadn't a clue as to what they said. I concealed it in my hands as the passengers formed a line to board the bus. I searched out the window for Pei Ling and spotted her with a bag of something. She stood out among the crowd, and I was relieved to see she was all smiles as she saw me through the window and waved.

"What did you get?" I asked when she sat down.

"A postcard for Ann. I think she misses home. And some candy."

"Well, I phoned Ro in there, and I don't think she misses anything, to tell you the truth. Happy as a lark."

"Lark?"

"Yeah, a bird. It's a saying we have. I guess larks are always happy."

"I'm happy, too, Aaron."

"Really?" I asked, doubtful after the stony conversation we'd just had.

"Yes. Really," said Pei Ling. I kissed her cheek and couldn't wait to reveal the little book I'd found.

She took it from my hand and examined it front and back and all over. "Oh, this is quite amazing. It is a book of imperial edicts. There are thousands of them, but this one is...let me see...the description of the beginning of our world. Where did you get this?" she asked in a very upbeat mood.

"I hoped you would know. It was in your seat when I got on the bus."

"It is not mine, Aaron, but this is perfect timing."

"Well, they say there are no coincidences, right?" I said.

"Who says?"

"They. I don't know who," I said. "It's just something we say."

"Who? You and who?"

"Oh for gosh sakes, just a saying," I said as it occurred to me that she was teasing again. "It means nothing happens by accident."

"Oh, yes. That is true. You found this book for a reason. Do you know what it says?"

"I can't wait," I said.

"Okay, let me read it...*The Earth was shaken to its foundations. The sky sank lower toward the north. The sun, moon, and stars changed their motions. The Earth fell to pieces and the waters in its bosom rushed upward with violence and overflowed the Earth. Man had rebelled against God, and the system of the universe was in disorder.* Sound familiar?"

There was no mistaking. This was a Chinese account of the flood that, as a child, I knew as Noah's flood. "When was that written?"

"Um, about 4,600 years ago," said Pei Ling. "A hundred years or so after the Deluge, when the Chinese calendar began to mark the beginning of the world in 2637 B.C."

"What year is it now on your calendar?" I asked.

"4695."

I ran the figures in my head. "Oh my gosh, this is all making too much sense," I said, and at once thought again about De Broglie's words on time and light years and distance.

"What do you mean, dear?" she asked.

"It coincides almost perfectly with our calendar! And I always wondered about, if man is millions of years old, why is there no written history older than about 4,500 years...like, boom, all of a sudden mankind got it all together?"

Pei Ling smiled at me with the smile of a successful teacher. "Yes, evolution is a rather dumb concept...but, good, dear, I think you're getting it. Maybe you *are* ready."

"Ready for what? You said that before when you were mad at me."

"I wasn't mad at you."

"But ready for what? What did you mean?"

Pei Ling smiled. "Andromeda. You will see. And don't worry about it...you are ready. I will make you ready."

I thought back to that first night with Pei Ling, about the incident with my leg and what I saw and how she kissed me out of my agony. Had it not been for the dreams, the times together, the passion, I would have thought her crazy. Or maybe I was crazy. But I loved this girl and crazy didn't matter. She was talking about what I'd only understood as theory. It looked good on paper. I considered that it was even possible. But actually articulating that it was possible, which is what I was taking her to say, was on the other side of my understanding. "Andromeda, huh? Isn't that about two and half million light years away? I just don't think we have that kind of time."

Pei Ling gazed out the window at an endless sea of sorghum. "Don't be funny, Aaron. You need to get serious. We don't need time. You've already seen Andromeda."

"What?"

"Do you remember when you woke up with the pain in your leg and I unwrapped your bandages? What did you see?"

My jaw dropped anticipating what she might say. "Well, I'm not sure. I'm still thinking it was a dream."

Pei Ling nearly glared at me. "I was there with you. Of course, it wasn't a dream. You saw another location in time...one outside the one you're in now...one a human senses, knows is there, but cannot quite comprehend it." I knew Pei Ling was exasperated with me when she said I needed to get serious.

"You mean about..." I swallowed hard. "...going to Andromeda?" I folded my hands on my lap and bowed my head like a coward to put some distance between me and the world.

Pei Ling ran her hand through my hair and kissed me. "I know, dear," she said. "I know. I didn't mean to be so hard on you. It is difficult."

Self-absorbed through this all, I'd completely forgotten what this trip was about, and I was ashamed and embarrassed. "Darling, do you know how ridiculous I feel? I am so selfish…I can't believe it."

"What?"

"Your father," I said. "You're going on so sweetly thinking about me when I should be thinking of you…I'm sorry, dear…so sorry."

"I'm okay, darling," she assured me. "Do not worry. I know where my father is, and he is happy you are with me."

Chapter Twelve

Ties That Bind

We arrived in Guanxian, a place where, from the stares of the children, I was apparently a stranger. A car pulled up that Pei Ling said was a taxi and we got in. We arrived soon enough at the village center, a small plaza that looked to be recently built with terra cotta tiles and a prefab fountain that looked like it could have come from the yard department of a big box garden supply store. Two very old people sitting on new benches looked like they intended to stay in place for the rest of the day. Peeking over the freshly planted landscape, I glimpsed a piece of the China I had imagined. A swift stream of icy mountain water flowed down a tree-lined aqueduct where in the western world would have been a street. On the walkways under the trees on each side of the aqueduct and the generations-old houses that lined them, clothes and colorful lanterns were hung out in a jaunty manner, and people were buzzing about, too busy to mind anything but their own business.

"This way, dear," said Pei Ling. "We can walk from here." Pei Ling was excited. I was nervous. I saw a flower vendor and asked Pei Ling to wait a moment so I could buy some flowers for her mother.

A couple of blocks from the plaza, we turned down a wide, shady street with a delightful park to the left and houses on the right. Gathered before a small entryway was a crowd of people some thirty or so in number. This must be Pei Ling's home, I thought, and I was right. What I assumed would be a somber crowd was a mix of young and old and little children, too, and they began to cheer and smile as Pei Ling came into view. "I guess they knew you were coming," I said.

Pei Ling, a little ahead of me, was caught up in recognizing faces in the crowd and smiling. I was fumbling with the suitcases when a teenaged boy ran to help me. He spoke English and said he was Pei Ling's cousin. I thanked the kid as he ran off with the suitcases to somewhere, and we made our way through the crowd and into an impressive, immaculate courtyard. The perimeter was lined with what I guessed where living quarters—small cottages with forest green walls, dark red trim, and azure stone roof tiles. Between the buildings and the courtyard were fastidious, tiny gardens of flowering plants, tightly trimmed bushes, and small shade trees. This was a wonderful place, peaceful, even with the crowd. My sense that this was the home of a rather well-to-do family was reinforced when I saw that an interior wall merely separated this courtyard, where an assortment of cooking apparatus had been set up with people busy preparing food, from another just like it on the other side where the crowd was moving to gather. I didn't understand what a happy hubbub of this extent was about, thinking it a bit overdone for a homecoming and definitely at odds with the recent passing of Pei Ling's father. As I entered the second courtyard, I assessed the crowd a little closer. Lo and behold, of all people, there was De Broglie, sitting alone, the bald top of his head shining like a beacon under a ray of sunshine shooting through the trees. He was smiling and clapping his hands with everyone else and looked straight at me. I was stunned, but glad to see a familiar face. Pei Ling greeted her people and I approached De Broglie. "What? What the...? What are you doing here?"

"Calm down, ol' boy. I'm glad to see you, too...I wouldn't miss this for anything."

"Well, yeah, but...what's that?" I asked. "Miss what?"

"Why, your marriage, of course!"

I almost fell over. "What? I'm getting married?"

"I knew you would take my advice," said the smiling De Broglie.

"Advice? I didn't take anyone's advice, and I don't know anything about a marriage...you knew about this?"

"Oh, yes," said the doc. "Pei Ling said it was a double secret big surprise...and asked that I would be here as your best man...if you'll accept me. What do you think all this hoo-hah is about?"

"Well, of course I accept you," I said, "but I thought this whole trip was to be with Pei Ling in her time of grief about her father and all...I'm totally in the dark on this."

"You didn't ask her hand?" De Broglie looked puzzled for a moment.

"Nope."

"Well, you should have," said the doc with a measure of well-meaning sarcasm. "You certainly are getting the better part of the deal."

"Oh, thanks a lot, doc." I knew De Broglie's point, and my spirits lifted thinking about this wonderful creature committing herself to me. I was watching Pei Ling move through the crowd, working it like a professional emcee. Turning our way, the wind seemed to come out of her sails as she morphed into a nervous amateur with each step closer.

"Excuse me uncle." She grabbed me from the doc to hurry me over to meet her mother.

"Uh, are we getting married or something?" I asked.

Pei Ling kept hold of my shirt sleeve and didn't say a word as she guided me to a woman who looked like she could be Pei Ling's older twin. I didn't know whether to extend my condolences for the passing of her husband, or plead my grateful thanks for her daughter, when I realized I didn't need to do either. We didn't speak each other's language. I offered her the flowers and bowed and smiled, and bowed and smiled again. She smiled, too. Everybody was happy.

The gathering was getting larger, and spilled into the first courtyard, where a thousand different scents rising from dozens of different foods wafted through the air, and the smell of sweet smoke from roasting duck and pork over an open fire could no longer go unanswered.

"I'm hungry, dear." I motioned to De Broglie to join us and we were directed to sit at the apparent head table.

Pei Ling grabbed my hand and looked at me with the saddest eyes I've ever seen. "I'm sorry I didn't tell you about this."

"You mean forcing me into marriage? Think nothing of it—just another day at the office." Pei Ling was relieved and I was glad to see her smile.

"Seriously, dear," she said. "Don't worry. Just go through with this today and you won't have to go through with anything else."

"You mean like fake it?" I asked rhetorically. "And not actually go through with the marriage? Not a chance. Think how disappointed De Broglie would be...let alone me. I've been waiting for you forever." Pei Ling grabbed my hand under the table with an I-love-you squeeze and said we could talk more about it later if I wanted, but I wasn't interested. The world was going on around me in spite of myself. Many drinks were raised in toasting Pei Ling and some seemed to include me, and even the doc. As twilight began to overcome the day, the crowd dispersed except for some hard drinkers who seemed to be having the time of their lives talking and laughing and becoming serious and laughing again. I was thoroughly enjoying everything and everybody and so was the doc.

"Well, my dear friends, I must retire for the big day tomorrow," said De Broglie. He shook my hand, placing his other affectionately on my back and moved to Pei Ling to kiss her cheek. I relished this sweet moment and remembered it for a long time, like her embrace of the doc at the airport. It's funny how things work out, I thought. After mom and dad died, I had no one who knew who I was anymore. De Broglie was beginning to fill that emptiness and, now, so was Pei Ling. A happy young girl showed the doc to his room and Pei Ling and I were alone at the table as the sun went down.

"I hope you're ready for bed," said Pei Ling. "We're going to do this again tomorrow in a bigger way after the ceremony."

"Oh, yeah," I said. "Where do we sleep?" I asked with conspicuous anticipation.

"We have separate rooms, dear. Mother sleeps in the main bedroom, uncle sleeps in father's room, and you will sleep in my brother's room."

"Your brother's? I remember you mentioned that he died some time ago?"

"Seven years," said Pei Ling looking down. "But don't worry. He is not a ghost. He is with my father in heaven and has no intention of returning to this world."

I didn't want to say any more on the subject, but it was a bit creepy to think I would be sleeping in what I guessed would be the same bed her dead brother slept in. "And where do you sleep?"

"I will stay in my mother's room. It will be a good time for us to talk."

"Sure, yeah...that sounds good," I said without a trace of conviction.

Pei Ling sensed my disappointment. "But I will come to you later in the night."

"That's fine, dear," I said glowing inside. "You should talk with your mother as long as you can."

Pei ling turned to me with a winsome look. “We have a lot to talk about, too.” I said I’d see her later and softly kissed her forehead. Pei Ling called to the little girl who showed De Broglie to his room and her cousin that helped me with the suitcases to show me to my room.

The cottage was empty of any reminders of her brother. It was beautiful, much larger than I had imagined—spick and span and free of clutter or personal mementos. There was an ancient, oil-burning lantern atop a small bookcase in which there were set some old books written, of course, in Chinese. Covering most of the wood floor was a colorful, rich looking rug of scenes denoting ancient China. The interior walls were lacquered in a deep forest green, and the windows to the courtyard on either side of the door were framed by shutters bearing the patina of dark, worn wood with a slight red tint. The faint, residual scent of a very appealing incense was evident. It must have been burned in this room not long ago, I thought, and it lent a warm, comforting feel. The boy showed me the closet and other appointments, and was especially excited to show me that this cottage was plumbed with its own running water and bathroom. “What is your name?” I asked.

“Li,” he said with a big smile. “My name is Li.” He pointed to the girl and said her name was Ching-Ching.

“Oh,” I said animatedly. “Ching-Ching is going to be rich!” The boy laughed as the girl turned to look at him and she laughed, too. “My name is Aaron.” I gave them each some Chinese money, how much I was not sure, but they seemed very happy and went on their way.

I put a flame to the lantern, slipped off my shoes, and settled down on the bed with a book De Broglie had given me, but soon found myself awash in thoughts of Pei Ling as I fell asleep.

"Dear?...Dear?" Pei Ling whispered as the door ever so slightly creaked open.

"Oh, hi, babe," I said in a lazy haze.

Pei Ling came in and gently closed the door and lay beside me propped on one arm and looking down at my sleepy eyes. She moved her head side to side so that her hair brushed across my face. "Are you too tired to talk?" she asked playfully.

"Oh, no...I'm fine. I'm awake."

"Let's get undressed and under the covers."

"Sounds good!" I said with hurry in my voice.

Pei Ling extinguished the lantern, as there was enough moonlight to navigate the room, and said she'd ready herself for bed. I would have some time on my hands.

I looked out the window into the night and the still, blue shadows of the courtyard and paused to take in this moment. De Broglie's room was catty-corner to ours and forty or so feet away. I saw through the trees a weak, yellow light appear. He must be up, I thought. I left a note for Pei Ling and made my way to De Broglie's quarters, passing by the remnants of the day's festivities, careful not to knock anything over or off the tables, and softly knocked on the door. "You okay, doc?"

"Yes, yes, I am fine," I heard him say through the open window as he walked to the door. De Broglie was surprised to see me and invited me in. "What? You have nothing to do at your place?" he chided.

"She's getting ready for bed," I said. "I looked out my window and saw your light flicker on and worried about you...it's late, you know."

"Say, you want a night cap?" asked the doc. "I have Suntory Old Whiskey. I picked it up on the Japan stopover. I'm too excited about tomorrow. I got up to get a shot...for relaxation."

"Yeah, I know what you mean. I can't really sleep, either...whiskey, huh? I'd really like to. But I better not."

"Sooo...this is a very nice place, yes?" De Broglie was as impressed as I was. "I thought my summer place was something."

"Yeah, very nice," I agreed. "This must be pretty upper class here."

"Maybe you will be marrying into money...or better yet, intelligence."

"You think she's smart?" I asked. "...not that I have any doubts."

"Very," said De Broglie. "And she's got the look."

"The look?"

"Yah, the look. You know the unique look on the faces of the ignorant?"

"I think so," I answered not knowing where he was going next.

"Well, Pei Ling *doesn't* have that look."

"Oh...yeah, well, intelligence is good." I changed my mind and asked the doc for a drink. We toasted and slammed down our shots in one swallow. "Wow," I said half responding to the whiskey and half to what was occurring. "This whole thing seems like I got caught up in some kind of unpredictable whirlwind."

"You getting the cold feet?" asked De Broglie.

"No, nothing like that," I said. "My feet are completely warm. I'm full speed ahead on this. I'm just confounded how things like this happen. You know, like the nature of the world...the nature of how things happen...the nature of existence, really."

"Leave the nature of the physical world to Eddington," said De Broglie. "Leave the nature of existence to Pei Ling." I declined a second shot as the doc poured himself one more, and turned to me with a serious look. "I think you ask too many questions."

"I think there are too few answers," I said.

"Hah-hah...touché on that one," said the doc. "Well, how things happen," began De Broglie like he was about to tell me a bed time story. "It all began billions of years ago when, by accident, nothing became something and finally a few millions of years ago, man popped up quite by accident and boom, here we are, mindlessly on our way to nowhere!"

"That's a funny one, alright," I said. "You know? I've been torn with the whole idea. That evolution doesn't seem to make sense anymore, and when I really give it some thought, it's actually quite preposterous."

"Of course, it is preposterous," said the doc sternly. "A bowl of sewage is set before the people and they eat it. You've been poisoned! It is why nothing makes sense to anybody. But let me tell you...the answers are there."

"Yeah. Poisoned," I said mildly feeling the effects of the whiskey. "How does a man who lives three score and ten, as the saying goes, expect to get his head around millions and billions of years?"

"He doesn't," said the doc. "My old friend Schweitzer, now there was a man...said it best...The greatest danger to modern man is his loss of rational thinking...and we have done it ol' boy! We have done it!"

De Broglie was almost jumping for joy. I didn't know if it was the booze or he was on to something or both. "Well, I don't know what you're so happy about," I said.

"I'm excited to be living during this time to see that what was written and foretold in the writings of the patriarchs is being revealed during our lives."

I was impressed with the doc's conviction and told him I would take what he was saying under consideration. For now, however, I realized I'd been gone long enough. "Well, doc, more on that later. I'd better get back."

"Okay, my friend, see you tomorrow." And De Broglie quietly and happily closed the door behind me.

Chapter Thirteen

The Obvious Becomes Evident

Pei Ling had relit the dim flame of the lantern and was sitting up in bed reading a book when I opened the door to her smile. "You're still up. Sorry I took so long, babe. You know those conversations with De Broglie..." I kissed Pei Ling, got ready for bed, and slipped between the covers, lying down with my face to the window so I could look outside. "De Broglie says you are smart."

"I am not dumb," said Pei Ling.

I turned over and looked at her. "You're the smartest person I've ever known, darling. When De Broglie says someone is smart, they are smart." I thought for a moment and added, "You know, I bet he's never said that about me."

"You are a son to De Broglie," said Pei Ling. "A son who is also a friend. Such a relationship could not be unless you had intelligence."

"What do you think is the difference between smart and intelligent?" I asked.

Pei Ling put down her book and removed her glasses. "Smart is learning things. Intelligent is knowing what they mean."

"Very good," I said. "I'll buy that."

"My advice is free to you, dear," said Pei Ling.

I laughed. "I think De Broglie must have meant to say you're intelligent."

"And I'll buy that," said Pei Ling. "It means a lot coming from him."

I looked out the window at the peaceful moonlit courtyard. "Really, though, there's no good reason for De Broglie to think much of my brain power."

"Why do you say that?" asked Pei Ling.

"I can't get my head around his work or world view…and I've had trouble with yours."

"Has he told you about his work?"

"Well, no," I said. "I just know about his invention. I have no idea how it works. It's almost embarrassing…although… although …" I said almost visibly thinking. "…between De Broglie's preaching about light and time, that imperial edict that showed up on the bus, and you teasing me about the Grand Canyon, maybe I'm beginning to understand."

"See how intelligent you are as you get nearer to life's end?" said Pei Ling in a wry, dry tone.

I turned from the window to face Pei Ling. "You know something I should know?"

"Of course not, dear," said Pei Ling quick to explain. "The end of life as we know it...our new life begins now. Together."

"Oh, if that were true, darling," I said with self-deprecation. "If only I could live up to my end of the bargain. Do you know that nothing in the whole wide world around me makes sense anymore except you?" Pei Ling kissed me sweetly and I kept on. "I had a talk with De Broglie about evolutionary cosmology. I tried to defend myself, the ideas I had learned..." I stopped and didn't know what else to say, but Pei Ling drove me on.

"And?" she asked.

"He got sarcastic. He was making a point. Read me the riot act about evolution and what an inane idea it is and all and that I was...well...fucked in the head."

"He said that to you?"

"Yeah, but in a good way....it's sometimes hard to understand how we talk to each other. It's the same with Ro. You know...we call each other every name in the book, but all in good fun. But, really, I think he could be right, and you, too. I've just never known anything else."

"What do you know?" asked Pei Ling.

"Seriously?" I had the greatest desire to spill my guts and hoped she knew what she was in for.

She moved closer and laid her head on my shoulder. "Yes, dear...I want to hear everything."

I looked out the window again at the moonlit sky. "I'm angry, dear."

"About what?"

"About everything and with just about everybody."

"Everybody sometimes gets angry, dear."

"Well," I said. "I'm really angry. Ugly angry. At this world and the people in it. Am I the only one who can't make sense of it? If God really made everything, he messed up, too. I mean, what is it with people?" I sat up on the edge of the bed. "The useless activity, meaningless conversations, obsessions with nonsense. Stupid music. Stupid movies. Perverts and degenerates. Pop culture. Schools graduating the ignorant. In De Broglie's day, a Nobel Prize meant something. Now they're awarded to anybody...there's a prize, in fact, for every fool who comes along. I mean...everyone's doomed and they're running around like everything's okay! ...everyone congratulating themselves on the great work they do...trying to fool everyone with double talk...I mean, if everyone's doing such a great job, wouldn't the world be a better place?" I stopped and turned to Pei Ling. "I guess I'm done...for now."

"You know something darling?" said Pei Ling. "You're not part of that world...not anymore. *We're* not part of that world. De Broglie, too. We hate the world and the world hates us. The world hates good because the world is evil...it hates the light because the world is dark. All those things you said. They are the evil in this world. Do you know that everything every one does is motivated by the desire to reunite with what we are separated from? Of course, most people don't even know they are separated from anything, but they know there's a void and they attempt to fill it, nearly always choosing darkness over light, evil over good...because it's easy. For people like us, it is no wonder everything here seems like a mistake. You are starting to make sense of this world, dear…it is no surprise that you are angry."

I felt great comfort in Pei Ling's words and thoughts, some of which I was aware and had been for most of my life but, still, there were the missing pieces. "Well," I asked. "What *is* everyone separated from?"

"If I thought you didn't know, you would not be here."

"You mean, God?" I asked. Pei Ling looked at me like what's the problem. "Well, I have some problems with that. Why did God let everything turn ugly in the first place?"

"He didn't," corrected Pei Ling. "Man caused it. The instructions were clear from the beginning."

"I didn't screw up anything," I said. "Well, I've screwed a few things up, but I didn't mean to."

"None of us means to, dear. But we all have, and we can't do anything about it. Good intentions are not enough to keep things going. This world has been running down and wearing out since the beginning…like all machines."

"Oh," I said. "That almost sounds like good news."

Pei Ling didn't reply, but asked a question. "Haven't you noticed how people are getting uglier?" She looked for my reaction and smiled. "Finally, you laugh."

"Well, I can't argue with that. I remember as a kid…my mom noticed some slob eating ice cream at the county fair. 'He sure is ugly' she said. Dad responded without skipping a beat. 'He's not alone.' I couldn't stop laughing. And now that you mention it, yeah, I could swear the adults I knew as a kid were better looking than now...you know, generally. And they certainly seemed smarter. Could it be?"

"You're not crazy," said Pei Ling. "The human race is becoming evermore genetically defective over time...as the world is running down and wearing out, so is the integrity of the human gene pool."

"Not that again," I said.

"Only if you want to make sense of it..." said Pei Ling.

"Well, now, wait a minute," I said. "I thought we were evolving? How can we be running down?"

"We are *devolving*," said Pei Ling. "Mutating upward is impossible. Mutations are *losses* of genetic information, not additions, and over time, they build up. It is why people are living shorter lives, overall, and suffering from new diseases. Remember the patriarchs I was talking about? They lived for hundreds of years. After the Deluge, the gradual corruption of our genetic code increased with each new generation and our life spans have been getting shorter...most of the world dies in their twenties and thirties, you know.

"Look what's happening...Western society has betrayed its founders...marinated in the labor of its forefathers, and have squandered their inheritance like spoiled children. Think about it. Your bellies have become fat while most of the world starves. Your questions of the day are rights for those who deserve none, the arrogant myth that humans can change the course of history or even the weather, celebrating self with self desecration, worshiping the creation instead of the creator..."

"And the many ways to wear a baseball cap," I added, but that didn't stop her.

"...Yes, and the media who fancy themselves as truth tellers tell lies. The sewer line from Hollywood to home fuels evil, raises up the least deserving and the least able, praises all manner of deviant behavior...demeaning decency and promoting destruction of all that is good." And then she took a breath and said "and there is more that we need to talk about."

"You've got to be kidding," I said. "You're not done?"

Pei Ling looked at me with a tired smile. "Yes, I guess I am. We need sleep for our big day tomorrow."

I was wide awake and couldn't let go without one more question...one more question out of many about the truth of what Pei Ling was now speaking. "What about the idea of a needy God, the selfish God who created man for himself?" I asked. "If he's so great, he wouldn't need anybody."

Pei Ling got up to extinguish the lantern's flame for the final time that evening and slipped into bed close to me in the darkness. We kissed a soft kiss and wished each other sweet dreams as we lay down with our backs to each another. Pei Ling reached over to put her arm on my side. "God," she said, "doesn't need you. You need Him."

Pei Ling had no trouble sleeping and nodded off in no time. I was keyed up about all the things we talked about and knew my knowledge was pretty lame. Her words rang true, alright, and I instinctively knew she made sense of the nonsense. The moon had shifted across the sky and poured its soft, blue light into the room. I noticed a Bible on the bookshelf by the bed and reached over to get it, remembering how I'd prayed as a child and stopped when I grew older because I learned from the secular world that such behavior was childish.

I was not feeling very confident right now, however, and it seemed like a good time to reconsider. I opened the book to no particular page and in the moon's light found Paul's letter to the Romans:

For the invisible things of Him from the creation of the world are clearly seen, being understood by the things that are made so that they are without excuse...they glorified him not as God, neither were they thankful; but became vain in their imaginations, and their foolish hearts were darkened. Professing to be wise, they became fools...God gave them up to their own uncleanness through the lusts of their own heart...and they changed the truth into a lie.

Talk about the world around me, I thought. And I lay down as Pei Ling's faint, sweet scent took me to dreamland.

Chapter Fourteen

A Formidable Challenge

If anything was traditional about our wedding, it was almost everything. I was left alone after a group of women knocked on the door and spirited away Pei Ling in preparation for the ceremony. A man who introduced himself as "Nelson" arrived soon after in an impeccable Western style suit to announce that he was Pei Ling's uncle and that he had wedding clothes for me. I was relieved they didn't include one of those garish red and gold nightgown get-ups with the matching head dress and gold ornaments that I had seen somewhere or another. I was outfitted in a traditional but classy looking black and gold ensemble, a style that might be best described as "formal ninja." I guessed that the outfit was something previously worn to a wedding or other important event. At any rate, it was a relief from what could have been, and after Nelson showed me the particulars of the clothing, he left to work the arriving crowd. I sat alone in the room awaiting further instructions. It wasn't long before De Broglie showed up, dressed exactly like me. "Where'd you get that outfit?" I asked.

"From Nelson," said De Broglie. "What do you think?"

"Stop with the modeling, would ya?" I said. I knew the doc was trying to lighten the day, and he did. I laughed like crazy, as a matter of fact, and asked him what he asked me. "So whattya think...just wait around for instructions?" The doc had no more ideas than I did and agreed.

I heard a short burst of the unmistakable bangs, clangs, and drumbeats one hears in Chinese opera and looked out the window. "Hmm...they must be practicing." De Broglie and I almost ran into each other pacing the floor. "I hope something happens soon. I'm going crazy confined to quarters."

"Is there a lock on the door?" asked De Broglie.

"No," I said. "But I don't know what else to do but wait." At that moment, Li knocked on the door and brought in a tray and towels, two cups, and a bottle of thirty-five year old cognac. I gave Li a tip as he left us with a smile and the goods.

"Geez, this stuff looks pretty good," I said.

"It is good!" said De Broglie. "I wish I had a cigar."

"I'm glad you don't...we'll stink enough with this on our breath." We'd had a few pops when Nelson dropped in to direct us to the ceremony. It was a good thing, too. A shot or two more, and the doc and I would have been in trouble. Nelson showed us to our seats just below a stage filled with flowers, burning incense, various Chinese things, and an altar type arrangement along the back. Nelson dashed into a room behind the stage and emerged with a big smile. Had he not been wearing a gold and white Chasuble with three Latin crosses emblazoned down the center, I would have thought he was going to introduce a group of acrobats, so great was his enthusiasm. I turned to De Broglie.

"I guess he does *everything*. You think he's legal?" The doc was puzzled. "To perform the marriage," I added.

De Broglie answered with a shrug as a lady at a piano near the back of the assembled crowd began to softly play the most beautiful rendition of a piece that was familiar, but which I didn't know.

"Ah," said De Broglie. "Rhapsody on a Theme of Paganini. Beautiful. Just beautiful."

A mysterious, unknown-to-me melody followed, and Nelson motioned us to turn around. Gorgeous in anything, Pei Ling shone like an angel dressed in a simple white silk gown with gold accents, and a small gold tiara atop an intricate hairdo that looked like it took a long time to do. De Broglie and I joined Pei Ling and I took her arm from the man who was standing in for her father. Pei Ling whispered to me that he was Li's and Ching-Ching's father and we all faced Nelson with proper sobriety. Nelson spoke in Chinese, but told me when to respond in English, and in a few short minutes, we were presented to the gathering as man and wife. I was certain this was the happiest day of my life, and supposed that it was just me, but a low, brief rumble shook the ground and the earth seemed to shift on its axis ever so slightly to let me know that a very special promise had just been made and that I'd better not let anyone down.

The musicians were hell bent on showing what they had and the traditional Chinese music banged and clanged in a furious up-tempo beat. Pei Ling led me through the required dances while De Broglie got help from several ladies. There were many toasts, kind wishes, and apparent great stories, based on the tears and laughter that I saw on the faces of the celebrants.

De Broglie told me he was leaving the next day and I said I didn't know our plans and that I'd check with Pei Ling and maybe we'd be leaving with him.

"I've had a wonderful time, Aaron," said De Broglie through the din. "So proud to see you off and into your new world. Whatever your plan, I hope to see you back in the states or at my summer place sooner than later."

The food, the clanging, the banging, the drums, the good wishes and the smiles faded into the background and Pei Ling and I ensconced ourselves in our room to change clothes and have a few minutes alone. "What now?" I asked. "Off to Andromeda?"

"Almost," said Pei Ling.

"You mean I haven't graduated yet?"

"You remember when I said you needed to get serious?"

"I am serious, dear," I implored.

"You are a willing student, but I am not yet sure that the foundation has set."

I admitted that I was yet to be fully formed, as the saying goes, "but how do I do that?" I asked. "We have a honeymoon to go on and all. Aren't you and your mother and relatives expecting me to whisk you off to some romantic place?"

"Don't worry about that, dear. My plan for you is what is important. Besides, you've already had your honeymoon with me," said Pei Ling with a smile.

"Hah!" I laughed. "Don't make it sound like that's all I want from you. I want to take care of you and do all those things I just promised."

"I know what you want," said Pei Ling. And I wondered, did she really, because, truthfully, I probably didn't know what I wanted myself. "I will stay here," she said. "And you return to study...it won't take long."

"What is it that I'm going to study?"

"The ancient writings."

"But don't I need you or someone to help? I mean, so I know what I'm doing?"

"The invisible teacher comes to the sincere mind," said Pei Ling. "You will see."

"I'm afraid it's going to seem like one big fairy tale to me, darling," I said, but I trusted her.

"Fairy tales! Delusions! Those are the realities of the atheist, dear, and you are not that. Here, take this." Pei Ling handed me one of the books I was to study and asked me to turn to a certain page.

"The atheist and evolutionist ask us to believe that we came from nothing and nothing created a mind with reason and logic, nothing without intelligence created understanding and comprehension, nothing without morals created complex ethical codes and legal systems, nothing without conscience created a sense of right and wrong, nothing without emotion created art, music, and drama."

Of course, I said to myself and assured Pei Ling. "I see what you mean." I opened the door with the intention to go see what De Broglie was up to and looked back to Pei Ling. "I'm anxious, though," I said. "I'm not going to like being apart from you and I'm going to miss De Broglie, too...geez," I remarked.

"...from the happiness of these past few days to saying goodbye to my most favorite people."

As it turned out, De Broglie was standing just outside coming to see what we were up to and overheard me. "Think of it as 'aloha'...until next time."

"Thanks, but that doesn't help," I said.

"I will be in Los Angeles for a week or so before going home," said De Broglie. "And you?"

"Pei Ling's staying here a few days with her mom. I have orders to study before setting up housekeeping with my..." I looked at Pei Ling and smiled at De Broglie. "...wife."

"Yes, indeed!" said the doc. "Um...study?"

"She won't see me again until I get an understanding of the scriptures...you know, as she put it, knowledge we know but which is not recognized by the earthly mind."

"Aha!" said an animated De Broglie. "Yes, I can imagine, with our talks and my observations...She is, after all, one of us, and soon you, too, will be."

"Well, that sounds like a strangely strange way of putting it, but, yes, I suppose that's where all this is headed. The problem is where will I study? I just can't see going back to my same old place."

"I know," said De Broglie.

"Somehow, I knew you would," I said.

"My place on the Urubamba," said the doc. "You'll have the place to yourself. It's quiet. It's beautiful."

"The Urubamba River?" I asked. "In Peru?"

"The Sacred Valley...yes," said De Broglie.

"Ugh" I groaned. "Any other time that would sound great, but the last thing I want is another endless flight to the other side of the world where when I get there, I'll still be on the other side of the world. Nope, and as a matter of fact, I just thought of it...Vegas!"

"Vegas?" said a horrified De Broglie. Pei Ling raised her eyes, too. "No!"

"Yes," I said. "It's the perfect existential city...surrounded by people, yet alone in a place buzzing with activity where nothing happens...and the food's great."

"Why," said De Broglie, stroking his chin. "I never considered that...yes...Vegas...that might work."

"Can we take a rain check on your invitation?" asked Pei Ling of De Broglie's offer of Peru.

Strangely, I thought, the doc's eyes seemed to peer over Pei Ling and to me. "Of course...whenever you need me...whatever you want."

Pei Ling turned a curious eye to me. "Las Vegas. Are you sure?"

"Positive, dear," I said.

De Broglie and I made it back to Chengdu, mercifully sleeping most of the way, thanks to the doc's back up stock of whiskey. And back home I went, thinking, wondering, excited with the most potent desire to know the truth and to know that the words of Pei Ling and De Broglie helped point the way. No wonder words were important. Wasn't the world and time *spoken* into existence? I got a room on the top floor of one of the better hotels in Vegas and lucked out with a corner suite that looked to the northeast and the most spectacular mountain range—a sparse, spare landscape of purple and pink that shown in the last light of evening as a soft, incandescent glow. Higher in the sky hung the astonishing full moon reigning over an indigo panorama. It was all far too vast and too deep to put into words, I thought, when an other-worldly presence made itself known high above the bright lights of this, the sinful city, and I realized I was becoming a new person, breaking the iron paralysis of Man's relative morality, situational ethics, and worship of earthly things. It occurred to me that truth existed, it was pretty straight forward, and life began to make sense for the first time since I was a child before I was ruined by the world.

And so I studied, and on the journey to who I was, I realized that almost everything I'd ever learned was a lie. The truth came to me as surely as Pei Ling said it would. By the act, the process, the reading and studying, the concepts and ideas of the wisdom of the ancient writings began to take hold and became part of me, and I came to know that modern churches, ignorantly or willingly, were apostate, accommodating the desires of Man over God, replete with do-it-yourself salvation plans, false doctrines, and marketing plans to attract the evil. There was no denying that leaders in this earthly realm had defaulted on their responsibility. The world was led by dead monarchs ruling over a dead earth with dead ideas. I thought back to earlier conversations with De Broglie and Pei Ling. That almost everyone on the planet was and believed they were mere animals of higher intelligence instead of creations in the image of God made sense. As the ancient writings declared and foretold, Satan is surely the ruler of this planet. How else to account for evil? How else to account for people going about like everything's normal or even good in an evil world? Pei Ling said a failed world is a comfort to the failed mind. And though the world was beginning to make sense, I still did not know who I was, and lay down to a dream that seemed to try to tell me.

It was on the street near the park at the end of Main Street. People were gathered, looking up into the evening sky, and I walked down to see what the excitement was about. It was dark enough to where everyone was a silhouette, though as I got closer to the crowd I could make out individual faces and saw that one was my father. He pointed to a place in the eastern sky and I looked up, but before I saw what everyone else was looking at, I noticed two small moons in the western sky and realized I was not on Earth. I turned to what everyone else was looking at...high in the heavens I beheld a city at night, in which I could see the smallest details—traffic, pedestrians, even the trees on the city streets stirring in a light wind. It appeared to be a miniature because it seemed close, but I realized it was a symbol. The real city lay beyond. I told my father, "Yes, that's where we're going." Others overheard me and everyone was happy. As we were about to rise toward our destination, a menacing drone helicopter was maneuvering as if to aim at us and it was---it started shooting massive bars of steel at us to interfere with our ascent to the city in the sky. For reasons unknown to me, I knew how to disable the threat by physically capturing and throwing the weapons of steel into a nearby wall. The helicopter observed my capability and gave up and left, and we rose into the heavens.

Vegas has a way of wearing out fast and I wanted to go home. I fumbled around to call Pei Ling in China to find out if she'd be back when I returned. After one technological misstep after another, I knew I'd gotten through when I heard an angel's voice.

"Hello?...Hello?...Darling?"

"I miss you," I said.

"Me, too, darling."

"Everything's good." What a stupid thing to say, I thought, but I had my "assignment" in mind. A girl in love wants her man to profess his love, and I told her again and again and told her once more.

"I cannot wait to see you, darling," she said.

They were the sweetest words, and I could see Pei Ling's smile in my mind as she said them. "When are you coming back?" I asked.

"Friday."

"Okay, day after tomorrow," I said with great excitement. "Where's our first night at home?"

"I think you like my place, dear...you have the key."

"Sounds great, baby. I'll get things together and see you at your place...our place." I said.

"Okay, darling," she said and spoke an air kiss over the phone. "Moo-wah."

I walked into the apartment where I first came to know Pei Ling. I looked around and tried to get a feeling that I belonged, but I still felt like a stranger. It would take some time to get comfortable with the idea that this was my place, too. Everything seemed to be in order, and I noticed that the plants looked particularly healthy. I guessed Ann probably had a key and had been watering them. I picked up the phone to call her.

"Aaron! Are you back?"

"Yes. I'm at Pei Ling's place. I'm going to move some of my things in today and be ready when she arrives."

"It's great you got married!" said Ann.

"Oh, yeah, I wasn't sure you actually knew about it. I was going to wait until Pei Ling got here to tell you herself, but I guess she called you with the news."

"No, I got a postcard from her."

"You did? Hmm, I thought she must have called you after the wedding."

"No, a postcard...anyway, we have something to celebrate. Let's have dinner on Saturday...you and Pei Ling and me and Ro."

"Yeah, sure, that would be a lot of fun. How's everything going with you and Ro, anyway?"

"It's going great, but we're not married yet."

"Well, maybe Saturday I can get him to hurry things up," I joked.

"I'll be fine, Aaron. It is my problem."

"Well, we'll see about that...anyway, Saturday. It's going to be great being all together."

"Yes, see you then," said Ann. "If you talk to Pei Ling, tell her I cannot wait to see her!"

"Me neither," I said saying good-bye and hanging up the phone. I moved my essentials to Pei Ling's apartment and gave notice on my own. It was a busy day. I showered and turned into Pei Ling's glorious bed early and reminisced, her scent still in the pillows. I was going over the events of the past week or so in my mind and remembered Pei Ling getting that postcard for Ann and I guess mailing it soon after that rest at the rest stop before we got to Guanxian. Did that mean she told Ann we were getting married before she told me? I guess it didn't much matter, but that was sure taking a chance. Or was it?

Chapter Fifteen

A Celebration of Sorts

Ever considerate, Pei Ling took a cab from the airport and arrived late Friday afternoon. We took some time doing what one would think two people like us would do after a few days apart, and I told her about the plan for Saturday dinner with Ann and Ro.

"I got the best table in the house, and we have it for as long as we want," I announced.

She was delighted. "Where are we going?"

"I'm not telling, and I didn't tell Ann or Ro, either. I just made sure they could stay all night."

"All night? All of us?"

"In separate rooms," I assured her. "I splurged, dear. Think of it as our U.S. wedding reception. We're even taking a limousine. I can't bear driving all the way to frisco and back."

"I thought you hated that place," said Pei Ling.

"Only the retro-grades that walk the filthy streets. Aside from the bums, meth freaks, and the people who think they're normal, we'll have safe harbor in the hotel and in the restaurant." She melted as I had hoped and I knew I'd done the right thing.

The four of us were escorted from the limousine by two doormen who took our bags and checked us into the hotel. We freshened up and met for dinner where the maitre d' showed us to a semi-private corner, isolated from the rest of the dining room by extra distance between tables. I wasted no time in ordering champagne. Ro turned up his nose in his inimitable way and announced that champagne was for sissies.

"Okay," I said. "See how many glasses you drink before you're on the floor, jerk." The girls were accustomed to our banter and knew it was all in edgy fun.

"Oh, man, this tastes like crap," said Ro. "What is this stuff anyway...I can't pronounce it."

"It's not Taittinger's, but it's not junk. I can't pronounce it either...voe-click-oh or something like that," I ventured.

"I love it, darling," said Pei Ling as she spoke in what sounded to us like perfect French. "Veuve Clicquot."

"Yes," said Ann. "Veuve Clicquot."

Ro and I enjoyed playing foils to the girls and I ordered a bottle of Taittinger's just to be ornery. "Okay, which do you like better?"

Ro took on a very serious and studious look. "I think the 'click-oh' is fizzier."

We were starting to have too much fun and I moved things along asking about appetizers and entrées. Ro and I got back to basics with 'Jack 'n' gingers' and a bottle of a library Cabernet. Pei Ling was finishing her savory custard with chunks of lobster, Ann, her abalone almandine, me with my black cod and shrimp, and Ro with his grilled rib-eye, when I seem to have changed the tenor of the evening. "Don't you think people are uglier now than they used to be?"

"You are," said Ro.

"Well, that goes without saying," I said. "But really, people are uglier, overall, than they used to be...like during our fathers' age...I swear, people were better looking then...and nicer."

Ann slipped a bone off Ro's plate and started chomping on the few vestiges of meat like there was no tomorrow. Ro wasn't doing badly himself, chewing on some unrecognizable but apparently edible delight.

"I think you're right, dear," said Pei Ling. "There's a scientific basis for it. 'Mutagenic accretion.' The number of genetic mutations increases in each successive generation."

"Mutagenic accretion" was new to me. "You mean like my father's generation had fewer mutations than mine and his father's generation had fewer mutations than his? And the generations after us will have more mutations than us?"

"Exactly," said Pei Ling. "It affects the entire body. Since mutations are losses of information, as a group, we're all dumber than our parents."

"Well, they'd be delighted to hear that!" I said. "No wonder schools have had to lower standards."

"Yeah," said Ro. "And why I see all those damn bumper stickers with 'My kid's an A student'...how can there be so many 'A' students these days?"

"Not everybody's dumber," said Ann entering the fray.

"Of course, not," agreed Pei Ling. "But as a group mankind is dumber and uglier than preceding generations."

"There are always exceptions," I said acting part moderator and part peacemaker. "Look at us...I take that back. Look at Pei Ling and Ann." Ro took another bite out of something and raised his thumb in support of my self-deprecating humor. The girls looked at each other and it was the first time I'd heard that precocious giggle since Pei Ling and her girlfriends came up the stairs that night at the Cuban International.

More seriously, Ro opined about the phenomenon being somehow associated with racial differences. I'd been studying. I knew the answer to that one. "Oh, you're a Darwinist. I'm not. Mankind came from one father and one mother. We're all one race."

"Oh, man, you believe that?" asked Ro.

"What do you believe? Evolution?"

"Yeah," said Ro quaffing a last gulp of cabernet. "Everybody knows it's true."

"Well, you can believe you came from a monkey if you want to...and in your case, maybe you did."

"Alright, wise guy," said Ro. "Douché." Ro gave me the evil eye. "You mean you believe that Adam and Eve stuff?"

“Let me put it this way,” I said. “The ancient writings...they’re history written by real people—primary witnesses to the events and people documented in them. Your evolution is theoretical fantasy, speculation, and bad science and you talk about it like is fact! Clinging to flawed ideas in the face of the obvious is what crazy people do. What do you think a sane person would believe? And let me tell you, like almost everyone who claims the ancient writings are poetry or some half-assed excuse for beliefs that make you feel comfortable—and I’ll bet you another night like this one—you’ve never opened a Bible and you’ve never read one sentence of it.”

“That’s because it’s BS,” said Ro.

“Ah, the great circular reasonist,” I said. “You don’t know anything about it but you *know* it’s BS...another sign of a crazy person!”

Ro went on to explain in a more temperate tone his view about all of us being on a prisoner planet or something or other, which I graciously entertained for a few minutes. “And if there is a God, why does he allow all this suffering?”

“That’s already been written,” I said. “You caused it...we caused it...a couple of liberals screwed up everything for all of us just after the beginning. Just like now...our people screw up everything, can’t do anything right and we have the temerity to call it progress, for crying out loud. We’re obsessed with pathetic, little rights...rights to abort troublesome babies, rights to stick a dick up some guy’s hairy ass, rights for reprobates to not be offended. I’m sick of all a ya...oh, one more thing...they call a fetus a blob of tissue...stupid a-holes....what else is it going to grow into?”

"You got a screw loose, dude," said Ro.

I looked at him with a half smile and raised my hand. "And so do you...why, I oughta..." And I put my hand down and lowered my voice. "I don't...I can't...go through life oblivious. I look at passersby, people standing on the corner, people doing their everyday thing, and I know I'm separate from them—a species apart. How can these people keep doing what they do like everything is fine? There is something very wrong with a society fixated on the comfort of the criminal, that justifies their evil deeds...a society that so easily adapts to the dress and manner of the profane, where fame is mistaken for intelligence and notoriety for leadership. All the signs are here...arrogance, depravity, and ignorance have finally reached critical mass. I don't know how anyone can deny it." I thought for a moment and looked at Pei Ling. "Actually, I do know...a failed mind is at home in a failed world."

My enthusiasm for conversation was dwindling as surely as the universe was winding down, and Pei Ling knew it. She affectionately grabbed my hand under the table and, as if on cue, the waiter stopped by to solicit dessert. We ended the evening as good friends always do and headed for our rooms.

Pei Ling and I followed Ann and Ro to the elevators. They were holding hands and I was glad. He deserved a good woman and some happiness, I thought.

"Hey, man," said Ro over his shoulder to me. "I don't know about your gal, but mine likes to sleep late. Let's get an early coffee."

"Yeah," I said knowing Ro was not an early riser himself. "How about the bar at eight...in the morning. Late enough for you?"

"Cool," said Ro.

We'd been in our rooms for a few minutes when the phone rang. It was Ro. "Hey, butt hole, how much did these rooms cost?"

"A lot," I said. "But nothing compared to our friendship."

"You mean the value of our friendship," said Ro. "So, okay, before you start blubbering, get your ass to bed and put it to good use...and thanks, you jerk. I appreciate it."

"I know you do," I said. "...but not as much as I like being able to do it for you...now shut your pie hole and I'll see you in the morning."

Pei Ling slipped into bed while I was on the phone and I couldn't wait to join her. "Back in a minute, dear. Let me powder my nose."

"What do you mean?" she asked.

"I mean I'm going to get ready for bed, but that's not what 'powder my nose' means."

"Then why did you say it?" she asked.

"Are you giving me grief?" I teased.

"Are you sad?" she asked.

"No, I'm not sad. I'm the happiest guy in the world...be right back."

Bed never felt so good. I took a big stretch and relaxed with my arms falling around Pei Ling. We turned off the bedside lamps as the light from the night sky and reflections from the streets below lit the room.

"Is Ann going to do to Ro what you've done for me?"

"I hope so," said Pei Ling.

"He's a hard nut to crack," I said and thought about a nugget of information I'd learned in Vegas. "You know, I ran across something interesting...Cain, who killed Abel...well, he and his descendants were inventors and discoverers of things having to do with earth. Things like building and constructing things. He and his people built the first cities, including the first city, Enoch...and you know what I say about cities."

"What do you say?" asked Pei Ling.

"When people get together, bad things happen," I said. "Once, a friend showed me a book with pictures of people dressed up in their Sunday best at a lynching in the 1800's. They had a kind of glassy-eyed, dazed look. There were whole families there...husbands and wives and little kids. Like it was some kind of pleasure outing. And there were two black men hanging from a tree, limp and lifeless as only dead men are limp and lifeless. I was horrified by the picture and thought about it for a long time, even now...that there were such people walking the streets, people I see everyday, today, entirely capable of doing the very same now as then. There is no evolution. There is evil and good.

"But, you know, I never pick up on the obvious, now that I think about it. And it has to do with what you said about Darwinism as justification for heinous acts. Few mention the subtitle of Origin of the Species... 'The Preservation of the Favoured Races in the Struggle for Life.' Darwin's theory holds that darker skinned people were degraded and closer in kind to the apes. I mean, he actually states this...is there a theory better to justify the most evil works imaginable against other humans?"

"Well," added Pei Ling. "His theory was supported by modern history's most evil men and embraced today by the evil among us now."

I took a frustrated breath in agreement and went on. "Anyway, Adam's third son, Seth, and his descendants, were inventors and discoverers of things having to do with astronomy, the heavens, mathematics...things like that. What do you think?"

"You *are* a man of the heavens, dear," said Pei Ling.

"Well, I keep looking for some connection," I said. "But I don't find any. I mean, it seems like there is a theme throughout humanity...like some people are predisposed to earthly, evil things, and some are predisposed to heavenly, goodly things."

"Isn't that direct enough?" asked Pei Ling. "Isn't it obvious? There are humans and roaming beasts that appear to be human."

"Well, that would explain a lot," I said. "So...so...are we really different from the beasts in disguise?" Pei Ling looked at me despairingly.

"Okay," I said. "Okay. Yes, I get it. We are, I would say, some mid-range being, like higher than the beasts and their human counterparts, but lower than the angels."

Pei Ling gave me a big kiss. "I like rewards," I said. We said our goodnights and I rolled over into a deep and dreamless sleep and I awakened early to call Ro.

The hotel bar was an odd place for us to meet. It seemed out of sync with guys who worked for a living, a group that Ro and I liked to think we were in. Trendy and upscale, it was a watering hole for heavy drinkers, power player businessmen, and small time politicians. Cold and spare in the fashion of the day, it was as sterile as a dentist's office. On the upside, the bartenders served the best drinks in town and the place was empty. I saw a familiar face from last night's dinner working behind the bar and apologized that we were early birds. He put down the glass he was polishing and welcomed us with a smile. "You're not early...you're really, really late." He put out some snacks. I ordered a martini. Ro justified a Bloody Mary in his effort to eat more vegetables.

"So you didn't take the money?" I asked. Ro looked puzzled.

"From Ann," I said.

"Oh, yeah...nope. Didn't take the money," said Ro swirling his glass and looking down at the bar.

"Well, I guess that's pretty decent of you...of course, she wanted to give it to you because she needs to get married. You gonna marry her?"

"Whattya think? I'm a whore? You think I can be bought for ten grand?"

"Hell, yeah," I said.

"But, you know?" said Ro. "I just might. The problem is she's talking the kinda stuff you talked last night...not forcing it on me or anything, but I have a feeling more is on the way."

"So what's the problem?"

"Hey, man. I gotta be me."

"Well, looking around, being one's self isn't all it's cracked up to be...what's so good about being you, anyway?" I asked.

"Let me think on that," said Ro.

"Maybe you just don't like going beyond the here and now, though if she's saying anything to you like Pei Ling has to me, it is the here and now that we don't see...the reality that you know is as real as right here, just beyond your grasp."

"Yeah?" Ro stared at me with a smirk, holding his empty glass in one hand and popping a smoked almond into his mouth with the other.

"Yeah," I said. "And I think you're considering it."

"I might be," said Ro.

"One more, gentlemen?" asked the barman.

"You certainly use the term loosely," I said, "but, yes, according to your kindness, one more...for both of us."

"*He* can have one more," said Ro. "I'll have another, but make it a Jack neat with a water back...lots of ice."

"Done with your vegetables?" I cracked, and pressed him about Ann. "So you're considering marrying her, right?"

"Let me ask you something." Ro looked as serious as I've ever seen him. "You put her up to this?"

"What?" I asked, incredulous. "I told her you could use the money, yeah. And you could and you knew about that. I was a friend pushing something along that I thought would help."

"Not that," said Ro. "The religious thing."

"What religion? There's no religion."

"The anti-evolution thing?" Ro insisted. "That's not religion?"

"I'm not anti-evolution," I said. "I'm pro-fact...it's called science. You need to tear away from the fraud that you've let determine your truth."

"And what's fraudulent?"

"Geez," I said feigning frustration but excited that Ro was at least interested. "Okay, I'll go over it again...media, pulpits, politics and academia...the 'MPPA.'"

"You think it's purposeful, or ignorant?"

"Sorry you asked," I said.

"Why?"

"Because now religion must come into it, and I know you have a panic attack anytime that's mentioned."

"Try me," Ro offered.

"Okay, but I'm really going out on a limb for you...if you study the scriptures you'll find the current state and the future of this entire world is all in there. Now listen, I'm not going any further with this...you'll need to find out for yourself."

"Why?"

"I don't know enough about it, myself," I said. "I'm still learning...but you're as interested in the truth as anyone, aren't you?"

"So what that everything's messed up?" said Ro. "I know it is and I'm good with it."

"Maybe you'd be interested in knowing why," I said. "It makes some sense of life when you understand why things are the way they are. But that's just me...if you don't care, I'm not gonna beat it into you."

"No, wait," said Ro "You got a point there, and if you comb your hair just right, no one will notice," he quipped.

"I mean, really," I said. "Doesn't your gut keep reminding you that everything is out of order?" I asked taking another swallow of my drink. "Yeah, of course it does," I said answering myself.

"Another drink?" asked Ro.

"Nah," I said. "Two of these zingers puts me smack in the comfort zone...but feel free, dude. I'll ride shotgun."

"Hmm," said Ro, pausing. "There's something going on with you...something weird. Like you're changing, or something."

"Because I'm not drinking another one?"

"Yes and no," said Ro looking at me askance. "I'll pass, too."

I was anxious to get back to Pei Ling, anyway, and told Ro as we headed for the elevators that I was going to stay another night and that he should take the hotel limo back to San Jose and put it on my bill.

"Helluva guy," said Ro. "Helluva guy."

"The least I can do," I said.

Pei Ling was in the shower when I returned to the room, and I fidgeted for something to do. I walked to the window overlooking the streets below. I looked around the room. Television, magazines, newspapers, room service, spa treatments, touring the wine country, shopping—Nothing intended to provide entertainment, pleasure, or information, even another drink, was anything I wanted. Pei Ling emerged with outstretched hands and put her arms around me. Talk about a light in my life.

"We're staying another night?" asked Pei Ling.

"Yeah, I thought it might be fun. Actually, though, I don't have a plan. There's really not much I can think of or want."

"Guess what a Chinese girl wants?" Pei Ling asked playfully.

"What's that?" I asked.

"Noodles!"

"That's a relief!" I said. "I'm glad someone knows what to do."

The sky was overcast and cold fog stirred through the streets. I grabbed Pei Ling's hand and slipped it with mine into the warm side-pocket of my coat. There were not many people out, but there were some. We came upon an old woman who had lost most of her hair, but who must have been beautiful to look at when she was young, and we passed a smartly dressed twenty-something girl with a grotesquely deformed foot that must have reminded her daily that she wasn't like other women her age, and I saw a teenaged boy with a disfigured face, perhaps wondering what it would be like to look like other boys. I couldn't bear the image of these sorrowful burdens and looked up at the gray sky with a broken heart hoping the tears seeping into my eyes would return from where they came, but to no avail, and I wept. Pei Ling put her cheek to mine. "I know, darling, I know."

I drew from my jacket a luxurious paper napkin that I'd stolen from the hotel restroom and wiped my face. "This is ridiculous," I said, embarrassed. With a forced laugh I said how good those noodles were going to taste. "What," I said blowing my schnoz, "can you possibly find to love in this blubbering fool?"

"Everything, darling." And that was all I needed to hear. I sobbed freely, remembering her in my arms when she shook with grief about her father. Pei Ling held me closer. "You confirm who you are, darling. I cannot help that I will love you always and I will never let you down or leave you...you worry about that...I know."

I felt like a child. "You're something else, babe...Okay, enough," I said, and gathered myself in the cool air that soon erased the visible signs of a sorrowed heart. We were somewhere on Washington around Kearny when we decided to turn into the first restaurant that was open. It was a good choice. Hot and steamy, it was as cozy as grandma's house. Entering through the door, we were faced with a tall, steep flight of stairs. To the left, an old woman was in the kitchen mixing and whipping and flailing as to prepare and concoct all manner of soups and dumplings and noodles. She looked at Pei Ling and motioned us up the stairs. A skinny, handsome man of forty or so met us at the top of the flight with a big smile and menus and sat us by the second floor window with a view to a narrow alley across the street. Colorful even in the fog, it was like an old Hong Kong street scene out of The World of Suzy Wong. I turned to the menu board, handwritten in Chinese characters. "That's why I brought you along, dear," I said jokingly. "I don't have a clue what it says, but it must be the good stuff."

"Oh, yes," agreed Pei Ling. "Let's see...whole lobster in ginger and garlic...and so cheap!"

"Sounds good," I said. "How about some dumplings, noodles...maybe some winter melon soup? I'm really ready for this."

"It won't be your last meal, dear," said Pei Ling.

"I know, but sometimes you have great expectations about the meal and the place...And you might go to the very same place another time and it's just another meal, and sometimes, just sometimes, on that very rare occasion, it's unforgettable. I'm thinking this might be unforgettable."

Pei Ling smiled. "Like my first dinner with you. That was my unforgettable."

"Really?" I said. "You know...it makes me think...there must be some mysterious goings-on that allow such times...some sort of combination of who knows what..." Pei Ling looked at me and I knew what she was thinking. "I know, I know," I said. "There are no coincidences."

The man who showed us to our table came over to take our order. As Pei Ling and the waiter briefly bantered in Chinese, she pointed to the menu and looked at me with a frown. "No abalone."

“No problem, dear,” I said. “I’ll eat anything but chicken feet and bladders.” The food soon arrived in a series from downstairs on a dumbwaiter and we began feasting on small plates of steamed buns with crispy duck and plum sauce, winter melon soup for me, wor wonton soup for Pei Ling, shrimp and chive dim sum, stuffed tofu, Chinese broccoli, and a most heavenly dessert of velvety tofu floating in a warm, sweet, simple broth. We never got around to the lobster in the holding tank and let it live for another day and another customer. It was a glorious meal. I couldn’t remember one as wonderful. “Unforgettable,” I said.

The waiter brought the bill along with some sliced oranges and fortune cookies. “There’s a custom to this,” said Pei Ling. “The cookie that points to you is the cookie with your fortune.”

I insisted Pei Ling open hers first. “What does it say?”

“Prepare for travel, soon,” said Pei Ling.

“Hmmm...that missed the mark,” I said.

“Maybe,” said Pei Ling.

“But you’ve just returned from traveling,” I said. “Anyway, okay, let’s see what mine says...‘Something you lost will soon turn up.’ Oh, well, that’s meaningless enough.”

“Are you sure?” asked Pei Ling.

“Let me think. Nope,” I said. “I haven’t lost anything that I know of...well, no objects or things or anything like that....oh, oh, I know. I lost my innocence a long time ago, but I don’t expect that to turn up anytime soon,” I joked. “When I think about it, though, that may not be exactly true. Ro said something weird. Something about me changing. And I suppose I have...but that's because of you, dear."

"Not me," said Pei Ling. "Well, maybe a little bit," she teased. "It's your recovery from ignorance."

"Hah," I said. "I couldn't avoid it, being drummed into me and everyone else who watched the tube, went to public school, or read a newspaper. My parents, God love them, were influenced over the years, too, though I couldn't ask for better. Did you know they sent me to parochial school?"

"Parochial school?"

"A private religious school. And boy, were they strict. Right and wrong were never so well defined. I talked my parents out of it when I was ten because I wanted to go with the neighborhood kids to the public school. It seemed big and impressive, but it wasn't long before I realized there was something wrong. I discovered I was smarter than anyone else, but I also learned to take the easy road and dumbed down to be like everyone else."

"But you are smart, dear," said Pei Ling "...and Ro was right. You have changed. Your rediscovered knowledge has changed who you were to who you are. And, now, finally you are able to see this world as it is."

"Then there's hope," I laughed. "Let's make an escape!"

Pei Ling excitedly took my hand and looked at me intensely. "We will, dear! Our cookies were right!"

Chapter Sixteen

The Big Mistake

It was easy settling in with Pei Ling. I loved seeing her asleep in the early morning when I got up, and I loved missing her when we were apart. She was like no one I'd ever known, and that was saying something. I wasn't proud of that, and wished she was the first woman I'd ever been with. But, well, there is life...a life I'd been rambling through, marveling how anything worked at all.

We were half way through the summer break and I used most of the time in research and study, realizing that if I was going to teach anymore, it wouldn't be the same. Understanding of time, space, and existence had new meaning. If I didn't share the same goals, values, and hopes as other people before, I certainly didn't now. 'Cosmology 101' would be a whole new story, well, the one it always should have been. I also knew that the university wouldn't put up with me for long once they got wind that my lectures might be based on reality written once in the ancient writings—not written, rewritten, and written again with every new textbook that comes along. It was no wonder the knowledge of the students of a few years ago conflicted with that of last year's students and would with next year's graduates. For all their efforts and spinning, nobody really knew what they were talking about, and it occurred to me that modern man is every bit as confused or more than those who experienced the confusion at the tower of Babel.

But this morning was a beautiful morning. The clear, bright sun streamed through the leaves of the towering, front yard oak, and through the windows along the east side of our apartment and into the kitchen. I sat at the big, yellow table as Pei Ling washed her hands over the sink and gathered some cooking tools.

"Poached eggs, dear?" Pei Ling offered to cook breakfast, and she was anxious to try some American standards on me.

"Sure, babe," I said. "...on buttered white toast."

Pei Ling looked at me as I raised my eyes above the newspaper. "I know how you like it," she said with a smile.

"So what are you doing today?" I asked.

"One of my classmates...she's rehearsing for a piano recital this morning and we are going for lunch."

"At the university?" I asked.

"The basilica...better acoustics."

"Wow," I said. "How'd she manage that?"

"She goes to church there," said Pei Ling. "You want to come?"

"Nah," I said, and thought of the irony of church goers who, however well meaning, hadn't a clue that the church age was over as the pulpits filled with apostates as surely as the scriptures said they would. "But enjoy the time with your girlfriend…I'll be here studying." I saw that Pei Ling was at a critical point in cooking and asked if she wanted help retrieving the poached eggs from the water without breaking them.

"No way, dear," she insisted. "I can do it."

Breakfast was perfect, of course, and Pei Ling left. I was enjoying the solitude when there was a knock at the door. Not good, I thought. I was looking forward to this time alone. I opened the door, and it was Ann with a downcast face.

"You look like a horse," I said joking.

"A horse?" asked Ann, shocked. "Really?"

"Yeah. A long face…like a horse, ha ha." It did not go over well, but I asked her to come in. She looked around and I took her coat.

"Is Pei Ling home?"

"She's out for a few hours," I said. "What…uh…what happened?"

"Ro," said Ann. "I cannot marry him."

"Hmm," I said, cautiously. "Maybe you should talk about it with Pei Ling."

Ann brushed against me on purpose, I thought, as she took a seat at the kitchen table. "I can tell you, Aaron."

"Well, I'm not exactly your mother, you know."

"But we are friends…good friends," said Ann with a pout. "I'm comfortable with you."

I sat down facing Ann in a bright stream of sunlight. "Don't get too comfortable, dear," I said out of empathy, followed by words I had no intention of saying. "I might do something I shouldn't."

"What do you mean?" asked Ann.

I looked at her uncomfortably frustrated and half joking. "Do I really have to say it?"

"What do you mean you might do something you shouldn't?" she asked.

"Okay, why did you touch me when you sat down? This is a big room. There's plenty of space," I said.

Ann paused for a moment with barely a hint of a smile. "I don't know what you're talking about."

"Okay. I give up," I said.

"Oh, don't give up, Aaron," said Ann. "Don't ever give up."

"Do you know what I'm talking about?" I asked, more frustrated by the minute.

"Not really. Do you know what I'm talking about?"

"Okay, great. Then we're both nuts," I said, breaking into laughter with Ann joining me. We composed ourselves, and I made an effort to hear out Ann's dilemma. "So what's the deal?"

"He wants me to do things...do things I don't want to do."

"Yikes," I said having a sense that it was some weird, sexual proclivity of Ro's. "I guess that's quite a shock...I mean, you don't seem like a girl whose had much experience in that department...which, of course, I'm saying is a good thing."

Ann bowed her head, embarrassed. “I haven’t had any experience at all!”

“Really?” I asked.

She was silent for a moment. “No. Never.”

I thought she was going to cry. “I can’t believe it. What about that time I called from China? He was going on and on about it and it sounded like you two were having the time of your lives.”

“He made it up,” said Ann. “He was joking. We were having a good time. But nothing happened with us...we just talked and drank...he didn’t do anything.”

“Oh, well good,” I said. “See, I told you he was a great guy.”

“But then he told me the rules if he married me...things I don’t want to do...”

I stopped her. “Are you sure he wasn’t joking and maybe you didn’t get it?”

“You think he should joke with me on that?” said Ann.

I felt stupid enough, and took a big breath. “Sorry...I guess the problem’s pretty obvious...to everyone but me.” I searched to say the right thing. “You know, there was a time, before I met Pei Ling, I thought of you.” As soon as the words left my mouth, I knew they were wrong, but I kept on, and they elicited all the wrong responses.

“Oh, you should have,” she said touching my hand. There was no mistaking her intent, even for me. “I would have been fine with that...I would have loved that,” she said.

My words certainly brought new life to the moment. Ann smiled warmly, still holding my hand, and I let her keep holding it. She looked at me with a girlish grin. “Oh thank you, Aaron. You are so sweet.”

I tenderly slipped my hand from hers, sensing this conversation was headed for a train wreck, and feeling I had already cheated on Pei Ling.

“Aaron?” asked Ann. “Are you okay?”

“Yes, yes. I’m fine.”

“Well, I have a lot on my mind,” said Ann.

“Yeah, I can imagine,” I said.

Ann looked at me with resolve. “Aaron, I’m tired...could I rest here for a while? I don’t want to go home right now...can I relax here?”

“You mean like take a nap?” I asked. “Lay down?” It seemed so transparent.

“Yes,” said Ann.

I didn’t exactly like the idea, but what else could I say? “Well, sure...I guess that’s fine. Do you want the bed or the couch?” Ann chose the couch and I brought a pillow and a blanket from the bedroom, and returned to the kitchen to make fresh coffee and read.

“Aaron?”

I looked up from my book. “Yes?”

Ann had a big grin on her face. “This must be your pillow.”

“Now how would you know that?” I asked.

"I can smell you in it."

"Impossible," I insisted with a measure of embarrassment. "They were just washed the other day."

"Don't worry," said Ann. "It's good. I like it."

"I know what you're doing, Ann." I said. She didn't answer and buried her face in the pillow and fell asleep.

I was miffed with Ann's interruption, at first, mildly flattered later, and finally, saddened. I felt sorry for her and wished I could do something about nothing I could do anything about. The complications of life are many and I thought about why things don't often work out well or even at all. I was concerned about Ro, too. Perhaps the whole thing between Ann and Ro was a misunderstanding. Even so, there was nothing I could do about it or should. They were my friends, and I could only offer myself in whatever way I could. Right now, that was suffering Ann's difficulties.

When Pei Ling returned in the afternoon and saw Ann asleep on the couch, she stealthily walked over to me and whispered. "Ann is here."

I whispered back. "I know."

"Why is she here?"

"I'll tell you later," I said softly.

"Did you have sex with her?" asked Pei Ling. I burst out laughing and Ann awoke, rubbing her eyes to see what happened.

"What time it is?" asked Ann.

Pei Ling told her it was three o'clock, and I didn't correct her. It was earlier.

"Oh, I slept for a long time," said Ann. Pei Ling took her hand and they went into the bedroom and talked for what seemed like forever. When they emerged, Ann's eyes were puffy from crying and she came out wiping tears from her face and attempting to compose herself.

"I am so sorry, Aaron, for bothering you," whimpered Ann.

I got up and put my arm around her. "Anytime you need us, we're here," I said looking at Pei Ling and turning to Ann. "Hey, are you going to be okay?" I asked.

"I'm fine," said Ann, as Pei Ling saw her out with a brief embrace and closed the door behind her, facing me.

"I hope she'll be okay," I said.

Pei Ling was sympathetic, but realistic. "She'll have to be okay. Maybe she learned something."

I looked at Pei Ling. "I know I did."

"Really?" asked Pei Ling. "What?"

"That it is hard to be a man. That with one small error I could have lost everything. I could have lost you."

"What do you mean?" asked Pei Ling.

"Well, Ann being here...vulnerable...and, well, she is attractive and sweet...and...geez...what am I saying?"

Pei Ling stopped me, taking my exasperated face in her hands and forcing me to look in her eyes. "Oh, darling," said Pei Ling. "If it is possible, I love you even more."

"I suppose it is possible," I said relieved and lightheartedly taking her into my arms. "Right now I want to...I want to...be closer to you than I ever have, if that was possible." I fumbled to explain as I saw Pei Ling thinking with a puzzled look. "I mean be super close...but deeper, more profound. Close to you through principle, righteously, faithfully...something like that," I said running out of words.

"Such closeness produces children," said Pei Ling smiling.

"Well, yes, that's possible, too." I answered. "But not exactly what I had in mind...at least right now. I know this sounds crazy, but I want to somehow meld with you to become another person, a new being separate but one."

"Like children," teased Pei Ling.

"Okay, yes and no," I went on. "A child is made from you and me, but I'm thinking a whole being transformed from you and me as we are rather than a child resulting from our biology...a science fiction kind of thing, but not science fiction...I'm trying to explain."

"I understand, dear," said Pei Ling. "Do you remember what I said about our motivations in this world coming from our desire to reunite with what we are separated from?"

"Yes," I said.

"Well?"

"I'm not talking about God, if that's what you're thinking," I said.

"No? That being, that person made from the two of us together...that longing cannot be satisfied in this world. But there is no emptiness in Andromeda… from where I've been and to where you are on your way."

"Okay, let's hash this out…"

"Hash?" Pei Ling asked. "Corned beef hash? I've heard of it before."

"No…discuss," I said. "Let's *discuss* this…I have discovered certain things in the ancient writings that lead me to believe I understand what you are saying. First of all, the knowledge in the scriptures is supernatural. One moment I was reading stories, the next I was reading history. By study, learning, and understanding we become new creatures, separate and apart from the human beasts roaming through a world that is…too much with us, to borrow the words of Wordsworth." Pei Ling looked at me approvingly as I continued. "What makes me mad, disappointed, angry…is that the supernatural side of our nature is so obvious, yet so totally ignored, even denied. And I've missed it all these years."

"Do not be too upset, dear," said Pei Ling. "This world is Satan's. Remember, it was given over to him after the Fall. Nearly all the people in it are deceived by him…but the wisdom of the scriptures was written for us who can receive it…be satisfied for the day that we are among them."

"You know," I said. "My thankfulness is beyond words, darling…beyond earthly expression…now how about some corned beef hash?" I was kidding, of course. We headed to a non-descript saimen shop in the golden triangle, where the noodles, we agreed, were probably better than Barney's.

"I'm having a time working on my new lectures for the fall," I said. "But enjoying it."

"How long before they fire you?" asked Pei Ling.

"I give it six months...the wheels of bureaucracy turn slowly. But my bigger decision is how long I stay to remain a burr in their ass."

"So you will have long enough to say what you need to say," said Pei Ling. "Then we will decide our future."

"I have to figure a way to earn a living," I said.

Pei Ling took my hand. "We will see."

Chapter Seventeen

Lair of Liars

I had been involved for several weeks, months if I count my time with Pei Ling and De Broglie, learning a true approach to cosmology. The day finally came on a cool morning in mid-September to deliver. The class was full, as it always was the first week or so before the floaters discovered they'd need to perform. After all, this was a public university with all the riff-raff that comes with being such an institution. I introduced myself, gave an approving look at the faces before me, and began. "This class is unlike any other. I expect that what you discover here will be antithetic to everything most of you have learned about cosmology, astronomy, and even human existence. Some of you...most...perhaps all of you will find that the ideas and knowledge conveyed in this room will be disagreeable, outlandish...even bizarre. Because you disagree or have acquiesced to ideas that are entirely different, however, your thoughts do not trump the truths of antiquity. And because you, from your world view, believe something to be true, does not make it so." I stopped. The room was still. I waited until the silence got uncomfortable before I asked for questions, and acknowledged a young man in the front row.

"Is there only that one old standard text assigned?"

"That's it," I said. "There are no books with new information...you don't even need to purchase the assigned text. You won't be tested on it. Most of what we will learn will be from each other and in books that are in the library here or downtown...and don't worry," I added. "...they won't be checked out. No one reads them. If you want to get a leg up, however, get familiar with Eddington's Nature of the Physical World, Newton's Principia, Chinese Imperial Edicts Regarding Creation, Kepler's Harmonies of the World, and De Broglie's Purple Silk in Andromeda. I'll put them on the board."

I dismissed the class, buoyed by their comments and questions, with a few of the curious staying behind. Some expressed relief that mine would apparently not be another boring class of the tired, ever-restructured teachings about naturalism and evolutionary origins. Still, I was realistic and no matter how supportive these students might be, speaking truth was taboo in the new Dark Age of politically correct America.

My first regulation class began two days later, using the time to look over my lecture notes and tie up loose ends. I was confident, and began the first lecture.

"Don't you get annoyed at injustice? Don't you get angry when you are lied to? Don't you become enraged when someone deceives you? What if I told you that all the big truths you've learned and believe in are lies? I expect the first thing you'd do is defend. It's natural...I understand. Changing is a hard thing to do. Your core beliefs are who you are. So let me begin with simple, elemental, fundamental facts. No theories or conjecture."

I paused a moment while several students repositioned themselves in their seats in what I'd guessed to be anticipation of what was to come. "From whom," I asked, "did we first learn the Earth is round?" As expected, the class en masse agreed that it was our Greek friend, Pythagoras.

"Wrong," I said. "Anyone else?"

A tentative voice rose from a girl in the back row. I recalled the first time Ann had spoken up, a little shy, but steady. "Well, mythically speaking, the prophet Isaiah said the world was round."

"As a matter of fact, he did," I agreed. "He beat Pythagoras by a couple of hundred years. And the prophet Job beat him by 500 years...by the way, why did you say, 'mythically speaking?'"

"Well, it's a myth. It's in the Bible," she explained.

"A myth is imaginary." I said. I looked across the faces of the collective brain trust. "I'm not teaching religion, you know. This is not a religion class. Scripture is history that conveys information key to our discipline of study. Its words did not appear without cause. It was written by real people who actually experienced what they reported and wrote what they saw, and I don't think sound science rests on denial of the obvious. Sane people don't, you know...so if this is uncomfortable for you, or you are delusional, I recommend dropping the class."

"Not a chance!" said the young man in a raised voice who earlier asked about the assigned text. I was mildly startled by the force of his voice and looked at the seating chart to find his name.

"This is wild," said Jeff. "It just takes some getting used to. I never knew that before...about Job and Isaiah beating Pythagoras to the punch. What else?"

"Oh, there's plenty," I assured him. "You know Wirtz and Hubble demonstrated in the 1920's that the universe is ever expanding, just as Isaiah wrote in 700 B.C. Our texts tell us that entropy, the Second Law of Thermodynamics, was discovered in the mid-1800's. Isaiah told us about it 2500 years ago."

I looked at the seating chart again to recognize Dan. "Well, who was Isaiah and where did he get his knowledge?"

"I wish I could say," I said, "but I'm not going to make it easy for any one of you or the administration to get me canned." The class laughed as I had intended. "We currently live in a nascent wave of tyranny growing stronger and more relentless everyday...if I discussed the origins of ancient knowledge, I'd be accused of proselytizing...you're going to have to study the facts and decide on your own."

Though I felt myself cowering a bit with those words, I no sooner felt the creep of doubt when I was renewed. "But let me ask where you get your knowledge? You get it from schoolbooks written by anonymous authors who have passed an educational litmus test, and for some reason, you inherently trust what they say. Isn't that odd when you think about it? I mean, really, why should you? You were first told the dinosaurs died from a comet impact, then they died from sunburn, then they died from greenhouse gases. The earth was ten billion years old then it was five billion years old, then it was three billion...no, wait...now it 4.5 billion. I mean, if you really have a mind, don't you kind of get the idea that no one knows what they're talking about?"

Dan spoke up. "It bothers me...a lot, now that I think about it. I'm a geology major, and one of the first things we discover is that carbon dating is useless past 50,000 years. The prof knows it too. But the four and half billion years is what we all go with. So, yeah, it's kind of weird."

There *is* hope, I told myself. And by the response I was getting from a few other students, they enjoyed the repartee and were sincerely engaged with the issue. "So that brings us to some bigger questions, doesn't it? This filter with which we view basic scientific and social structures must be based on at least some false premises. I mean, everywhere you look, things are a little off don't you think? We're supposed to be evolving, aren't we? If you really think about it, we, as people, as humans—and I challenge anyone to scientifically prove otherwise—are no better than generations past, and likely worse. Were it not so, wouldn't the world be a better place and wouldn't we be a better people? I mean, we've had millions of years to get on with it, right?"

The inevitable question came at last from the girl who reminded me of Ann. "Well, how old do you think the Earth is?"

"I know how old the Earth is," I said. "How old do you believe the Earth is?"

"What everybody knows...four and a half billion years," she responded. I realized I'd seen her on and off campus for a few years. She was either a career student or taking what she thought was a throw away class for credit...one of many a lifetime non-achiever. “Do you know how dumb that sounds? You didn’t hear Dan?” I felt some turn against my blunt questions like a mob of dolts, while some others chuckled. “What everybody knows? Who knows? The faceless, unaccountable academicians who put their personal consensus down in a text book? You took *their* word for it?”

“Well, come on, Mr. Grey,” she said. “Everybody knows it’s true.”

“You’ve interviewed everybody?” I asked. “Have you?” The answer was, of course, was no, and I seized the moment to make a point. “You people just sit back and digest the conventional wisdom of the day and walk about life, secure in your idiocy. What, in God’s name, is wrong with you? Do you not know that everything you do, see, experience, embrace, reject, love and hate is built on a supernatural foundation? You are the physical manifestation of that foundation, and for those of you who deny it, or choose to ignore it...well...you’re in either no position to know truth or you’ve placed your bets on the side of darkness. I call it ‘tiny mind syndrome’...Just enough capacity to reject truth and replace it with the most ridiculous arguments, posits, premises, and concepts that, to the tiny mind, seems profound...”

“But, Mr. Grey!” Dan interrupted my rant before I said something I would have really regretted. “We never learned anything else.”

“I know,” I confessed, and after realizing how I must have sounded, I was contrite. “Actually, I’ve been in the same boat you are now, but for an extra twenty years. I’m...I’m sorry for seeming to be an asshole."—a line that broke the tension with a moment of laughter. "I'm not, really," I said. I want so much for you to have the benefit of the truth...I get frustrated once in a while," I said as to excuse my behavior. There wasn't a peep from anyone in the class for what seemed an eternity. Finally, the girl who challenged me spoke up.

"I know what you mean, Mr. Grey." Jeff and Dan and some others in the class agreed.

"Well," I said. "I appreciate that. There are those who will never see truth, and I guess, ultimately, we have to follow through with teaching the mandated course so everyone can pass the exams and be wards of the state. As you might imagine, I won't be teaching that."

Jeff looked dismayed. "You're quitting?"

"No point spending any more time here," I said.

"Well...when?" asked Jeff, drawing in his classmates. "I'm not done with this...I don't think any of us are."

I asked for a show of hands, imagining some were curious to see a grown man's wheels fall off before them, and of forty students, eight apparently agreed with Jeff. "Okay," I said. "But I'm warning you. This is going to be a discussion about why everything you've ever learned or thought you knew about where you and the world came from is wrong...one huge error...without scientific evidence of any kind. So, if you're willing to listen, we can use the remainder of this period. For the rest of you, I formally and insincerely apologize. You may as well leave now...and for those of you staying? Congratulations."

The pop-cultured witless, the uncurious, and the purposefully ignorant shuffled out as fast as they could. The eight clustered together in the front row. I was moved by their loyalty or, at least, willingness to learn. "There's no time to waste," I said. "So why don't we just start with some topics to get us thinking. There's so much we could talk about, but since this is astronomy, perhaps we should stay focused on the heavens." I was about to pose my first posit when the girl who earlier argued with me volunteered to get coffee for us.

"Seriously?" I asked.

"Sure," she said with a smile and a wink. "We'll think better with coffee." I agreed and took her action as a kind of empathy for the stress I was probably not hiding very well. Dan called out as she got to the door to be sure to return with plenty of cream and sugar.

"We'll fill you in," I said. She smiled and said she'd be right back. I scoured my thoughts, searching for a show stopper that I hoped would live up to everyone's expectations. "Did you know that Venus spins in the reverse direction of the other terrestrial planets in our solar system?"

"Well, sure," offered Jeff. "That's not news."

"Do you believe in the big bang theory?"

"Of course," said Jeff.

"So being the smart lad that you are, you know that the situation with Venus is totally inconsistent with a big bang...yet you go on...you know, this is why this is hopeless," I said out of frustration, but continued. "Okay. Wait," I said closing my eyes and holding my finger in the air to reprimand myself. "I'm sorry...but let's say a big bang began this world billions of years ago...There's something else going on out there in our little corner of the universe that doesn't make sense. I'll give you a hint...Neptune and Jupiter."

Jeff jumped at the question like it was a no-brainer. "Oh, yeah. They radiate more energy than they receive from the sun...and...well..." he thought for a moment. "...that would be impossible if the universe was as old as we've been told."

"Good man," I said. "And the implication?" I gave him some time and he took it.

"It means..." said Jeff. "...that...that if the universe evolved over billions of years, at the known rate of energy loss, Neptune and Jupiter would have stopped radiating surplus energy eons ago."

"Yes, of course," I said. "And the problem is reconciled by the laws of physics as we all know and love them when the universe is a few thousand years old...does everyone get that? And while I'm at it, you know that spiral galaxy we live in? The same kind we see in countless numbers in the Hubble deep field? The centers spin faster at a known rate than the spiral arms—phenomena we observe right now—if such galaxies were really billions of years old, the spiral appearance would not hold over time—they would be twisted beyond recognition...and one more thing. If the universe was born from one cosmic cloud...how it got here, of course, science cannot explain...if the universe was born from a singularity, one cosmic cloud burst, why are the planets so entirely different?"

I noticed movement outside the classroom door and walked over to open it for our coffee volunteer, who kindly laid out the goods and everyone helped themselves.

"Okay, I said noticing our time would soon be up. "I've saved the best for last...the horizon problem. Everyone seems to avoid it, hell bent on believing in and fruitlessly trying to prove a scientific theory by avoiding facts that conflict with it. I mean, don't you have to ask yourself what kind of science is that? And worse, what kind of scientist would you be? So, we have the horizon problem. The universe is a really big place...really big. We think we measure the end of the observable universe, but we have no idea what's beyond...not that we have much of an idea of what's going on here...anyway, big bang requires that at the center of the universe, the point of the big explosion, the temperature must be very hot, indeed, and incrementally cooler in the regions of expansion...as we move away from the point of the original event. Yet *all* areas of the universe are virtually the same temperature...no matter where we look. Even if the universe were 20 billion years old, there would not have been time to exchange enough energy to result in the same, ambient temperatures we see across the universe. So, why do we see the same temperature across the universe?" I looked at the students and looked at my watch. "Think about it...and that's about all I have to say."

"Wait!" said Dan, with the others in agreement. "Where are you going?"

"To Andromeda," I said, realizing they had no idea I thought I was half serious.

Dan jumped up, almost frantic. "But how will we keep in touch?"

I said I'd leave a forwarding address with the administration and I walked out of the room and down the hall.

The truth was, I had their addresses and I intended to write each of them a personal note of thanks for putting up with me and invite future discussions at a time and place to be determined. When I got to the stairway, I looked back on the chance that anyone was rushing to implore me not to quit, like in the movies, but no one was.

Chapter Eighteen

A Lonely Road

I arrived home, coat draped over my shoulder in one hand and my briefcase in the other. Pei Ling saw me coming up the walkway and met me at the door. “Well, I did it,” I said.

She smiled and put her arms around me. “Congratulations, darling.”

“Thanks, babe,” I said. “It wasn’t easy.” I took off my shoes and put my coat in the closet. “You know, you might think I’m crazy, but I got to thinking on the way home…I want to visit a place that I haven’t been since I was in school.”

“L.A.?” asked Pei Ling. “That’s not crazy, dear.”

“No. A field in the Central Valley. There’s a Poplar tree there.” I thought this could sound foolish and looked at Pei Ling for some indication of doubt, but she continued to listen. “It’s beaten and worn, and still it survives. Well, at least I think it does.”

“Did something happen there?”

"Yeah," I said wistfully walking over to look out the window. "I never told you about it. It was a low point in my life...the lowest. I was driving back to L.A. for school. My mother had died a few days earlier and I was with her. She lay unconscious on her side with her head bowed downward and her arms stretched out above her with her hands and fingers curled inward in the pathetic and heartbreaking pose that only those who have seen it know. I looked at her in all her human frailty, imagining her as the little girl she once was, full of smiles, joy, and hopes and dreams that must have mostly passed her by. I couldn't shake that image or the sorrow that goes with it.

"Well, I decided to take the long way back to Los Angeles, following the grid of lonely, narrow two-lane farm roads that stretch from Highway 99 in the east to I-5 in the west. For whatever reason, I always found comfort driving those empty old roads. Well, I came upon a stunted, tattered Poplar tree and, I don't know why, but I stopped and turned off the ignition and got out of the car. I walked over to the tree with nothing particular in mind...and what I'm trying to say is there was just something in that spare, forlorn landscape that drew me. The tree was rooted on the bank of an empty irrigation creek, and as far as the eye could see, were tilled, dry empty fields all the way to the southern horizon, with the coast range to the west silhouetted in parched, dusty air. The sun was about eleven o'clock and it was hot, burning into my forehead like a pin. I had to put my hand up to shield my face, it was that hot. Well, that stunted little tree with a handful of leaves on its disjointed, haphazard limbs seemed like an oasis in the middle of all the nothingness. It was as quiet as a void and still as a portrait when an odd wind came up and swirled about me and went away as soon as it had come. I don't know what it was, but it said to me that everything would be okay…and it was and has been ever since." I turned from the window to Pei Ling whose soft smile was as comforting as the sheltering wings of an angel.

"I think you were in the presence," said Pei Ling. "Like Andromeda, it is something we cannot know, except indirectly. About which we cannot speak, but only hint. Yet as real as you and me at this moment looking into each others' eyes with a love we cannot express."

"Yes," I said, endlessly comforted by her words. "I know what you mean, dear…why would an unremarkable, common, stunted old tree be anything?" I looked down, lost for a moment. "Yet…yet, for me, throughout my life, now and again, it has been everything."

"You see?" said Pei Ling.

"What?" I asked half puzzled and not really expecting an answer. "So what is this Andromeda, you talk about? I mean, I know Andromeda, but I get the feeling you're talking about something other than the galaxy."

"Yes, I am, dear," said Pei Ling. "It is the evidence of things unseen…do you want to go on your trip alone?"

"Oh, not at all," I said. "I don't think you've seen that part of the country, and you might find it interesting, especially if you've read Steinbeck."

"Really?" asked Pei Ling. "He is one of my favorite American authors. East of Eden. When I got to page eight hundred, I was disappointed that it would soon be coming to an end."

"Well," I said. "The story continues in one way or the other, and maybe you'll recognize parts of it on our trip."

"How exciting, dear!" said Pei Ling. "How long will we be gone?"

"Well, I don't really know...maybe a few days...until my episode at the school filters down and the shit hits the fan in the offices of the dean of dunces. I don't have to be there when it does. How about you, dear? You have any plans?"

"Nothing I can't change," said Pei Ling.

"Well, then, let's start driving," I said. "Maybe we'll go all the way to L.A.—see what some of my old haunts look like these days." And it occurred to me for the moment how little I knew about Pei Ling and her about me. There was a whole range of reality about each other we didn't know, and I was at once excited about new discoveries, but tempered by things that perhaps we'd rather not know about each other. Well, mainly about me and some of the things I'd done in the past. These things had started to bother me...like once watching ants devour a writhing grasshopper, or when some kids put a firecracker in a frog's mouth, or dragged an opossum behind a motorcycle—I didn't intervene. Not great sins, but sins nevertheless. People do those things to other people, for gosh sakes. But they were monumental sins to me. On the other hand, I couldn't imagine Pei Ling ever doing anything she was ashamed of and for the first time I considered that maybe I was not good enough for her. "You ever been to L.A., dear?" I asked.

"No. Actually, I have been to no place except here...and Hawaii," she said with a soft smile.

"Well then, we should enjoy this trip," I said.

“Yes,” agreed Pei Ling with glee rising in her voice and showing in her smile, and I was certain I was undeserving of this wonderful angel.

We packed enough for a few days on the possibility of traveling beyond the Central Valley, and left early the next morning just before dawn so I could see the sun rise in the east. This time of year, entering into fall, the valley would often be cloaked in fog for most of the morning, and on a good day, mere turn to gray skies by late morning and reclaim the land in deep, gray mist by late afternoon. As it turned out, this morning sky was clear. We dropped down Highway 152 into the valley. Far to the east, the sun rose through clouds over the Sierras in a brilliant, radiant display of thundercloud-filtered sunshine...the kind you see in paintings and pictures that evoke the presence of God and a world beyond this one.

There are stretches on south Highway 33 to Manning Avenue east that are, in their own way, among the most melancholy places on earth. Here and there, off in the distance, twisted and barely recognizable old tractors and farm implements sit, useless and broken among tattered fences, and the remains of old, ramshackle out-buildings, some of which must have been homes a generation or two ago.

“My!” exclaimed Pei Ling in a whisper. “Look at those old buildings...I wonder who lived there.”

“I know,” I said. “This whole damn world is a symbol, isn’t it?”

“Yes,” said Pei Ling still looking out the window. “A metaphor of this broken world.”

I was delighted with myself for understanding what she was saying. "I remember going on road trips with mom and dad...we would sometimes pass by an old shack, a homestead, some old place like we're looking at right now, and dad would say something that only now I realize was kind of profound. He'd say that what we were looking at was not a shack, but a good dream gone bad. And that's what it was. And that's what those buildings are. Remnants of the dreams of the people who lived in them. Where life happened. Where people lived and cried and laughed and worked hard, eking out another day and hoping for a better one the next." Pei Ling reached for my hand and glanced at me with a smile and then in silence out her window.

After some hours, we arrived at a junction and pulled into a touristy, upscale hotel and restaurant. "I guess we can have lunch here...Do you want to go with me?"

"Yes, dear," said Pei Ling. "Of course."

"I mean to the tree."

"How long will you be?" she asked.

"Oh, I don't think more than a couple of hours."

"I can stay here," said Pei Ling. "It looks like I can spend some time in the history museum and souvenir shop."

"Okay, let's eat." And we went inside and we did. I also got to thinking that I was unsure of exactly where that tree was that seemed so precious to me at the start of the trip, and like a deflating balloon, I was rapidly losing my desire to seek it out. "You know, dear? This really is a pretty nice place. I don't feel like going on to L.A. today...let's maybe stay the night here and leave in the morning. What do you think?"

"Are you worried about finding your tree?"

"What?" I asked. "How'd you know that?"

"I know."

"Hmm," I said looking at her with a suspicious smile. "Must be that woman's intuition or something."

"Yes, something like that...I know where your tree is."

"Oh, come on," I said. "Impossible."

"I can see it in my mind...it's the same little tree you remember."

"Okay," I challenged. "Where is it?"

"I'll know when I see it."

"Sounds like a magician's trick to me," I said. "You're going to ask me questions that seem innocent enough to me, but that will tell you where the tree is."

"But you don't know where the tree is," she said with a good-natured chide and, speaking of her offer, telling me to take it or leave it.

"I'll take it," I said, and we set off. Some distance east, I was inclined to turn south, but Pei Ling said it was too soon. "Are you kidding me? You're that sure?"

She kept silent, looking out her window, watching the passing landscape when we approached an unremarkable road. "Turn here," she said. We drove a mile or so south and I looked off to the left and felt some familiarity. I sensed we were close.

"Turn there," said Pei Ling. And up ahead stood the tree I remembered from so many years ago.

"I'd like to learn how to do that sometime," I said.

Pei Ling looked at me. "You already know."

I didn't say anything and we got out of the car and walked over to the tree, where I generally surveyed it, the sky, and the surroundings. "Hmm. It doesn't look quite the same as I remember. The weather's much better today and the soil in the fields is dark from rain. It's clear and beautiful now. But this is surely the same tree, and it even looks a little healthier."

"Are you disappointed?" asked Pei Ling.

"Well, whatever it was that was here is gone now. I wonder where it went."

"This place served its purpose," said Pei ling. "...when you came here the first time."

I looked around for a moment in silence. "You're right. I got what I needed then." We went back to the hotel, stayed the night and returned home in the morning. Pei Ling agreed that we'd go to L.A. some other time.

Chapter Nineteen

Trip of a Lifetime

Another day suffering sycophants and fools, and I was glad to get the university off my back, except for the severance pay. I'd made an appointment to meet Ro at a dive on San Fernando Street. The bar was old and dark and smelled like years of spilt liquor. Overhead, a crummy black and white television was blaring election results. "Look at that piece of work," I said. "If you had any doubts just how stupid people are, there's your proof."

"His supporters are well-intentioned just like he says *he* is," remarked Ro sarcastically and swilling a shot. "Good intentions...it's all you need now."

We were living Spengler's prediction, except it was once and for all, not a cycle. Western society's downward spiral was irreversible and there was no point in commenting further. I let it go and instead asked Ro if he'd come around yet.

"What? Whattya talking about?

"To the light," I said.

"Oh, you're fuckin' crazy," said Ro with the humor of a good friend. "Whattya bringin' that up for?" I followed him to the pool table. With a cigarette hanging from the corner of his mouth, he grabbed a pool cue and chalked it to break. "Okay, I'm drinkin', shootin', an' listenin'."

"Look, you," I said. "Now listen."

"That's what *I* said," answered Ro.

"Okay, yeah. Funny. Now this is deep, real deep... but first get me a beer...I'm going to the head."

Ro was leaning on his cue and staring at the television when I returned. I looked up at it too, and neither of us said anything for a minute or so. "You know," said Ro, glued to the box. "I might believe in karma...you know, coming back according to what you did in life."

"That means the world would be filled with shit," I said.

"Oh...yeah...well, true," said Ro. "But I'm good with just dying. Beats this never-ending grind—and finally I'll get a rest!"

"Can you be serious about this stuff?"

"I am," said Ro.

"So all this...this world...you...came about by unknown means...and accident. Don't you ever wonder why?"

"I don't think about it." said Ro.

"Well, we're here, aren't we? You don't have any curiosity about that? You see a building. Even it has a reason for being there. You drive a car. It has a purpose. There just happens to be food for us to eat. I mean, you idiot...ever wonder why there's something instead of nothing?"

Ro turned from the television to me. "You're crazy."

"See? You're thinking about it," I said. "And, yeah, maybe I am crazy, but we still need to make sense of this mess we call living."

"Why?" asked Ro, rhetorically.

"I know when I'm talkin' to a wall," I said exasperated. We ordered another round and I figured there's always tomorrow to start cutting back. "Say, what's the deal with Ann?"

"She ain't my type," answered Ro.

"Broads," I said with a disapproving nod of approval.

"No," Ro corrected. "Broads *are* my type. Ann's not my type."

"Ann's a broad," I said.

"You jackass," answered Ro. "What's wit' you?"

"Well...actually...I quit my job...or maybe it quit me."

"What?" exclaimed Ro. "What the? How you gonna pay for another weekend for me and the chick?"

"I thought she wasn't your type?"

"I'm thinkin', I'm thinkin'," said Ro.

"Seriously, though, that was a good time," I said. "We'll do it again." Ro paused for a moment and said that we would never do it again, and I knew he was right.

"Well, anyway," I said. "I just quit. Couldn't stand the hypocrisy...ignorance of the obvious...root word, 'ignore!' It was like I was the last man awake in The Invasion of the Body Snatchers. If I stayed any longer, I woulda fallen asleep and lost my soul. I'm telling you, something is systematically, organically awry in the world."

"I got that," Ro agreed. "Like we're swimmin' our way through a vat of swill."

"I mean, is there one leader or institution with any credibility or respectability whatsoever?" I asked. "Even the guy who did that movie about doing the right thing can't do the right thing." Ro didn't answer.

"See? No one. Remember when there were guys like our dads? Who were like...like men? Guys who bucked up and did what needed to be done. Excuses...that's all people have these days. Awarding and congratulating themselves for things they're supposed to do. Well, I'm telling you, people are weird...and I guess I've had enough." My head was spinning pretty good and I knew it. "Is this just whiskey?"

"Yeah...whattya think, I slipped ya a mickey so I could take you back to my place?"

"Well, I sure am lit," I said.

"You're reverting to amateur status," said Ro. "You been on the wagon?"

"I've cut back a little."

"That's you're problem," Ro assured me, and I could see he was getting plastered, too. "But there is one more thing, not that I really care, but once and for all, I gotta ask you...Do you really think the world is only a few thousand years old?"

I thought for a moment, a shot glass in one hand and my eyes on Ro. "To tell you the truth, I don't know, *exactly*, but it's in the thousands...it's the only thing that fits. And if you're so sure it's millions, show me the money, dude, as in proof. You don't know," I said sarcastically. "It's only *what you've been told...get it?*"

I was starting to roll with the drinks, but I knew what I was saying and Ro knew I knew what I was saying. "You've also been told," I said mockingly, "that Man's been around for hundreds of thousands of years or whatever the latest guess is...Why isn't there any recorded history older than 5,000 years? Where are the transitional fossils from amoebas to Man? Millions of years? The world's a nut case. No empirical, scientific evidence. None. Nada. Zip. Get it? Evolution is the doctrine of Mao, Stalin, der fuhrer, the malformed jackass in North Korea, racial warfare, fear of the future, mind-numbing stupidity, and earth worship...say *that* after one more whiskey!"

"What? Darwin?" asked Ro.

"Yeah," I said. "He legitimized racism for the masses. You *do* remember the title of his inglorious, seminal work of insanity, don't you?"

Ro feigned offense that I would think he might not. "Of course...'Origin of the Species'."

He reminded me that I told this story at our celebration weekend in frisco, but I went on anyway. "Nope. *Origin of the Species: The Preservation of Favored Races in the Struggle for Life.* When he says 'races,' he means the color of your skin. Yet he says we all evolved from the same single cell. So even *his* ignorant ass makes no sense. His version of science says we came from a single cell, which means we're all the same race, and then he talks about favored races. *Your* people are nuts."

Ro took my insults without animus. We broke up the drink fest and said we'd see each other around. I walked home through the mostly vacated section of old downtown. A storm was rising, and warm, surly winds were blowing across the street from the west. The mix of booze and quitting my job felt like paradise, and I anticipated a great storm with lightning and thunder and rain and I thought if I got caught in it, I wouldn't care. I'd embrace it, looking up into the sky and having a first hand encounter with God himself. I almost made it home before the downpour began and I changed my mind about staying out in the weather.

"You're wet!" Pei Ling exclaimed. "And drunk."

From anyone else, calling me drunk would be an insult. Typically, an argument might ensue. But Pei Ling was not typical. She was happy to see me, even in my inebriated state. I can say that because she loved me, but more to the point, she was happy when I was happy...and I was happy when she was happy. What a break. I flopped on the bed, and Pei Ling dutifully stripped me to my shorts and got me under the covers. Yes, I thought. I was the luckiest man in the world.

I slept through a dreamless night, and in the morning I awoke to soft murmuring and the sound of boiling water. I lifted my head to see steam coming from a tea pot on the stove and heard Pei Ling's whisper coming from somewhere in another room...something about a place where time flows. I was sure that's what she said, but I wasn't quite sure. And who was she talking to? I remained in bed, straining to understand her conversation. "There is no place where time does not flow, and there is no flow of time where there is a place where time does not flow." Was that what I was hearing? I thought, damn, if I had not been drinking I could probably make it out. It was driving me crazy. I got up quietly and walked to the open door and peeked into the living room. My heart sank in an anxious kind of way. Pei Ling's back was to me and she looked like she was talking to someone, but no one was there. She was talking softly to the air like a crazy person. "...spoke the world and time into existence, a place where no time flows and where no time flows where there is no place." I tiptoed back into bed and waited a few minutes before saying something.

"Pei?" I called, and realized I never called her "Pei." It was always "darling" or "honey" or "babe," and I wondered if she noticed.

She was at the door in a moment. "Yes, dear?"

"Um, would you mind getting me some tea?"

"Tea?" asked Pei Ling. "You never drink tea. Sure you don't want coffee?"

"Well, I don't want to trouble you. You already have hot water, don't you?"

"It's no trouble, darling. I will get your coffee."

I wanted to get up, but lying down felt too good, and I pulled the covers up to my neck.

"Dear?" Pei Ling called from the kitchen. "You called me 'Pei'."

"I know...I don't know why."

"Yes, that is unlike you," she answered.

She brought the coffee bedside and asked if I wanted anything else. I said no and got the nerve to ask. "Dear, who were you talking to in the living room?"

"No one, dear," she smiled.

"Yes, something about time flow and place...I heard you."

"Oh, that," she said stroking my forehead. "I was praying."

I'd never considered that, and felt a twinge of guilt about asking. "Oh...what were you praying for?"

"For you, dear," answered Pei Ling. "I was praying for you."

"Really?" I asked. "Why?"

"I was praying that you will make it to Andromeda."

"You mean there's a chance I won't?" I asked trying to sound absolutely serious. "I thought it was more or less a done deal." On one level, I was entertaining Pei Ling on the idea that we could really leave this world. I wasn't sure she was serious, but she must be. She was praying and someone must have heard her, because she was in no mood to consider my doubts.

"Oh, you're going," she assured me. "By the grace of God, my prayers are answered."

And with that, I was at once disquieted with an unsettling, intense awareness of sensations, physical and spiritual, that seemed vaguely familiar somewhere, somehow in the past. The last words I remember were Pei Ling's, smiling with tender encouragement and saying, "We're leaving now."

In an instant, I was bathed in the last mellifluous light of a morning that I thought would be my last. I swirled from this world into another in a backwards spiral of voices and visions, through fathomless darkness and a strong wind blowing me toward a point of light in the far away distance. The mighty forces shut my eyes, shielding them from an indescribable, pleasant terror, if such a thing can be imagined. The wind subsided. The darkness withdrew. I opened my eyes to an unspeakable, unfathomable beauty and sitting on a bench with my hand in Pei Ling's and hers in mine. We were in a wondrous setting of trees and grass and hills in the distance, but this was no place like the Earth I knew. Every blade of grass, every leaf on every tree, everything everywhere I looked shimmered in a nearly white gold so bright as to be almost blinding.

I could see what was near, but whatever was in the distance was washed out in the brightest of golden luminescence. A very distant sound of singing birds and, closer, the rustle of leaves in an easy breeze were all that broke the silence. I looked down to see what I was wearing, what I looked like, but could not make out any vestiges of clothing, for everywhere I looked out of curiosity, my sight was over shone by bright, streaming light. It was as though only what I needed to see, I saw, and I looked at Pei Ling. She was beaming with happiness and seemed almost unable to contain her joy. I imagined I appeared the same to her, and a shared, comforting spirit at once resided in us together.

"We are here, darling," she said. "What do you think?"

"What do I think?" I asked.

"No, what do you think?" she responded.

If I had any doubts, I knew now that this was not my imagination. It was Pei Ling and this was real. I was stunned and speechless, for a time, and said that this place was the most remarkable thing...that I could not imagine anything as glorious, peaceful, or as utterly beautiful. And while I had at first thought that it was the brightness of the light that prevented me from seeing the details of our bodies, I realized these areas *were* light, light itself. Movement was effortless, and out of curiosity, I asked Pei Ling if we could leave this spot.

"Sure, darling," she said. "Where do you want to go?"

"Well, I don't know, exactly. It's really quite satisfactory to sit here and experience this wonder."

"Me, too," said Pei Ling.

I looked to see what was around us. Back over my shoulder, a shiny gold two story building materialized as I began to adjust to the light. I shuddered, recognizing the building as the one in a dream I'd had after my mother died. As I remember, my brothers and sister were with me in a type of waiting room on the second floor. My father, who had not yet passed away, was in a room being tended by cherubs with fluttering wings who seemed to be making a fuss among them about how to prepare him for eternity. I went from the room and spoke to, for want of a better description, the station nurse and asked if I could see my mother. She said only I could see her, and that I would need to be disinfected, as mother was in a critical healing stage before she would be ready to pass into heaven. The nurse disinfected me by waving a kind of wand around me and pointed to a room near the end of a hall. I knocked on the partially open door and there was mom, standing stiffly as if in pain, bracing herself on the edge of the bed. She told me that she wasn't quite ready and that it would be a couple more weeks before she was, but we could take a short walk outside and talk for a while. The bench Pei Ling and I were sitting on now was the bench I sat on with my mother. I looked at Pei Ling through the shimmering light. "Are there other people here?"

"Only people you know," said Pei Ling.

"Really?"

"Well, not all of them," she said. "Just those who are here. In fact, hardly anyone makes it here. That's why we don't see anyone but us. The population is rather sparse."

"Can we check in that building?" I asked, motioning to the building where I'd seen my mother and father in the dream. Pei Ling said we could, and I saw that in this effortless world, we needed nothing more than to will ourselves toward wherever we wanted to go. We moved up the first landing on the stairs and to the door on the second floor. I opened it to a long, empty hall and we went in. I passed by the room mom had been in and the empty nurses' station and to the room where my father had been. It, too, was empty. "There's no one here...not a soul."

"Yes," said Pei Ling. "It appears to not be in use at the moment."

"But this is where I saw my mom and dad. I wonder where everyone is."

"The angels have done their work, and your parents have ascended from here."

"But isn't this heaven?"

"No, dear," said Pei Ling. "Not even close, but as close as we will get for now."

I was disappointed and amazed at the same time. Could there really be even something higher than this? We returned to the outside and I paused by the railing on the stairway. Below me, I saw the bench on which we had been sitting and the path along side it, lined with golden poplar trees, and leaves stirring lightly in the soft breeze. Off to the right was a vast expanse of golden fields that reached to the other side of a great valley, ending at the bottom of a tall mountain range, far greater and grander than anything I'd ever seen or could have imagined. I was overwhelmed with the sheer size and beauty of all that my eyes and senses feasted upon, and I looked at Pei Ling. "I saw a path leading away from our bench past the building, dear. Do you think we could go down that way?"

"Sorry, dear. We have to be getting back soon."

"We have to go back?" I asked, fearing what might be involved in our return. "I mean, why? Is it going to hurt?"

Pei Ling laughed. "No, it's not going to hurt. But we cannot stay in this light much longer."

"What?" I asked. "It's infrared or something? And where is it coming from. There's no sun...I mean, I can't see any sun...just everything is bright, like a super luminescence."

"That's the reflected light of perfection. As it is, we're going to look a little different when we get back."

And I had an idea of what she meant. "Like sunburn or something?"

"Not exactly," said Pei Ling. "Our bodies will glow a bit."

I was fascinated. "Really? How long will that last?"

"We've been here longer than usual...maybe a couple of days."

"Longer than usual?"

"You're surprised I've been here before?" asked Pei Ling with a smile.

I thought for a moment. "Not really. I remember seeing you asleep one night and thinking I must be seeing things or going crazy...light emanating from your gorgeous mouth and cute little ears. What a relief to now know why."

"Let's go back to the bench, dear," said Pei Ling. And with that, we returned from where we came, but without the voices and visions...only the soft murmur of a gentle breeze and a faint flush of home sickness.

I found myself in bed in the same position as I was when Pei Ling took me to Andromeda and she was bringing me coffee from the kitchen. Only now, I wasn't drunk or hung over. I never felt better, though I was a little disappointed in gravity. Bed continued to feel like the right place to be and I asked Pei Ling to join me.

Chapter Twenty

As Bad As You Think

"Hey, man, let me beat your ass in pool." Those were the first words Ro said to me when I met him a day later at the dive bar we seem to have made our meeting place. I agreed to his game of pool, and while I was reluctant to tell him what happened, I also couldn't keep it under my hat. We brought our beers to the dark corner in the back room and chalked our sticks. I moved away from the table and out of the overhead light to let Ro break. The 8-ball teetered on the edge of a corner pocket, but didn't drop. Ro remained in shooting position as he took a long look at me to take my shot.

"What's with you?" he asked.

"What?" I said, thinking he was impatient. "I'm coming!"

"What's with your face?"

"What, I got a face made for radio?"

"No! You're glowing in the dark, dude."

"What?" I said hearing his words clearly.

"Will you stop saying 'what'?" demanded Ro. "I said you're glowing in the dark!"

I realized it must be the latent effect Pei Ling talked about. "I think I got burned from a sun lamp...I found one in the closet the other day and...you know...I was screwing around and fell asleep under it."

"Oh, yeah?" said Ro. "What, you're sunning yourself now? Like a fairy?" Ro was unconvinced. He came over for a closer examination and I thought he was going to have a heart attack. "Geez!" he exclaimed, and jumped back, almost falling to the floor.

I laughed. "You got the heebie-jeebies?"

"You're fucking glowing, man!"

I shrugged. "No one else seems to notice."

"Are you kiddin'? Look at their mugs," said Ro. "The guys in this joint don't notice anything...now, what's the story with your face?"

"Okay, so I'm glowing a little bit," I said. "But you won't believe why."

"Oh, yeah? Try me," said Ro. "I never saw anything like it."

I took the cue from Ro's hand and placed it with mine back on the wall. Ro ordered a couple of whiskies and I told him the whole story. He was speechless for a time, itching, I thought, to tell me I was full of it. But he knew I wasn't making this up, and you don't tell your best friend he's full of it unless you're pretty sure.

“So,” I said. “You’re skeptical. You should be. Pretty amazing story, though, huh?”

“Hah! So you *are* conning me.”

I looked down, smiling, and swirled the last swig of Kentucky corn mash and swallowed it. “Well, I don’t care if you believe me. Makes no difference, does it?”

“No,” said Ro. “Unless it’s true. But you were glowing, man. What kind of trick was that?”

“I’m done explaining,” I said. “It was what it was...is. What you do with it is up to you.” I walked out to the street to the nauseating crowd, who were shuffling mindlessly through the day with no clue who they are or where they were going. Ro followed and grabbed me hard on my shoulder.

“Wait a minute, man,” he implored. “You were glowing in there for real?”

“What do you think?” I said, turning to survey the street. “Look at this town...a billion dollar renovation, new streetcars, beautiful masonry, artful landscaping. And who’s here? Crazy people in rags, street toughs who measure life in a can of spray paint. The city can’t keep up with the puke, the two-legged defecators, and chewing gum on the sidewalks...”

“Hmm,” puzzled Ro. “The world’s bad, but not that bad.”

“Oh?” I asked. “What are *you* looking at? Lollipops and candy canes? Come on...Death? Destruction? Heartbreak? Hypocrisy? War? Despair? What? You think we drink because we love hangovers?”

By the time we wound down our walking conversation, we found ourselves in the early afternoon outside the Cuban

International. “Hey, the place is open,” I said. Ro agreed it was time for lunch and we went in.

Maria met us at the top of the stairs. "My boys, my boys, where have you been?"

“Busy,” I said kindly.

“Yeah,” said Ro pointing to my head like I didn’t see him. “He’s been busy.”

We seated ourselves and ordered the usual. The lunch crowd was on their way out and Maria stopped by with a couple of beers. “Where’s the girl? The pretty one?”

I looked at Maria with the look of a happy man. “She married me.”

“Oh, my!” Maria took a deep breath and put her hand to her chest. “Holy mother....Oh, I knew there was something. You were meant for each other,” she said in a tone more sincere than cliché.

I delighted in Maria’s approval, while Ro insisted that Pei Ling got a raw deal. “It’s a guy thing,” I said to Maria. “He’s jealous.” She rushed into the kitchen to tell Joe who told Maria to tell us that lunch was on the house. I would tip appropriately.

“Whattya do now?” said Ro. “A married man.”

“Same as you, I guess...live one day to the next and see what happens.”

Ro looked at me, suspicious. “Oh yeah?”

“Are you kidding?” I exclaimed. “After what I’ve been through?”

“Yeah, I kinda had a feeling something changed.”

“What really changes,” I said, “is finding that I owe others something now. Knowing how everything began, where we came from, knowing what lies outside this world does that. I owe those kids that I walked out on a chance to know what I know. They’ve learned all the wrong stuff. They think we’re born, we live, and we die. That’s it... What a crock.”

“You talkin’ religion?” asked Ro. “That’s a mistake. Hell, people have killed more people in the name of religion...”

“No! I’m not letting that go,” I interrupted. “Death is on the hands of your pagan, earth-worshiping environmentalists...a million people a year die from just your ignorant-ass ban on DDT. You need to check your facts, dude. But say what you want, stick with what’s comfortable, and tell me how that works, anyway...you don’t believe in God, but you blame God. You see why I can’t stand your people?”

“Well,” said Ro changing the subject. “The first thing I’d do if I were you is get a colonoscopy.”

“I’ll pass,” I said. “George and Ben did without one and that’s good enough for me.”

“George and Ben?”

“George Washington and Ben Franklin,” I explained.

“Oh, well, what kind of sense does that make?” said Ro.

“Look,” I said. “If I got ass cancer, I’d have it with or without getting a probe up my butt...I’ll take what’s comin’ to me. I’m playing the hand I was dealt...and why would a person be so hot to stay around here for long, anyway? Ignorance is all over the place...every hour an affront to courtesy, everyday an insult to decency, a state of never-ending disappointment.”

"Then how do you explain Pei Ling?" asked Ro.

"She's an exception, of course. And so are you, you idiot."

"Yeah?" said Ro swigging a beer. "Kind of strange the way that all happened with her and you. Maybe she's a guardian angel."

"Could be," I said. "Until her, I'd been searching solo, despairing in the world. Suddenly, she shows up from across the sea, on one particular day, at one specific moment in time, in the same place as me, and the rest is history, as they say. Could it be true there are no coincidences?"

"Got me," said Ro. "But if true, if there were some way to prove it, now that would make your case."

"You know," I said with a measure of reluctance. "I had a hell of a dream the night after the morning I met her. It was a thing about her choosing me...where I had no choice in the matter...not that I wanted it some other way," I said and doing my part to finish the beer and also noticing Ro's curious look. "You've had dreams?" I asked.

"Yeah. Crazy ones, too," he said. "But, you know, they're just dreams."

"I wouldn't be too sure about that," I said. "I know, your people think they're just psychological curiosities. On the other hand, they might be messages."

"You think so?" asked Ro. "I had a dream where a rabbit chased me up a tree. What about that?"

"I think it means a rabbit chased you up a tree...Not every dream has meaning, dipshit. There are tares among the wheat. You gotta be able to discern...get the message...maybe your receiver is on the fritz."

Ro offered to pay the tip and I let him. On the way out, I saw Maria and Joe had posted some well-meaning signs—Conserve Water, Conserve Energy. "See?" I said to Ro. "That's what I'm talking. The amount of water on earth has never changed. Energy is limitless. Everyone's crazy."

Chapter Twenty-One

Hope After All

"Good morning, darling." Pei Ling's words were sweet and pure like the glittering yellow sunshine and early morning air on this Saturday morning. "Poached eggs on toast?"

"No, thanks, dear," I said. "Just coffee and a kiss. I need to get going to meet with the students—the ones who stuck with me after my exile from the university."

"Really no time for breakfast?" asked Pei Ling.

"Really. They know my affinity for good food and they want to make a day of it in Frisco—it's going to take me a couple of hours to get there."

"Taking the train?"

"And a cab," I added.

"Can't they pick you up?"

"They offered, but, really, I'd rather take the train. You know...time to think."

Pei Ling took her eyes off the eggs she was scrambling and looked over at me in the bedroom as I fumbled to get dressed. "That is so like you."

I looked up from tying my shoe. "Where'd you get that one?"

"What one?"

"'That is so like you.' You've been watching too much teevee?" I joked.

Pei Ling smiled and continued tending breakfast, placing bread in the toaster. "Where are you meeting them?"

"The place at land's end…by the ocean," I said looking at my watch. "I better get going."

She sent me off with a kiss, the kind you remember all day and maybe into the next. It was nine in the morning and the train was pretty much empty. The only soul to pass through for the first hour was the conductor. The journey was cerebral, the train gently swaying with the lay of the track and the plaintive crossing bells clanging every so often as we passed through the towns going north. I looked out the window the whole way, watching life go by and thinking how fortunate I was and how sure that whoever was watching over me must have a good reason.

The agreeable sense of journey changed downtown. Rising up the escalator to Market Street, I was reminded I was in San Francisco. The sour odor of the never washed and the smell of urine rose from the streets like the fetid odor from a decaying body. People dressed like bums. A man in a doorway at Front and Market was just pulling up his pants after defecating in front of an oblivious crowd of what, passersby? Barnyard animals were cleaner and better mannered. I could only imagine the extent to which this city had given itself over to willful depravity. I hailed a cab, thankful to be heading to a more civilized area west of downtown.

Fortunately, I was dressed for the elements. The cliffs and the sea were shrouded in fog, and I wondered how many of the students might have used the weather to cancel. I opened the glass doors and walked through the entryway to the hostess and said what I was there for, and she kindly directed me to the far end of the dining room where familiar faces greeted me. They had even placed a name card on my place setting.

A waiter with a drinker's face took my coat and, seeing that the time was a few minutes before noon, asked if I'd like an eye opener, to which I surely agreed. I sat down, all of us reacquainting ourselves and updating one another with the latest goings on, when my turn came.

"Mr. Grey, how about you?" asked Dan. I appreciated that he was the first to stand with me during my final lecture, but I was in a pinch. Andromeda would be the biggest news at this table but, at this point, it was too big.

I stammered a bit with nervous laughter. "Oh...well...I'm enjoying married life...and looking for a job."

I looked at the group and with some embarrassment realized that I couldn't recall the names of the others with Dan and Jeff. The girl who had volunteered to get coffee at the lecture saw that I was lost. "I'm Susan," she said with a smile. "And this is Ron and Trish."

"Yes, yes, now I remember," I said rising to shake their hands. I sat down and said five was a good number and that I never expected all eight of the original group to show anyway.

"Yeah," said Jeff looking at Dan and Susan. "We're the stalwarts...and I think Ron and Trish are just looking for an excuse," he joked.

"An excuse?" I asked.

"They don't get out much," continued Jeff good-naturedly.

"Well, this a good place to get out to," I said. "You're here and that's all that matters...let's order and get started." And we did.

"So I've been thinking about it...this lie we live in," Jeff began. "I have the pieces to a puzzle, but I can't put them together."

"Well, then...you're most of the way home," I assured him. "Who among us understood everything on the first day of class? And you won't this...but when you do, you will suddenly discover how fundamental it is."

I was probably getting ahead of myself, I thought...too hopeful and too optimistic that my message would be heard. I was aware of the long odds of truth surviving in a world of lies, but I was willing to give it a try. I was obligated, in fact, that because I knew the truth I had to speak the truth. I could only take these kids at their word, and they seemed sincere enough. I decided on an idea that had been accepted without question by everyone at the table, including myself before Pei Ling.

"Well, okay then...something you know well enough...There are more than one hundred million galaxies...*more than one hundred million,*" I repeated for emphasis. "Each with more than one hundred million stars...*each one.*" I paused to let the number sink in. "We're used to throwing around big numbers, but that's one hundred million times one hundred million...Can anyone seriously get their head around those numbers? Of course not," I said after a pregnant pause. "No human mind can grasp that number. We have no idea how many stars or galaxies are out there. Not a clue."

"Well, how many stars do you think are out there?" asked Jeff.

"I don't know," I said. "But let's say we did...then what? It's a distraction."

"From what?" asked Susan.

"From what's going on in this world," I said. "Where you are this minute and where you came from. Who you are and where you're going you'll have to figure for yourself." I was in a mood, both foul and compassionate, as it seemed I often was on this subject. "Now, look, courageous or a coward, look at it this way...the courageous can admit what you've assumed as fact is wrong...the cowards can claim they're victims of the tyranny of unexamined assumptions. One thing, though...you're all lucky to be here at this moment in time. I should have been so lucky to have someone reveal the truth to me at your age."

"You know what I think?" said Jeff. "I think it's always been there...you either didn't or couldn't see it until now."

"Hah," I said appreciating Jeff's comment. "You're singing to the choir."

"Preaching to the choir," said Susan joining in.

At any rate, we three were of the same mind. I had an audience more receptive, more knowledgeable than I'd anticipated.

"You think we'd come here if we didn't already know we'd been screwed with?" asked Jeff. "We're here because we think you know something about this...the particulars...you don't need to convince us of the basics...I mean," said Jeff with a self-deprecating laugh. "How dumb do you think we are?"

"I won't answer that," I joked.

Ron and Trish, who had been enjoying the meal and taking everything in without comment, spoke up. "What are you all talking about? Can't you just come out with it?"

I saw Ron's point, of course, and questioned my own courage once more as I second-guessed how they would receive what I was about to declare. No, I thought, substituting a measure of disdain for valor. Whether they rejected my words or embraced them, truth is immutable. I grabbed a slug of my drink so big it dropped down to the safety zone just as the prescient waiter stopped by and suggested another.

"Look," I said. "This world, the universe, and time, were spoken into existence seven thousand years ago, give or take, the worldwide deluge, separation of the continents, the forming of mountains and canyons occurred five thousand years ago in one fell swoop, Man's earliest writings began a hundred or so years later when the people dispersed from Babylon to the far flung continents, diffusing and separating the genetic matrix, causing racial and language differentiations...and here we are today...and being told that none of that is true."

Ron and Trish discreetly slipped money on the table and left without a word. "I guess we're supposed to think they went for some fresh air?" I remarked.

Jeff looked at me smugly. "Like I said, we're the stalwarts."

Dan contemplated for a moment and fiddled with his finger, drawing some imaginary thought on the table. "About that...the timeline. It makes all the difference."

"Mr. Grey," said Susan. "Do you know that Dan and Jeff and I...we've been looking into this, too? We had to because we know that, until now, we really have been living the lie of others. And until you, we thought we were alone...isolated...fearful to question."

"Well," I said. "There is no doubt you should be fearful...you saw what happened to me at a modern day bastion of free speech."

"You're a pariah at the university, alright," said Jeff. "But we'll be okay. They take our money. In your case, the university is a crack whore, and you shook the habit."

Dan lifted his glass of orange juice in a toast. "Here's to all of us making it through this mad world."

"Yes," said Susan raising her glass also, and turning to the window to look out to sea. "This mad, ghastly world."

At the same moment, Ron returned with a sheepish grin. "You're back!" I said with a welcoming smile and at the same time wondering what was going on in Susan's mind.

"Yeah...Trish went downtown to shop. I'll meet her later. I didn't want to miss this."

"Very good, then," I said. "Perhaps you're one of the stalwarts like us."

"Well, not sure about that," said Ron. "But the timeline, like you said..."

"You mean carbon...radiometric dating?" I asked.

"Yeah. It's goofy," said Ron. "You give a specimen to one lab and they come up with twenty million years...give it to another and they come up with a million...then there's the helium thing...there's too much of it."

De Broglie had talked about that to me and I delighted in finding someone else bringing it up independently. Dan turned to Ron for an explanation. "Helium escapes from rock at a known rate...and it escapes rapidly...if Earth was, say, more than about 10,000 years old, all of the rock bound helium should be gone...it isn't, of course."

"Well, there you go," said Jeff.

I looked at Susan, who had run with Dan's comment that the world had gone mad. "Ghastly? I'm not disagreeing with you, but I'm interested in knowing how you...well...know."

Susan leaned over the table. "Signs...mannerisms... people spit in public now...they walk the Thorazine shuffle...they swagger like they had something to be proud about."

"And they're just plain dumber," said Dan with rising passion. "...that people believe atmospheric gasses essential for life are toxic, that the beheading cultures are equal to those that go to the moon...I mean...we're surrounded by idiots! You can see it in their empty eyes...they believe that changing words changes facts."

"Words," I said. "How incredibly important they are. You've heard people say 'they're just words,' but they are everything. According to Man's first written words, our world was spoken into existence."

"That's a tough one to grasp," said Dan sitting back and stroking his chin in thought.

"Do you have a better answer?" I asked.

"If I do, I don't have it at the moment."

"Let me ask," I said, "Have you considered it outside the realm of human understanding? You can fiddle around with physics and philosophy all you want and no one's come up with a satisfactory answer. You can describe life, observe its mechanisms, see it work, but you don't actually know what life is. To know the truth, doesn't it make sense to begin with what's already been revealed instead of making up something to fit modern humanity's limited comprehension?"

"Well, I can't argue with that," agreed Dan.

"Let's knock down another lie," I said to a skeptical looking Ron. "Carbon dating. The method starts right off with false assumptions, beginning with the idea that we could possibly know the level of elements originally locked up in the earth's crust at creation—and ending with the preposterous and wholly unsupportable notion that the earth is billions of years old. The assumptions merely accommodate man's hubris. Even if it were true, no mechanism or process can measure billions or millions of years in a physical world only thousands of years old."

Ron thought for a moment. "So the earth isn't full of gas...science is," he joked.

"*Pagan* science," I added. "Dan, you're the chemist. What was it that Boyle said?"

"Who's Boyle?" asked Jeff.

"The father of modern chemistry," I said. "...the guy who changed the hocus pocus of alchemy into the science of chemistry."

Dan took the lead. "Well, Boyle said that conflicts between scripture and science are due either from a mistake in science or a misinterpretation of scripture."

"In other words," I said. "Going forward, like Boyle, Kepler, and Newton, you're going to need to check everything against the truth revealed in scripture instead of the self-serving ideas of modern man."

Susan spoke as we wrapped up the meeting, and by the expressions of those around the table, she spoke for all. "Think about all this, all the lies we've been told over the years...well...I just don't know now who we are."

I stowed my papers and led the group out the door into the cold. People outside winced and held their coats tight against the furious swirls of damp wind. None of us were doing the same, and I guessed that the fire of truth was keeping us warm. I heralded a cab and looked back at the group. "Stay together," I yelled, and wondered if I would see them again.

The cab driver looked to be of Middle Eastern descent and I heard some uncharacteristic but rousing choral music playing very low on the radio. "You can turn that up if you want," I said. "I'm usually forced to listen to jazz, oldies, or sports."

"You like it?" he asked with a thick accent and glancing back with a smile.

"Yeah, I think so...what is it?"

"Handel. Unto Us A Child Is Given," said the driver. "The words are from the great prophet Isaiah...750 B.C.," he said turning the music up a bit. "Oh...oh...listen to this part," he implored, interrupting himself to turn up the volume again as the radio poured out the lyrics across a thunderous, gleeful blast of musical notes that had been written and placed in just the right sequence: "He shall be called Wonderful! Counselor! Almighty God! The everlasting Father! The Prince of Peace!"

As the song ended, we were nearly at the train station. "Where are you from?" I asked.

"Middle East...I know what you are thinking," he said.

"I'm sure you can guess," I agreed.

"There are many of us...from everywhere...we have been saved from the lie of this world and live in the promise of the new."

It was a story I'd heard many times in the past. Now, it had meaning and truth and I wondered why that was. What was the nature of this change in understanding? Certainly Pei Ling was a messenger, but all the messages in the world hadn't impressed me until now. And what did Susan ask? Who are we? Now, there was a question.

Book Two

Chapter One

An Effect Is Not Greater Than Its Cause

South of the equator, Dr. Emile De Broglie was driving up the Pan American Highway to Chancay in Peru. Along the way, north of Lima, scrap wood and tin shanty towns covered the rolling hills to the east as far as the eye could see. He wondered about the little girl who served him almost ten years ago going south along this route. She was the sweetest thing, he remembered. It had been a long day. A tiny roadside shack caught his eye by the rusted Coca-Cola sign hanging from a tired, crooked pole along the highway. On a quirk, he pulled into the gravelly driveway and waited a moment for the dust to settle to get out of the car and walk over to the hut.

A pretty girl of twelve or so years got up from a stool where she was reading a magazine and smiled. She didn't speak Russian, German or English and De Broglie didn't speak Spanish and it didn't matter. She understood the language of a thirsty man. De Broglie, cola in hand, returned to his car and stopped halfway, retracing his steps back to the girl and her happy smile. With the best hand and facial signals he could muster, he asked for a napkin. She nodded knowingly and returned in a minute, happy as a sprite. As if to surprise De Broglie, she hid what she had behind her with perfect dramatic timing and with the stroke of a magician drew up a half dozen sheets of toilette paper. He got what he needed and returned to the car. Looking back, he saw the girl looking at him and he waved good-bye with a warm smile. He sat in the car for a moment before starting off, looking at the toilette paper and thinking of the girl and her ingenuity and grace in answering his mundane request. She must live in one of the nearby shanty towns, he thought. And he wondered and worried about the life she lived and the future she looked to, but he couldn't take care of the world and drove off.

As he passed the area today going north, he saw the shack still there, barely changed, the same coke sign, now more weathered and broken, hanging from the pole by a thread of rusted wire, and a new one nailed above it advertising Inca Cola. A less curious man would have made a note to check back on the return trip, but De Broglie made an abrupt u-turn just after passing the shack and pulled in to park his car. In the years since, he had learned some rudimentary Spanish and asked the young woman sitting on the stool behind the counter how long she had worked there. She answered in English with an accent that made it almost Spanish.

"Oh," said De Broglie with engaging timidity. The girl had the same kind look he remembered of the girl who served him years ago, and questioned her answer to be sure of what he heard. "Eight years?"

The girl seemed puzzled, and began to empty some boxes and stock the shelves behind the counter with cigarettes and candy. "But I think I saw you here ten years ago," De Broglie said. "Certainly, you do not remember, but you sold me a coke and gave me napkins...uh, '*papel higiénico.*'"

The girl thought for a minute and came from behind the counter and looked at De Broglie. "I am sorry, senor. That was my sister."

"Oh, how is she?" inquired De Broglie, happy with the familiarity. "Please tell her I remember her kindness."

De Broglie saw that she was earnestly following his every word and turned sad when she understood what he was saying. "I am sorry, senor. She is...she is gone from us."

"Gone?"

"Yes. I am here now...she died." De Broglie took a deep, a labored breath, the kind one takes when hearing such news and the girl reached for more words. "You knew her?"

"I got a coke from her and I remember her and I will never forget her," said De Broglie. The girl explained that death came bearing a child and she began to cry and in her grief rushed into De Broglie and De Broglie embraced her. "I miss her so much," said the girl.

"I do, too," said De Broglie, as he released his embrace and didn't know what else to say. He bowed his head and thought how he should exit the situation. "And about you..." asked De Broglie. "How are you?"

"I am fine," said the girl, her spirits lifted by the question and gathering herself.

De Broglie did what he could think of at the time and extended his sympathies and left twenty dollars and his card. "Please tell me about your life someday. I do not know what you will write to me, but please write to me if you will."

De Broglie departed from the girl and continued on to Chancay. I should have done something for the girl all those years ago, he thought. Perhaps she would not have died, and he wondered what kind of life she had lived, if she had joy, his mind racing with thoughts of what he should have done then and what might have been now.

Bearing up, De Broglie drove a while north, and off to the left, saw the curious old castle at Chancay and knew he was close to his destination, a place far enough away from the noise and nonsense that attracts weekend tourists and the curious. He passed the town square, which was once immaculately landscaped but which was now overgrown with weeds, and turned right a few blocks down the street to the ocean. He parked his car and entered the courtyard to the restaurant where he was to meet Dr. Hernando De La Croix, a long time friend and colleague.

Nothing at the restaurant had changed over the years. A barely serviceable tin roof was held up on stilts over some old wooden picnic tables covered with blue and white paint freely slathered over and over again as to make a slick, almost cushioned surface. The place was nearly empty and De Broglie sat down alone looking out to sea. Before long, a slightly plump man, impeccably dressed, walked briskly toward him. "Emile! Emile!" It was Dr. Hernando De La Croix in his signature white suit, silk tie, and fedora in hand.

"Yes, yes, how are you?" exclaimed De Broglie, embracing his old friend. "I'm so glad you could make it."

"And if I didn't?" asked Hernando.

"I would have had the best ceviche in the world alone."

"Hah. Indeed," said Hernando, observing a barely perceptible slur in De Broglie's speech. "You've been drinking without me!"

"Oh, yes," answered De Broglie, mindful but not embarrassed. "I will watch myself."

"Oh, please don't, my friend," said Hernando. "Let me catch up." Hernando signaled the waitress and asked with his irrepressible smile for a Pisco sour "...with some booze in it," he added. She brought the drink in a flash and Hernando surveyed the surroundings and turned to De Broglie. "So tell me, how is your work going?"

"Wait, wait...not so fast. A topic that big now is like a shot of early morning whiskey," exclaimed De Broglie, laughing.

"Yes," said Hernando. "I mustn't be too hasty. Apologies all over the place, my friend. But I could not wait to see you!"

"Nor I, you," said De Broglie.

"So what brings us together?" asked Hernando. "Wait! I know! But first allow me my drink." Hernando raised his glass in a silent toast to De Broglie and took a first sip, delighted with the fine balance of sweet and sour over ankle deep booze and nodded approvingly. "We are here because you want my help...your call was not as mysterious as you think," said Hernando in a good-natured chide.

De Broglie smiled. "I was testing you."

"I have shut down my project, you know," said Hernando.

"I suspected as much," said De Broglie. "When you wrote that the government was getting in your business, it was merely a matter of time."

"Hah! The *bane* of my work, I should say!" said Hernando raising his voice and just as soon lowering it to an intimate whisper. "But I needed their money."

"Hah! It's why I work alone," said De Broglie. "You would be surprised what a mind alone can do in a small laboratory."

"You'd be surprised what a *small* mind alone can do in a laboratory. Nothing!" exclaimed Hernando. "You are a genius!"

"You flatter me, my friend," said De Broglie. "I am no greater thinker than you. I do admit, however, I have a keen awareness of the unseen. Your hurdle, you know—and it was insurmountable—was moving mass in time...far too costly, far too inefficient...impossible, though I suspect you thought you were close." De Broglie looked into the distance and back to Hernando, briefly scratching his head the way a man does when he has a profound thought and he's going to surprise someone with it. "Why travel in time when you can peer into it?"

"You are saying quantum theory is useless?" asked Hernando.

"Oh, much worse, my friend," said De Broglie. "The conclusions...foolish babblings of vain men! Wasn't it you who called me to report from that conference you attended some time back that to a quantum physicist, nothing is something?"

"Hah. I know of whom you speak," said Hernando. "He maintains to this day that something can come from nothing..."

"...and betraying his stultifying arrogance," interrupted De Broglie, "that an effect can be greater than its cause."

"Yes, yes," agreed an increasingly animated Hernando, "and yet his books are required reading in schools the world over!"

De Broglie stroked his chin, intensely looking at Hernando. "I am very familiar with quantum theory's foolish notion that in a vacuum, things can materialize out of nothing, with the caveat, of course, that it has never been observed...and that while the average person cannot conceive of it, nothing is something to a quantum physicist...do you understand how astonishingly ignorant that is? I ask you, what accounts for such thinking?"

"Well," said Hernando, trailing off as if to disagree, "The way you put it..."

"The way I put it?" asked a slightly agitated De Broglie.

Hernando nervously adjusted his tie, knowing De Broglie would not appreciate his response. "I submit, a case can be made for evolutionary cosmology and quantum theory."

"You too?" De Broglie frowned. "Like the rest...ever yearning, never learning."

"But the tide of humanity is not with you," retorted Hernando.

"And when did I ever care what humanity thinks?" demanded De Broglie. "The humanity that swims in a sump hole and thinks it's the Riviera?"

Hernando shrank at De Broglie's words. "Perhaps you don't want my help."

"One deluded with evolutionary nonsense is no help at all," affirmed De Broglie. "It means you cannot think."

Hernando stared at De Broglie and continued to entertain his words. "You claim to know the earth is billions of years old, know where we came from, how we got here...and you cannot even explain the workings of a single human cell, how the sun shines, or why a seed sprouts!" De Broglie took a breath and Hernando took a drink. "This would be comedy if it weren't so irritating," added De Broglie.

The waitress laid out a spread of food and refreshed the drinks. "Shall we eat?" asked Hernando not letting on that De Broglie hit a deep note.

"Yes, by all means," said a calmer but still disdainful De Broglie. "Let's eat."

Unfazed by this serious but friendly confrontation, Hernando started in, joyfully hunting and picking his favorite morsels...chopped seafood and fish roe marinated in lime juice with diced red onions, giant kernels of purple corn, and delicate strands of seaweed and fresh coriander artfully placed in a trio of pristine scallop shells. The two men did not talk for a long time, and no one can be sure if it was De Broglie's taunting, a third drink, or a message from God himself, when Hernando stopped, focused on De Broglie with the startled look of a man taking his last breath and said, "I got it."

No teasing, no antagonism, De Broglie understood what Hernando "got" and smiled. "Welcome to our world."

Chapter Two

The Works of Man Come To No Good End

"What am I going to have to do?" asked De Broglie. "Kill you?"

It was a matter of expression, of course. De Broglie and Hernando had just arrived at the doc's compound along the Urubamba, the place I turned down for Vegas. It was, indeed, gorgeous—a group of three modernist cottages, connected by walkways leading from the grand house to the guest house to the laboratory, where, just outside its door, the flowing Urubamba cascaded in a comforting reverie. The walls to the west were entirely glass, and the floors of the cottages were particularly immaculate, shiny with heavily lacquered wood hewn and polished with the mark of local craftsmen and, in the entryway of the grand house, De Broglie's prized alpaca throw rug.

"Come in, my friend," said De Broglie. Hernando entered and stepped on the rug and was duly impressed with the surroundings, smiling dutifully in awe and appreciation when De Broglie turned to looked at him. "You smell."

“Me?” Hernando thought it was something in the house, thinking he had merely the good manners to say nothing.

“Look at your shoe,” said De Broglie. “I believe you have something stuck to it...look, there is something hanging there.” Hernando grabbed De Broglie’s shoulder to lift his leg and examine the bottom of his shoe. Sure enough, it looked liked the cause of the putrid offense and it was.

“Can you not look where you’re stepping?” insisted the furious De Broglie who, as soon as the words left his mouth, felt for Hernando’s embarrassment and pointed to a water hose near the side of the house.

“I’ll get you another one,” offered Hernando walking over to wash his shoe.

“The rug? Don’t bother,” said De Broglie. “I’ll have it cleaned.” He had no intention of having it cleaned, of course. He could not bear that the rug had been tainted and hauled it out back for disposal at a later date and quickly ran a mop over the area where the rug had been so that the entire floor shown in its polished splendor.

The two had agreed that Hernando would stay for a couple of days to observe and get a handle on De Broglie’s work. If all went well, Hernando would send for his personals in Lima and stay for an undetermined time. Late in the afternoon, Hernando asked De Broglie what they would be eating for dinner and the doc explained that his chef would be coming soon to prepare whatever she was going to prepare and that Hernando would be sure to like whatever it was. De Broglie looked out the expansive glass wall of the sitting room on the west side of the grand house. “It’s time for cocktails, my friend.”

And the doc broke out his wet bar on wheels from an ante room and marshaled the unit between the easy chairs where De Broglie invited Hernando to sit and enjoy the view.

"Unfortunately, I don't see this in Lima," said Hernando.

"I know...I know," agreed De Broglie looking across the wide valley to the snow capped Andes in the distance. "It's always dreary in Lima...but you wanted to be where the action was, right?" Hernando, taking a drink and looking to the mountains, agreed.

"I have all the action I can handle right here," said De Broglie. "No one to bother me, no unexpected visitors."

There was movement in the kitchen where the chef had let herself in as was her custom. After a short while, scintillating aromas began to fill the air, delightfully tempting the two men. It was a relaxing time, especially for Hernando, who was grateful to find relief from the stress to which he and his work had been subjected by political forces in the country.

The men gazed quietly as the long shadows of late afternoon moved across the landscape. "Ah, ol' boy...Where has freedom gone?" opined Hernando looking into the distance.

"I'm afraid Orwell's time of universal deceit is upon us," said De Broglie. "Certainly, we are moving into the dark era of ignorance foretold in the scriptures...a time when people would embrace tyranny and oppression over freedom and liberty...a time when nearly the entire world would work in opposition to truth and light."

"Fortunately, you are apart from it here," said Hernando.

"Yes, this place does put us some distance from most manifestations of human evil...for how long, I do not know." De Broglie picked up his drink. "I'll not be here much longer, just the same."

Hernando looked at De Broglie, shocked. "What? You are sick?"

"Nothing in particular...though, at my age, one never knows." De Broglie looked at his watch. "Time to eat."

"Do you always eat at the same time?" asked Hernando.

"Yes. At exactly the same time every evening so I can be in the lab at seven."

Hernando commented to De Broglie that it appears he allows one hour for dinner. "Yes. More than an hour, you are eating too much. Less than an hour, you are eating too rushed."

They walked into the dining room with their drinks, where two formal and very intricate place settings had been set. Hernando picked up one of the forks and held it to the light. "What are these?"

De Broglie ignored Hernando for the moment and called for Isabella to come into the dining room, where he introduced the two. When Isabella returned to the kitchen, Hernando could hardly hold his excitement. "How beautiful is your housemaid!"

"She's not a housemaid," declared De Broglie. "She's a talented girl of infinite potential who has graciously accepted my offer of employment...a housemaid I tell what to do, she tells *me* what to do...and she certainly has...I, in fact, attribute my good health thus far to her."

"Gazing on her sweet countenance is sure to help," said Hernando in a moment of whimsy.

"Compose yourself!" said De Broglie good-naturedly. "About the fork...what was your question?"

Hernando lifted the utensil to the light again, and then a knife. Between the handle and the tines on the fork and the handle and the blade on the knife was fixed a tiny transparent glass bulb, amber in color and containing a curious mechanism that seemed to be suspended by no visible means. "What is inside? There is something in there, but I cannot make it out."

"Put on your glasses," said De Broglie. "It's a miniature clock work...an homage to time."

"Where on earth would you find such a thing? It's beautiful!"

"I made them," said De Broglie. "In my lab...I will show you later."

"But first you will eat," said Isabella, rolling in a cart covered in white linen on which sat individual portions of enticing English cut ribs of prime beef, buttered carrots and peas, steaming popovers and butter, roasted duck, chow fun, Chinese broccoli, and a bottle of inky, cabernet franc from the states. De Broglie and Hernando smiled approvingly at Isabella and dug in as soon as she left the room.

"Of course, I don't eat like this everyday," said De Broglie. "But you are a special occasion." The doc also made an exception to his rule of being in the lab an hour after dinner, and instead, after dinner, directed Hernando into the library for rare brandy and fine cigars. The two sat silent and sated, looking out to the panorama now immersed in the last bit of deep, azure twilight, and to the first stars revealing themselves in the evening sky.

"I've been thinking," said Hernando with a pause long enough to compel De Broglie to ask about what.

"About the mass in time problem," answered Hernando dropping some ashes into the ashtray. "I should have known, but I was so taken up with trying to deal with draconian bureaucracy and the politics of evil that I never had the chance to focus."

"Yes," said an understanding De Broglie. "You were sabotaged by the limiting idiocy of your colleagues and culture." Hernando smiled and appreciated De Broglie's empathy and recommitted to learn everything he could from his old friend.

De Broglie looked at his watch. "It's almost eight...shall we retire to the lab?" Hernando was excited to see De Broglie's work and helped him clean up the remnants of the cigars and empty glasses. "Remember," remarked De Broglie holding a glass in one hand and an ashtray in the other. "Though she were a housemaid," stressed De Broglie, "I would not leave my mess, just the same."

"Certainly not for Isabella," said Hernando following De Broglie to the kitchen. "By the way, has she left?"

"Yes," said De Broglie.

Hernando frowned. "A shame I did not have a chance to say good bye."

"She'll be back," assured De Broglie. "...off to the lab?"

"Yes, and we'll make it on time," said Hernando with a wry edge.

De Broglie motioned Hernando to follow him. "Can I take my drink?" asked Hernando.

"And what do I have in my hand?" asked De Broglie. "Of course, you can!"

The soft rush of the river played like white noise in the breezeway leading to the lab. The air was pungent with jasmine and honeysuckle. Had the two men been boys, an outside observer would think they were up to no good as they approached the door to the lab in silence and almost on tip toe. But, alas, they were men—two of the brightest in their fields. Neither had reached this point in their lives by following the conventions, consensus, or cultural buffoonery of their peers.

It was night and the lab was like no other room in the compound. An eerie light that seemed to come from nowhere in particular got Hernando's curiosity. "What is this luminescence? We almost don't need lights."

"Hah," exclaimed De Broglie. "Had I operated Beula more recently, we wouldn't need the lights at all."

"Beula?" asked Hernando.

"Yes, my fully functional, perfectly perfect, efficient masterpiece mechanism to peer into time," said De Broglie. "But to answer your question, the glow is a kind of residual dusting of, as far as I can guess, light-emitting neutrinos...yet they are not neutrinos. I don't know what they are. In any case, they flow into the room after operating Beula...not always, mind you...just sometimes. And sometimes much more than others. At any rate, it does not seem to be dangerous."

"And when do I meet Beula?" asked Hernando.

"Soon enough," said De Broglie with almost a measure of disappointment. "Are you not curious about the glow? I was hoping you might have some idea."

"I'm more curious about Beula," answered Hernando.

"Let me tell you something, first," said De Broglie. "I don't think even my protégé has an idea...at least not yet...but I believe I have discovered time."

Hernando looked puzzled.

"The essence of time," said De Broglie. "The very nature of time! Until now, all have failed on the assumption that the world has existed for millions of years. If there were only one remaining fish in all the oceans of the world, I would more likely catch *it* than stumble upon time using such nonsense."

Hernando thought for a moment and looked De Broglie in the eye. "But you had only to find the fish in a pail of water?"

"Yes, not an ocean!" said De Broglie excitedly. "I knew you were the right man for this."

"And how did you come across such an idea?" asked Hernando.

"From that pop culture astronomer in the 80's," said De Broglie. "That is, his mistake, I should say. You remember his book. I threw it in the trash after reading the very first sentence. *'The cosmos is all that is or ever was or ever will be.'* How would he know, I asked myself? How would anyone know? I was astonished at the hubris, the lack of scientific rigor. I was so angry that this man represented science to the masses. But in my anger, I recalled what was to be the foundation of my success...Do you want a drink?"

"No, no," said Hernando. "What was it? What did you recall?"

"A passage in the scriptures," said De Broglie.

"Really?" asked a nearly agitated Hernando.

"Are you sure?" asked De Broglie.

"Sure of what?"

"That you don't want a drink?" De Broglie knew he was getting Hernando riled.

"Why you son-of-a..." said Hernando laughing. "Yes, give me a damn drink."

"Okay, okay," said De Broglie handing his friend a short brandy from the bottle he kept in the lab. "As I was about to say, the scriptures...there are two references written by separate scribes of the Word, hundreds of years apart but saying the very same thing...'everlasting to everlasting.' This means, of course, there is something in between, don't you see? Time exists between the first everlasting and the everlasting to come. We are in that time now!"

"Aha!" said Hernando, fascinated. "So you also have a primary source for your time line!"

"Precisely!" said De Broglie delighted but just as soon fretting. "There is one thing that bothers me about this science business, though...How is it," asked De Broglie, "that working with the same data we scientists draw different conclusions?"

"You *would* bring that up," said Hernando drawing back contemplatively. "I have an idea about that...but one I have been reluctant to reveal."

"To me?" asked De Broglie.

Hernando took a deep breath. "To anyone...that is, man is inherently evil, my friend. The natural scientist chooses evil, arriving at unscientific conclusions naturally. Take the DNA similarity between monkeys and men...the foolish mind, embracing evil, sees shared DNA as evidence of evolution. The wise mind, the sound scientific mind, understands shared DNA as evidence of a common mechanism of creation."

"Yes," said De Broglie. "But unlike the beasts or other living organisms, Man was created in the image of his own maker...it is so plainly stated."

"That is a difficult difference to explain," said Hernando. "The evil are easily conned."

"Because they want to be," agreed De Broglie. "So many of my weaker students went into government work," said De Broglie alluding to Hernando's confrontation with politics.

"Yes, you have to wonder what awaited them there." said Hernando.

"The easy life of the idiot," said De Broglie. "Renewing the unrenewable, sustaining the unsustainable, working to make permanent a temporary world."

"Evil has great sway over the dim mind," said Hernando.

"Well, I suppose you are right...it comes down to that, doesn't it," said De Broglie sipping his brandy. "Certainly, it is fortunate that our outward personas are congruous enough with society. If they really knew who we were, I would never have been able to finagle the money and equipment to support this."

“As a scientist,” said Hernando looking around the lab, “I would certainly never assume anything other than we do our work because we seek the truth...but, I sense there is something more in it for you.” Hernando paused for a sip of his brandy and looked at De Broglie. “What exactly is the purpose of your work?”

“It is a gift,” said De Broglie.

“For whom?”

“For those aware of the eternal worlds but who are bullied by their failed culture into denying them...they need something undeniably obvious,” said De Broglie.

“Hmm,” said Hernando. “You know very well what the scriptures say...I, too, have read them.”

“What’s that?” asked De Broglie.

“If I have told you of earthly things and you do not believe, how can you believe of heavenly things?”

“Oh, yes,” said De Broglie. “A profound wisdom, for sure...exactly the reason for Beula!”

“My friend,” said Hernando in a sober voice. “The people of this world are dead. You are too kind. Let them enjoy their ignorance.”

De Broglie sat back and sighed. “That would be truly depressing. I have put so much work into this only to realize it is futile?”

“Not futile my friend,” said Hernando. “You know as well as I that those who can see will see and those who do not cannot. Do you think that the wicked read Jeremiah and understand that the almond tree is the watcher or that the

Psalmist precisely described the crucifixion 700 years before the event? No. Your work is already seen and understood by those who desire light and truth."

"You think so?" said De Broglie ready to move on from the conversation.

"Tell me," asked Hernando. "Does anyone else know about your Beula?"

"Only one other person," said De Broglie. "Aaron."

"What is his understanding?"

"Well, he was certainly impressed," said De Broglie. "Understand? I don't know."

"If he's of the right mind, understanding will come," said Hernando. "And in so doing, your intent has already been accomplished," he said attempting to lift De Broglie's mood.

"Perhaps you are correct," said De Broglie. "I should not worry...a wonderful girl found him to keep him and guide him. It won't be easy, though...his culture and education turned him originally into a fool..."

"...Yes, as we all were," Hernando interjected.

"Yes...well," De Broglie continued. "I'm not sure about that...certainly I was a fool once, but Pei Ling?"

"Pei Ling?" asked Hernando.

"His wife," answered De Broglie. "Aaron's wife...I think she has always known" said De Broglie pondering his words. "Anyway, if he could meet the least of my hopes, it would be to plant the seeds of what he has learned."

“Well, we do our best, don’t we,” said Hernando. “...though the works of Man come to no good end.”

“But mine is not a work of Man,” said an emphatic De Broglie. ‘Mine is a work of God.”

“I understand,” said Hernando, and he did. “Now, are you ever going to show me Beula?”

Chapter Three

De Broglie's Algorithm

"How did it go with your students?" asked Pei Ling stirring something over the stove that smelled fantastic.

I greeted her with a brief kiss and hung my coat in the closet. "Well enough, I think...you're home tonight, aren't you?"

"Yes, dear."

"Good. I'm going to get a shower and relax."

"You're in a rush?" she asked as I hurried into the bedroom to change. "Are you going somewhere?"

"I just said I'm going to relax tonight."

"Maybe you were going to relax somewhere else," said Pei Ling.

"Is that an edge I hear in your voice, dear?" I came quickly from the bedroom and slipped my arms around her waist. "I am in a rush...for you...I haven't seen you all day. You think I could manage another moment away from you?"

Pei Ling pursed her lips in an unconvincing pout. "I wasn't sure."

"Nice try, dear." I said. "You're sure of everything." And she was. "Say, what is that?" I asked unable to resist the delightful aroma of whatever it was that she was cooking.

"Dim sum."

"You can make that?" I asked, surprised.

"It's not difficult...just takes time."

"Smells delicious," I said. "I hope you don't mind that I'm not hungry...I had a big lunch."

"Are you sure?"

She asked the magic question and I rethought my answer. I was not hungry, but I could not overcome the enticing aroma and submitted. "Just a couple," I said. She prepared tea and condiments for us to dine in bed while reading and listening to music together, which had become our custom—the reading and music, not the dining in bed.

"Dear?" I asked motioning to the music. "Would you put on *Feel the Moon*?"

"Oh, you want something depressing!"

"What's to be happy about," I said. "I never got around to Pascal's wager or De Broglie's algorithm."

"With the students?" asked Pei Ling slipping into bed next to me as the music began to play softly in the backgroud.

"Yeah...kinda feel like I failed them again."

"You can't teach them everything, darling," she said. "They have to invest their effort, too." Pei Ling took a sip of tea and put down her cup. "What is De Broglie's algorithm?"

"A mathematical proof of why we don't belong here…why this place is not our natural home," I said taking a bite of dumpling and looking straight ahead with the stare of a thinking man. "Indeed, we are strangers here."

"Really?" asked Pei Ling seeming to be genuinely impressed.

"Well, *you* know that," I said.

"Yes, I know we don't belong here…but De Broglie's algorithm," she implored.

"Well, as I remember it, the doc said that taking all identifiable factors into account, there are perhaps only one in a thousand or more of us who are even open to…even have any desire for truth…he said the algorithm is based on the ancient writings…the scriptures." I paused a moment to let my thoughts catch up with my words. "No wonder I'm inclined to avoid people."

"What are the identifying factors?" asked Pei Ling.

"As De Broglie explained…it's funny how I'd forgotten this until now…anyway, he explained that the weightiest factor was pride…people who do things of and for themselves to show to others…like self mutilation, bizarre personal behavior, bumper sticker mentality…you know…sharing meaningless opinions as if they were meaningful."

"They are interested because they are of this world," said Pei Ling.

"Well, if I were to draw my own conclusion, the fundamental problem seems to be that people choose the made up history of man over the real, cosmic history of existence in the written words of the patriarchs and prophets—people who actually witnessed the beginning."

Pei Ling looked at me, engaged. "The life we live here and now is foretold in their writings. There is no point to worry, dear. Those who are given to the truth receive it intuitively. Remember Pascal...'there are those who are afraid to lose God and those who are afraid to find Him.' There are few who want to find Him."

The conversation was a heavy one for the moment. "I still think we should just go back and live in your little village in China." Though Pei Ling knew I was not serious, she said it is getting close to the time we recede from this world...before it consumes itself in its own evil. "You think the day is coming soon?

"There are signs," said Pei Ling.

"Such as?" I asked.

"Look around, dear."

I couldn't deny it and agreed it can only get worse. "Speaking of which, things are going to get worse if I don't get a job soon."

"Why don't you call uncle?" suggested Pei Ling.

"De Broglie?...I don't know what he could do...I don't want to teach anymore, and even if I did, I'm blacklisted."

"Blacklisted?" Pei Ling new what it meant, but was reluctant to believe it real.

"Oh, yes," I said. "It's a firestorm. Everyone knows about it, but no one talks about it. Any world view outside of evolution, secularism…the slightest reference to religion…is not tolerated."

"But evolution is religion," argued Pei Ling.

"They think it's science…we've fallen that far," I said.

"But there is no scientific basis to it," Pei Ling exclaimed.

"I know…I know dear, thanks to you." I looked at the time and thought that perhaps I should give De Broglie a call if only to keep in touch and describe to him the circumstances of my firing, which I guessed he would find very entertaining. At the very least, I was curious as to what he was up to and picked up the phone. I guessed right. De Broglie almost couldn't stop laughing.

"You…He…You…You mean he said you'd never…oh…oh…that *is* funny."

I let him have his fun and waited for the last laugh. "I'm quite happy you see the humor in this," I said with a measure of sarcasm.

"Stop!" said De Broglie. "You'll get me started again." And I could hear him trying to stop from laughing aloud. "So you *are* out of the indoctrination industry!" said a composed and supportive De Broglie. "Good for you."

"Yep, I never thought it would come to this," I said. "It took me a long time to realize the insanity of idiots as intellectuals, and the simple-minded as scholars."

"It is the way of the world, my friend…your courage in standing up to fools is greatly satisfying," said De Broglie. "I like to think I had something to do with it."

"You did…and, actually," I said. "I don't feel like it took any courage at all. It was what a man is supposed to do."

"All the better, Aaron," said De Broglie, pausing to fully gather himself. "On another note, I am not going to ask about your financials…they are beside the point…this is just how things work out…I want you to come down and work for me…with us…with my colleague, Hernando, and me…work with us on the most fantastic, universe-shaking project in the history of Man…besides the Creation, of course."

It was quite a claim De Broglie was making, and I understood that a man of De Broglie's stature walked in, well, a different circle of friends than me, and I couldn't help but be curious about his colleague. "Hernando?" I asked. "Hernando De La Croix by chance?"

"Yes," confirmed De Broglie. "The very same."

"I thought he was an economist?"

"Hah," said De Broglie. "That's his cover…he's a brilliant scientist…like yourself."

"Alright, alright…don't embarrass me. I'm not nearly in the same league as you guys."

"The point is," said De Broglie. "I'm not doing you a favor. You're the right man for the job."

I told De Broglie to hold on for a minute, covering the phone's mouthpiece and turning to Pei Ling. "He's offering me a job in South America."

Pei Ling looked at me like she knew something good was about to happen. "In Peru? The Urubamba?"

"Let me be sure," I said and thinking it wouldn't make a difference because I was running out of money, and I asked De Broglie.

"Yes, yes...my compound on the Urubamba...the place you turned down for Las Vegas."

"Okay, okay, don't rub it in. Pei Ling will be very happy," I said, pausing to catch up with the excitement of the offer. "Um, the job...what job? What is the project?"

"Don't you want to talk about money?" asked De Broglie.

"I don't care about the money...I know you'll compensate me more than I'm worth....I mean, all expenses paid to one of the most beautiful places on earth from what I hear..."

"Oh," joked De Broglie. "You think I am going to pay your way down here?" De Broglie paused to see if I was going to answer, but I didn't. "Yes I am," he said. "How soon can you start?"

"Whenever you want me," I said.

"Good. There will be two flight vouchers in the mail in a few days and you can redeem them when you are ready...but make it soon."

I agreed to De Broglie's terms and told Pei Ling the good news. She was elated and said she'd plan a celebration with Ro and Ann.

"I don't know if that's a good idea, dear," I said. "I think they're on the outs."

"Nope," said Pei Ling emphatically. "They're on the ins...Ann straightened him out."

"Hmm," I said. "That's hard to believe, but if you say so..." Ro wouldn't get that other weekend in the city at my expense that he'd chided me about. And if I were to die now, I thought, I would come very close to fulfilling the notion of a friend who once said the worst that could happen is to die and have money left over. I planned to get down to De Broglie as soon as we could, and suggested that we do any celebrating with Ro and Ann at home.

"Great idea, dear," said Pei Ling. "Something simple with a great bottle of wine and...and...voilá! Right?"

"Yes," I said. "Voilá."

Chapter Four

Fear of The Perpendicular

"I'm not even going to ask," I said to Ro as we washed dishes while the girls chatted in the other room.

"About what?"

And I knew he knew what I was asking. "You and Ann!"

"Yeah, yeah..." said Ro. "...that's all fine now...wanna know if she paid me the money?"

"Nope, and even if I did, it's none of my business."

"Hmm," said Ro with a hint of suspicion. "You're sure agreeable. You've been agreeable all night. We never even talked about the religion thing. You didn't even bring it up."

"It's up to you," I said. "I'm done arguing with people."

"I don't believe that for a minute," said Ro.

"You either get it or you don't. I'm exasperated arguing with idiots...present company excepted, of course."

Ro dried the last dinner plate. "That move to Peru...I don't know about that...sounds risky."

"Risky?"

"It's a helluva long way away," said Ro. "I didn't even know it was south of the equator until I looked."

"It's a ways away, alright, but closer than China," I assured him.

"The problem," said Ro "is you're going down instead of sideways."

"What the hell are you talking about?"

"Here, I'll show ya." I followed Ro into where the girls were and the globe on Pei Ling's desk.

Ro held it up. "Look! See? Peru is down here, and China is over there."

I looked to Pei Ling and Ann who continued to be engaged in a conversation I could only imagine, which I had to, since they were speaking Chinese, and turned back to Ro. "What difference does that make?"

"It makes a difference," said Ro. "Hey, I gotta smoke. Take your drink outside."

It was a temperate evening with a light breeze rustling through the trees and strong enough to keep Ro's cigarette smoke out of my face. He took a forceful drag from his cigarette, so intense that it lit his face with an orange glow, and he exhaled a long, satisfying, thunderhead-sized cloud of smoke. "So this is it?" he asked with a mix of melancholy and finality. "You won't be coming back?"

"Well...never say never," I said.

"I never said never."

"You jackass," I said with the affection of a friend. "Pei Ling said she's going to pay the rent on the apartment for a couple of months until we see what happens...so...I'm sure we'll be back...I can't imagine not coming back here."

Ro's next drag on his cigarette burned away nearly an inch of tobacco. He seemed to enjoy it so much, I almost thought about taking up smoking. "Sure you'll be back?"

"Well, yeah," I said. "After we settle down and I'm situated with the job."

"What are you going to be doing down there, anyway?" asked Ro.

"I'm going to be working with De Broglie...you know, the scientist dude...major league scientist dude," I said making light of the topic.

"But what are you actually going to do?" asked Ro. "...like be his secretary?"

"I don't think so," I said with a laugh. "Actually, I don't know, exactly...But I need a paycheck."

"Hope you're right," said Ro unconvinced.

"Hey...you and Ann can always hop a flight to see us...De Broglie tells me it's beautiful down there."

"Me?" asked Ro incredulously. "I wouldn't survive...no smoking on airplanes, remember?"

"Buy a couple packs of those nicotine patches and wear 'em like a belt," I offered.

"Are you crazy?" said Ro. "But that might be an idea," he said dismissively. "Let's go in."

The girls were wrapping up the evening, and to tell you the truth, I was feeling a bit melancholy myself about leaving these familiar surroundings and two good friends. When Pei Ling and I finally hit the sack, she knew I was bothered.

"And I never found out from De Broglie what he expects me to do," I said.

"I wonder," said Pei Ling, "what he has in his mind?"

"'*On* his mind,' dear, '*on* his mind,'" I said good-naturedly and kissing her forehead.

Pei Ling chuckled. "Oops...yes, 'on his mind.'"

"No matter," I said. "Now that I begin thinking about it, I'm getting pretty excited with the idea. I'm anxious to meet De La Croix, too." I paused for a moment in thought. "You know...I almost can't believe...out of all the people in the world...that me, a farm boy from no-where's-ville...could be working with two..."

"...men whose last names begin with 'De'?" asked Pei Ling.

"Well, now that you mention it," I said with a laugh. "But, no...two of the most eminent scientists and thinkers in the world...I mean, what are the odds?" Pei Ling stared at me. "I know," I said. "There are no coincidences."

Chapter Five

An Inviting Place To Be

We were an hour or so between planes in the late afternoon at DFW, an opportunity to try the much heralded Texas barbecue. It was good, for airport fare. Pei Ling looked at me and took a napkin from her purse to wipe the corner of my mouth.

Evening was coming on as we boarded the flight to Lima. An hour into the air, the sun yielded to the lesser light of a half moon in the night sky. I looked at Pei Ling who was sleeping like most of the other passengers and I enjoyed this time alone with my wandering thoughts. Looking down over Central America, the cities glowed in a tired, yellow light. It was very different from the bright, white light of North America and the cities of Asia and, in its own way, and at this time, more comforting. It was near midnight when the captain announced that we were on approach and the plane began to nose slightly downward to meet the fog and haze of coastal Peru. As the wings disappeared in the weather, I joined the other passengers as we tensed up a bit, hoping to break through the mist and see some sign of the earth below. We did, just as the wheels hit the runway and some of the more enthusiastic applauded the pilot and crew.

We stayed the night for a flight to Cuzco the following afternoon, where De Broglie said he would have a driver waiting for us. Outside the terminal, a man was holding a sign with "Arin Gray" on it. He appeared to be Chinese and he was. He also spoke English.

"How are you folks today?" he asked pulling out of the airport and looking at us in the rearview mirror with a welcoming smile.

"Doing well, doing well," I said taking in the unfamiliar sights. "How long is the drive?"

"An hour or so," said the driver. "The doctor said to take the scenic route." I looked at Pei Ling and doubted that there was a route that was not scenic.

"Do you work for De Broglie?" I asked, wondering if the doc had a full time staff, which wouldn't surprise me, though would seem rather extravagant.

"A contractor," said the driver. "He calls me when he needs someone picked up at the airport."

"I see," I said, and asked his name.

"Pablo," he answered. "I know...you think it is funny a Chinese man with a Spanish name."

"More interesting than funny," I said. "There is something about 19th Century immigration to Peru, but I don't know the details."

"Oh," he said with a continuous smile. "You know something of the history! Yes, you are right. My great-great-grandfather came as an indentured worker. Somehow he survived and here I am."

"Well, we're certainly glad," I said.

Some time passed without conversation as we motored along the lazy curves of the majestic mountains and through the pristine Sacred Valley when Pablo continued. "You must be a very important scientist."

I winced, looking at Pei Ling. "Not really," I said. "Just a good friend....how'd *you* meet De Broglie, by the way?"

"My brother in Lima," said Pablo with a proud edge. "He's a lawyer for the government. He got me the job with the doctor... maybe ten years ago."

"I see...does he, De Broglie, keep you busy?"

"Maybe two...three times a year."

"That's all?" I asked surprised.

"Oh, I am very busy with other customers," Pablo assured, "but when the doctor calls, I drop everything...he pays very well."

"Yeah, that sounds like him," I agreed. I was a bit reluctant to ask the next question, feeling it was none of my business, but curiosity was getting the better of me. "So...two or three times a year...who are the people you take to see De Broglie?"

"I don't know for sure. But mostly I hear their conversations...they talk about history and philosophy and I think 'physics' is how you say it? It's why I thought you were a scientist."

"So sometimes there are several together?"

"Yes," said Pablo. "Sometimes I need to get the big car. Sometimes there are three or four. Once I drove five people." I was taking all this in and looked at Pei Ling who now seemed to be interested in the conversation. "One thing," added Pablo. "I never take them back to the airport. I always wonder how they get back, but, of course, I never ask."

"Well, we will be sure you take us back when we return," I assured him. "...though that might not be for a few weeks or more...so you've worked for De Broglie for ten years and in all that time, you've never taken anyone you picked up at the airport back to the airport?"

Pablo looked at me in the rearview mirror. "Never."

Pei Ling pulled me closer to offer privately that De Broglie probably uses someone else as his generous way to give some business to another deserving fellow. I considered and thought it a possibility, however odd, and wasn't sure I was buying it. "Well," I said. "I'll find out what gives when I talk to De Broglie."

We pulled into the circular, paved driveway and to the front door at the main house. Pablo put out our bags and I offered a tip.

"Oh, thank you, but the doctor pays for everything," said Pablo. I insisted and said De Broglie would never know, and Pablo took the money with a grateful smile and pulled out of the driveway, gracefully accelerating down the road and disappearing into the distance.

We stood where Pablo had left us and looked around for a few minutes, puzzled at not finding a soul to greet us or any sign of activity. It was certainly beautiful, but a bit unnerving coming all this way to find no one home. “Geez,” I said. “You'd think he'd be here to meet us.”

Pei Ling was silent as I set our bags on the doorstep and we ventured onto the grounds of the compound. There were many meandering paths encircling the structures and bursts of explosively colored flowers here and there in a very precise, professional looking landscape, perfect as perfect can be. I mentioned that it was like a five-star resort, and looked up at the tall trees as a wispy breeze rustled the leaves and Pei Ling took my hand and we continued around a corner to the edge of the river.

“Wait a minute,” I said. “This place reminds me of Andromeda...almost a perfect replica, but an earthly version, smaller in scale and without the grandeur and gold, white light.”

“Yes, dear,” said Pei Ling in a whisper. “It does. It does.”

“Except, of course, I can see all of you...and if I took off your clothes...” Pei Ling hit me with a playful slap and we went on. Maybe fifty yards away was a weathered wooden outbuilding. It looked shabby compared to the living quarters, but sound. A light column of smoke was coming from the chimney.

“A sign of life!” I said. “I'm going to peek through the windows and give De Broglie a start. He deserves it for not meeting us...watch, this is going to be fun.”

“No, dear,” said Pei Ling. “Maybe it's a neighbor's house.”

I ignored Pei Ling and told her to wait while I played my mischievous trick on De Broglie. I put my face close to the window and tapped. A girl who had been just out of my view appeared on the other side of the glass and let out a short, but blood-curdling scream. I'd made a bad choice. In a split second, I heard the door unlatch and ran over to lend my apologies and suffer the upbraiding that I deserved.

"Who are you?" asked the girl, calming down as Pei Ling approached.

"I'm Aaron Grey and this is Pei Ling, my wife," I said taking Pei Ling's hand.

The girl relaxed and smiled in a complete and welcoming turnabout. "I am Isabella...please come in."

"I'm, I'm really sorry," I said.

"Think nothing of it, although you did scare me almost to death!" said Isabella, now with a laugh.

"Yes, I know. I certainly didn't mean to...I thought you were going to be De Broglie...it was meant for him."

"You know him very well, then," said Isabella.

"Yes, we go back a long way."

"May I get you some tea?"

I looked at Pei Ling and declined for both of us. "Is De Broglie around?" I asked.

"I'm not sure," said Isabella. "He wasn't at the house?"

"No. No one seems to be there," I said concerned about leaving the bags at the front door. "If you don't mind, we'll head back to the house and check again."

"Yes," said Isabella. "I should get busy with tomorrow's supper...I didn't know you were arriving, but I now know why the doctor told me tomorrow's meal is for a special occasion...it will be fun."

"Oh, good," I said. "I guess he didn't forget us."

"Can I come back and help?" asked Pei Ling of Isabella.

"If you really want to," said Isabella. "I could use extra hands."

Pei Ling agreed and told Isabella that she would return soon and we headed to the main house. From a short distance away, I saw that our bags were gone and assumed that De Broglie must have arrived and I hurried the last few yards to knock on the door. The doc came in a moment and welcomed us like the good friends we were.

"Hah!" exclaimed De Broglie. "Wonderful to see you! I put your bags in the middle house where you will be staying...come, I'll show you."

Pei Ling and I looked at each other as we followed in near amazement at how everything was perfectly in its place, uncluttered, like new, and almost appearing to be untouched by human hands. Yet it was inviting and warm with an unmistakable sense of the doc's touch.

"I know, I know," said De Broglie. "You're thinking it looks more like a movie set than a place someone would live...but, you know I'm a bit persnickety about cleanliness and order."

"Yes, I *do* know," I assured the doc with a smile. "Pei Ling is very happy that some of it has rubbed off on me."

"Well, here we are," said De Broglie opening the door to our quarters.

We marveled at the gorgeous room lit by a huge skylight. The natural hardwood floor had been worked to a high sheen and in the center of the self contained room with kitchen facilities and its own bathroom stood a large, four-poster bed on a very large and expensive looking area rug. De Broglie rushed over to the west wall and drew back the curtains to reveal floor to ceiling glass with a sliding door that opened to a tiled patio. Outdoors, a small immaculate lawn was set off by ornamental bushes, colorful flowers, and trees trimmed like umbrellas to shade the delicate, pastoral delights from the equatorial sun.

"I could stay here forever," Pei Ling swooned.

"You can," said the lighthearted doc.

Whatever small embarrassment I felt in accepting De Broglie's kind offer of work left me with his expressions of genuine happiness on our arrival and his sincere effort to make us comfortable. I was as happy as Pei Ling seemed to be and half jokingly asked De Broglie what price I'd have to pay for all this.

"Nothing," said De Broglie. "You've already earned it, I believe."

"Really?" I asked curiously. "And what do you mean, you 'believe?'"

"I have devised a test for which you already have the answers...you merely need to match what you know with what I ask." Like De Broglie, I didn't like surprises either, and he sensed the seriousness of my curiosity. "Don't worry, you won't be alone...De La Croix...Hernando will be joining you. I suspect you and Hernando are on about the same learning curve for the task at hand."

"Me and De La Croix on the same learning curve? You've got to be kidding...he's a Nobel laureate."

"Yes, and he received it when it meant something, too...but don't be so impressed," said De Broglie. "On the subject we'll be discussing I suspect you might even have an edge. For now, relax. Walk the grounds and explore...oh, and one more thing...there's booze and a wet bar in each of the living quarters."

"As long as there's one in ours," I joked.

Pei Ling, standing next to me, put her head on my shoulder and smiled at De Broglie. "Isn't uncle sweet, dear?"

"I can't argue with that...should we take doc up on his suggestion to explore?"

"I promised to help Isabella," said Pei Ling. "You go have some time with uncle."

"You met Isabella?" asked De Broglie.

"Yes, we both did," I said. "When we arrived there was no one here...her building was the only one showing signs of life. I scared the hell out of her, too. I thought you were inside and tapped on the window. When she saw my mug, she freaked out."

"Oh," said De Broglie. "I should have told her to be expecting you."

"Well, I'm going to get going," said Pei Ling and with that she was off to help Isabella.

"A bad sign," said De Broglie shaking is head in fun. "She's starting to talk like you."

Chapter Six

One of Us

"Where is De La Croix, by the way?" I asked De Broglie as we walked a pathway through the grounds.

"Moving his belongings to a house up the road."

"He's staying for a quite a while then?" I asked.

"Yes, while we work on the project."

"Well, I haven't passed the test yet and, I guess, neither has he?"

"No matter," said De Broglie. "I wouldn't have dragged you both here if I thought you couldn't handle it...really, it is more conversation than test. You already know the answers...it's all a matter of sequencing time for context so you'll understand what you will be doing."

"Well," I admitted. "You didn't exactly drag me here."

De Broglie laughed. "You may think I did you a favor, but there are not many people in this world that I can count on...who have the potential to understand the project as you and, I believe, De La Croix."

While I had doubts about my potential for whatever the project was that De Broglie was talking about, I assumed some measure of confidence with his faith in me. "It certainly does sound interesting," I said. "So when will De La Croix and I take the test...or, engage the conversation?"

"Tomorrow after supper," said De Broglie. "...after a good night's rest and a great meal...and another thing, don't call him De La Croix...it's too long...call him Hernando."

I didn't argue that Hernando's first and last names were both three syllables, though "De La Croix" did somehow seem longer. Maybe he had a point. We walked for a time in silence and my mind again started rushing with thoughts, not the least of which was the curiosity of being here, at this time, with these people, for a project I could only imagine, in a more or less isolated area along the Urubamba River in the Sacred Valley in Peru. How in the world did I ever get here?

"Doc," I said with an emotional edge, "I just want to thank you for everything...even during the early years when I took your first lecture...your mentoring, even when I didn't get it...it all led me here."

He put a fatherly arm on my shoulder. "Do not sell yourself short. Do you know? I take credit for nothing. It is all the work of the invisible hand of God, an unfathomable idea for the willingly ignorant, I realize, but not to you and those like us."

"Why *do* you think people reject knowledge?" I asked contemplatively.

"The easy answer," said De Broglie, "is that they are ignorant...the larger question is how they got that way...certainly, not without help...a topic best left for tomorrow night."

“Yes,” I said, his words reaffirming what I had come to know. “Well, I guess I’ll see what Pei Ling is up to, unless you have something else.”

“By all means, Aaron, go on,” said De Broglie. “I’ll see how Hernando is coming along.”

The grounds between the main house and the outbuilding where I was headed to see Pei Ling and Isabella was not landscaped, but rather overgrown with wild oats, now dry and golden after yielding their seed, but upright and strong in the light breeze that would occasionally sweep across the field. It was a pleasant area, a kind of oasis in reverse from the severely manicured flower beds and lush landscaping that surrounded the main house. I followed the path that had worn its way to the outbuilding with no small sense of wonder and entered when Isabella answered the door. “And how are you girls doing?”

“Isabella is going to show me how to butcher meat,” said Pei Ling washing her hands over the sink and turning to me excited to learn something new. “See? Look through the window...our dinner is out there.”

I peered through the window over the sink to a short distance away in the field where two recently dispatched steers hung upside down near two men who were about to finish the business of turning the animals into food. The men each took the largest knife from their holsters and gutted the animals from stomach to sternum. The warm viscera and blood spilled and splashed into a pit beneath the animals and steamed in the cool air. Next, the men took smaller knives to make a few strategic incisions to separate the hide from the animals and in a matter of little more than a few minutes the carcasses took on the familiar look of meat. It was a somber and surreal transition, but a transition nevertheless.

"Well," I said, "at least you didn't have to do that."

"We get the easy part," said Isabella. "They will bring in the biggest best pieces and we will break them down...the rest will go to the market in town."

"Oh, you're a poet," I said in a lame attempt. "Down? Town?" Gratefully, all of us ignored me as the two men carried in a half side of beef and placed it on the large wooden cutting block in the middle of the kitchen.

I looked at Pei Ling. "Are you sure you're up to this?"

"Yes," she said. "It is fine...now that it looks like meat."

"Or you can continue with the vegetables," offered Isabella.

"No," said Pei Ling. "I really want to watch you and learn."

"Okay," I said heading toward the door. I was glad to see that Isabella and Pei Ling seemed to be hitting it off, and grabbed a cup of coffee. "I'm going to wander around outside for a while."

"Your husband is very nice," said Isabella grabbing the chine of the carcass and beginning to carve from the rib section.

"Oh, he's the best," said Pei Ling. "Uncle...I mean...Dr. De Broglie...is fortunate to have him."

"You call Dr. De Broglie 'uncle?'" asked Isabella. "That is cute. He told me about the wedding and how he surprised your husband."

"Yes," said Pei Ling. "It was wonderful that uncle could make it...we all are very close in spirit...I knew it when I met Aaron and I knew it when I met uncle...and as I get to know you, you are one of us, too."

Isabella, pleased by Pei Ling's words, was putting the last touches on a rib steak. "Here, now you try." After having watched Isabella closely, Pei Ling sliced off a couple of steaks from the rib section, scraping the meat and cartilage from the last four inches or so of bone to form a kind of very large meat lollipop. "Perfect!" said Isabella.

I found myself near the main house as an old but serviceable, faded red pickup pulled in with De Broglie at the wheel. I went over to see if he needed help unloading anything, but there was nothing. "Where's Hernando?" I asked.

"He has much to do," said De Broglie. "It looks like he won't make it until tomorrow...just as well. We can catch up and you and Pei Ling can start to make yourself at home."

"But I have to pass the test, first, don't I?"

"You're going to pass the test," said De Broglie. "Relax...you are here for the duration."

"That sounds a bit ominous," I said. De Broglie was into one of his weird moods where he was unintentionally short-tempered and to which I'd become accustomed to just letting it go. It would pass, as it always had, and I knew better than to ask if anything was wrong.

"It *is* ominous," he said. I remained silent. He caught himself and his temper and made amends in a softer tone and I let him talk without interrupting. "I'm frustrated...frustrated! Maybe I brought you here only to have some friends with me."

"Well, two things," I said out of my own concern. "When did you ever need anyone around you, which you don't have to answer because we both know the truth on that...and you're telling me that getting me down here was a whim? You have no real job for me?"

"No, no," said De Broglie with his emotions in reverse.

"Then what's the problem?" I asked.

De Broglie grabbed my forearm and stared into my eyes with a tear almost seeming to work its way out of his. "My work...sometimes I think what good is it, really?"

"Oh," I said. "You've been looking into the maw of reality?"

"Yes," he agreed letting free of my arm. "I've spent my entire life on this and now, for what?"

"Well, you're right there," I said. "The space between birth and death is filled mostly with noise, as far as I can tell...it all turns to dust...into existence, three score and ten, then out of existence. Boom. That's it."

"A lovely thought," said De Broglie. "But true."

"Since when did I need to teach *you* that?" I asked.

"I wanted to be sure you knew it," said De Broglie. "The test...the discussion...you'll need to know tomorrow night...I wouldn't want my favorite student out-distanced by my favorite friend."

"If that's all it is, I've learned to be pretty good at that," I said.

"Don't be so sure," said De Broglie. "Lies come fully formed with a small peg of truth and people see the lie as truth."

"Hmm," I thought. "Like a grapevine...the lie is grafted to a cane of truth but people see only the fruit, accepting it as a miraculous gift from their version of a god instead of Satan himself."

"Ha-ha," laughed a delighted De Broglie. "You will have no problem."

Pei Ling caught up with us in the garden and said that she and Isabella were done with the prep for tomorrow's dinner. I put my arm around her shoulder and asked how the butchering lesson went.

"I liked it," said Pei Ling. "Did you know Isabella was a vegetarian?"

"She is?" I asked surprised.

"No," said Pei Ling. "She was."

"And what changed her mind?"

"The ancient writings...she discovered that we humans became omnivores after the Fall...and came to realize she could not be something she is not."

"Indeed," said De Broglie suddenly tired. "Shall we go to the main house?"

It was a welcome suggestion. I looked forward to settling into a comfortable chair with good whiskey, which De Broglie had outfitted the place with both. Pei Ling and I went to our quarters to freshen up and met De Broglie in the sitting room of the main house with its grand view of the Andes. Pei Ling made herself at home as De Broglie had suggested and prepared some light hors d' oeuvres of local cheeses, cured meats, and vegetables from Isabella's garden. De Broglie lit a cigar for himself and was pouring drinks when Pei Ling and I walked in with the food.

"What? No teevee?" I joked.

De Broglie looked up, taking me seriously at first. "I think we can get something on the satellite." When he realized I was joking, he came back with a joke of his own. "There are some game shows you would enjoy or perhaps the world news with one of your three national idiots." The doc saw the silver tray that held the food Pei Ling had prepared. "Oh, that looks good! Perfect for a smoky bourbon."

"Well, let's get started," I said.

With a glass of booze in one hand and a tidbit in the other, De Broglie, as was his custom, walked to the window and looked into the distance. "How do you like the place so far?"

Pei Ling couldn't wait to answer. "I've never been in a more beautiful, more relaxing, more comfortable place in my life...the views, the river...it's unlike anyplace."

"Me, too," I agreed in a light mood.

"I'm going to miss it," said De Broglie turning to us somberly and heading over to his easy chair.

A quiet came over the room and I got to the point. "Okay, what's the bad news...is there's something wrong with you I'm going to be really angry about?"

"It's okay, uncle," said Pei Ling. "That's him when bad things happen to people he loves."

De Broglie smiled. "I know, dear," he said as if I weren't in the room. "...but I'm really rather appreciative...his is a righteous anger, not a selfish one."

"Which brings us to the point," I said impatiently. "Is there something wrong with you? Are you about to bite the dust, or what?"

"One never knows at my age," said De Broglie. "I have a vague sense of urgency. I've just not felt quite right for a very long time."

"Well?" I asked. "Is there pain? Where is it? What exactly is the problem?"

"Nothing in particular and everything in general," said De Broglie. "You will know if you are lucky enough to get to my age...a persistent sense of not feeling well...but that's not what I want to talk about. Besides," he said wryly, "I'm not planning to leave this minute." De Broglie took a small, deliberate sip of his bourbon and turned to me. "But I've wanted to tell you...I have no heirs, as you know...when I leave this world, I'm leaving the remainder of my work to you...this place, the lab, the old truck...to you."

I looked at Pei Ling, stunned, and it showed, and to De Broglie. "*Verklempt*, I think it is in the language of your relatives," I said in a way that made sense to De Broglie. "I...I don't know what to say...and yes, you jackass...I'm about to blubber like an old fool...not as old as you, but like a fool just the same...and put your damn drink down, would ya?"

De Broglie looked half startled at my order. "Don't worry," I said. "I'm not going to French kiss you." He laughed and the three of us embraced as one.

“Whew! That was some news!” I said. “The truck, too? Is all the paper work done? If not, let’s get a rush on it.”

De Broglie laughed along with his assurances that it was. “Yes, all taken care of. Another load off my mind.”

“You are very, very...very kind, uncle,” said Pei Ling.

“So are you and Aaron...it’s just the right thing to do...well, now, let’s get back to eating and drinking.”

I looked at De Broglie with profound appreciation. “This news certainly changes the evening...I feel more like celebrating than serious talk.”

“Yes,” agreed De Broglie. “Let’s celebrate...Pei Ling, would you see if Isabella can join us?”

The sky was darker than it was light as Pei Ling carefully made her way along the footpath to Isabella’s door. As she approached, she saw through the kitchen window Isabella talking with an older, slightly round man. She was tempted to stop and watch the two, but continued to the door and made herself known because watching people who don’t know they’re being watched is wrong.

“Oh, do come in,” said Isabella.

“Yes. Thank you,” said Pei Ling with a smile and turning to look at the distinguished looking man in the room.

“This is Doctor De La Croix,” said Isabella introducing the two. With his customary ebullience, he briskly walked to Pei Ling to kiss her hand and said to call him Hernando.

“Oh,” said Pei Ling. “We’ve heard much about you. Uncle...I mean, Doctor De Broglie, says you’ll be working with Aaron, my husband.”

"Yes...I'm very much looking forward to it," exclaimed Hernando.

"Well," announced Pei Ling. "Uncle has invited you to the house for a celebration."

"Perfect!" said Hernando. "Emile will be surprised...he thinks I'm still busy moving in! Very well, then, shall we go?"

The three followed the path back to the main house and walked in to greet De Broglie and me.

"Hello! Hello, my friend!" said Hernando to De Broglie. "Are you surprised to see me?"

"Not really," said De Broglie. "I had an idea." And his idea was that Hernando, so obviously enamored with Isabella at their first meeting, would sooner than later find a way to meet her on more personal terms.

"A cozy little fivesome with me the odd man out," said De Broglie jokingly.

Pei Ling affectionately took De Broglie's arm and announced that we were the odd ones because we...all of us...were here because of him.

"Thank you, my dear," said De Broglie patting Pei Ling's arm. "But we are here...really...because of Aaron...you and I in a supporting role, Isabella in a functional role...Hernando as foil."

I was humbled. Hernando was puzzled. The celebration seemed to be turning into the talk I'd hoped to avoid at least until tomorrow.

"Foil?" asked Hernando.

"First get a drink, my friend," said De Broglie.

"I'll get it," interrupted Isabella and she did.

"What do you mean, foil?" asked Hernando again. "I expect to contribute importantly to the project."

"There is no question," said De Broglie. "On the other hand, to manifest knowledge into reality is a formidable task. I would guess you and Aaron to be of roughly similar understandings...you with the scientific edge and Aaron the spiritual. We need both...one playing off the other will strengthen the project."

Disinterested in what the "boys" were up to, Pei Ling and Isabella discreetly left to another part of the compound. As I watched them go, the air in the room seemed to tighten and I felt keenly alone. It was a feeling I'd forgotten for a long time. The banter of De Broglie and Hernando drifted into the background and I became absorbed with the incredible good fortune and people in whose lives I found myself—Pei Ling, De Broglie, mom and dad, a few special friends, and now Hernando...There is a responsibility one has to good people and I wanted to be someone they could be proud of. Until now, I was very sure I was not. Though not understanding where or who I was for most of my life, I was beginning to have a grasp.

"Aaron!" De Broglie beckoned me with an attention getting voice as Hernando looked on. "Aaron!" As if coming out of a trance, I heard De Broglie's call, looking at the two men from behind the haze of a kind of coherent stupor.

"Yes, doc," I said. "That will be fine."

De Broglie glanced at Hernando then fixed his eyes on me. "What will be fine?" he demanded.

“That we get on with the discussion now…the discussion we’d discussed that you had intended for tomorrow.”

“Oh,” said De Broglie somewhat timidly. “Well, let me think…yes…I…I see no reason to wait. Very well, then, shall we retire to the library?”

I signaled De Broglie and Hernando to go ahead as they seemed to be not-so-discreetly sizing me up as if to discover something they didn’t already know. I dutifully followed the older men, though Hernando wasn’t much older than me—he merely looked that way—and I made a quick detour to the kitchen to replenish the hors d’ oeuvres. Entering the library, De Broglie and Hernando bookended the large mantel over the burning fireplace with cigars and drinks, intensely discussing something about which they both must have felt very strongly. So rabid was their conversation that the day that started out with sunshine and anticipation seemed to be disappearing into the long, dark shadows of late afternoon.

Chapter Seven

When It All Went Wrong

"Gentlemen!" I said with an insincere smile to cover my discomfort. "What goes on?"

"Hernando is not prepared," said De Broglie impatiently. "Can you imagine? A Nobel laureate?"

I almost thought De Broglie expected me to answer and attempted to broker a peace. "Well, he got it when it meant something, didn't he?"

"It *never* meant anything!" De Broglie shot back. "No prize means anything...they are awarded by other men! Don't you get it? Either of you?"

I looked sympathetically at Hernando and answered De Broglie. "As a matter of fact, yes," I said. "We both get it." Knowing De Broglie as I did, there was no need to say anything more.

Hernando and I sat down and De Broglie walked away from the fireplace to the panoramic windows and a long, quiet look out to the mountains. "When did you first notice that things were wrong?" he asked taking a sip of his drink.

"You know, Emile," said Hernando. "I hadn't realized it until Chancay…I am embarrassed…no, I regret that it took me so long."

"None are righteous, my friend…not one," said De Broglie continuing his gaze into the distance. "We all have regrets, but we are not chained to them. There was a time, you know, when I, too, poisoned the minds of my students."

"Meaning?" asked Hernando.

"Meaning that I marched in lock step with my contemporaries…preaching that earth began billions of years ago with the big bang and life started to evolve a few hundred million years thereafter and we're the sum total of that process," said De Broglie, still looking to the mountains and sipping his whiskey. "It was the biggest lie I ever told."

"When you think about it," I ventured, "if it were true…if we really were the result of billions of years, we're not much to write home about."

"Indeed," agreed De Broglie turning from the window to Hernando and me. "That's one way of looking at it. Another is that you know when you talk about such periods of time, one instinctively understands the impossibility of it….and, sure enough, the science bears that out…do you know why?"

"Now, wait a minute," said Hernando. "Yes, it is true that the idea of millions of years, really, is impossible to grasp, but distant stars support it…it would take light from the most distant galaxies billions of years to reach earth…so the earth must be, well, billions of years old, yes?"

"Yes, that is the foolishness that is taught," said De Broglie. "Shameful!"

Hernando was at a disadvantage in a conversation about cosmology and I defended him. "He wouldn't be expected to know what we know," I said to De Broglie.

"No one's on trial, here," said the doc. "We just have to mete this out among us. So what would you say in answer to the distant starlight problem?"

"It's not a problem," I said. "The problems are the idiots who accommodate implausible ideas...a leap of faith, as it were. They assume the universe it infinitely expanding, infinitely big with no supporting data...their theory requires that the temperature at the starting point must be hotter than the infinite outreaches of the universe, but the cosmic radiation background shows the temperature identical everywhere. The big bang is idiocy."

"Ah," remarked De Broglie with a laugh.

"Well, it is," I said getting pumped up for a final blow. "No one in science tells you, of course, but operational science, observable science, coincides with the writings of the ancients...that the earth was created a few thousand years ago. I'm not sure even Einstein realized it because he never alluded to it in any papers that I know of, even though it was right in front of his face."

A knowing smile came over De Broglie. "Einstein's been wrong before...remember, he said the reason for time is so that everything doesn't happen at once...not true...the reason for time is so that something happens at all."

Hernando seemed to be on the edge of his seat waiting for what we would say next. "The gravitational well...are you familiar with it?" I asked.

"No," said Hernando with excited anticipation.

I was delighted to explain. "Gravity slows time. A clock at sea level where gravity is stronger ticks slower than a clock on a mountain top where gravity is weaker. The clocks are not defective...the flow of time itself is dependent on gravity. Since we know this from operational science, we can apply this data with a good measure of certainty to time flow here on Earth. If our earth and galaxy are in a gravitational well—which would make sense if everything began here as the ancients said it did—we are, indeed, at the center of the universe—time flows slower for us than it does outside our galaxy and much slower in the outer reaches of the universe. I haven't run the numbers, but a million years outside our galaxy could be something like a few thousand years on earth." I looked at Hernando. "You're not getting a headache, are you?"

"No...not at all," said Hernando urging us on.

De Broglie added that while we can measure time dilation precisely with atomic clocks here on earth, when we start looking outside our galaxy, things become less certain. "It is never said and never found in a textbook, but the measure of distance between earth and Orion varies by more than a factor of four. Depending on what method we use, earth to Orion spans a distance of from three hundred light years to fourteen hundred light years with many estimates in between."

"In other words," I said. "No one knows for certain...it's basically a guess...like so many things...why everything is a little off and nothing works quite right."

"The well," said Hernando. "How could we be in a gravitational well if the universe is infinite?"

"That's a wrong assumption," said De Broglie. "There is no observational science to actually substantiate or suggest it in any way...it's merely someone's idea that took off into popular culture and has become fact through the influence of...and I cannot help that it makes the most sense...Satan."

"Satan's influence?" asked Hernando.

"Yes," said De Broglie. "Certainly, you don't think humans could be as ignorant as they are without help, do you?"

"I suppose not," said Hernando.

De Broglie continued. "The greatest of Satan's achievements is having convinced the malformed of spirit and the misshapen of mind that there is no evil...thus, we are burdened with living in a society of confused fools." De Broglie took a satisfying drag on his cigar and exhaled. "We, fortunately, are a unique group."

"Those who are aware of the truth," declared Hernando.

"Yes," agreed De Broglie. "In the very biggest, all-encompassing meaning of the word. We see the world very differently from the pagan. They say 'look, there is no proof of God,' but those who live in truth, see the proof everywhere. For example, the evil man sees chemical similarities in all things earthly, and believes we came from stardust while to the man of light, it is evidence of a single creator using similar mechanisms to form all things."

I began to realize what De Broglie was talking about. That in order to achieve correct results, I needed to start with correct assumptions—where we came from, how long we've been here, and what actually operates the physical world we live in. Unless Hernando and I understood this, we could not carry on with De Broglie's project. We would not be capable. But I had another question. "Why doesn't everyone recognize the truth of the ancient writings?" Or, perhaps the better question, "Why do they deny it?"

Engrossed in conversation, none of us heard Isabella and Pei Ling walk into the room, but there they were, and they had apparently overheard at least the latter part of what we were talking about. "You are having a time understanding all of this," said Pei Ling looking at us with a sympathetic smile.

"...and trying to explain it, too," added Isabella.

De Broglie suggested that everyone could not be held accountable, since not everyone is aware of the ancient writings. I didn't know if Pei Ling was not buying that or if she was merely adding to De Broglie's point. "You really frustrate us," said Pei Ling. "Isabella and I overheard you and, well, we couldn't take it anymore...It is an apocalyptic war between good and evil...isn't that right, Isabella?

"A light has come into the world but people love the darkness rather than the light because their deeds are evil. Those who do evil things hate the light and will not come to the light because they do not want their evil deeds to be shown up. But those who do what is true come to the light."

De Broglie paused. “Yes, in so many words and in a lot fewer than mine.”

“So,” ventured Hernando. “A fundamentally different way of thinking,” said Hernando.

“More than that,” said De Broglie. “We are fundamentally different. Period. We experience life through ideas and concepts. The evil experience life through the physical world and the made up reality of the defective mind—it is quite limiting, you know.”

Hernando and I were silent for what seemed a long time. “Very well, then,” said Hernando looking at me but talking to De Broglie. “I believe we’re ready...let’s get started.” Hernando did not mean that we would start right then, but rather to assure De Broglie that we understood. I could tell by De Broglie’s manner and essence of a smile that he was satisfied, too, particularly with the words of the girls.

“I hope you are finished,” said Isabella to De Broglie. “It is past your bedtime.”

“Yes, yes...I know,” said De Broglie with almost the tone of a child talking to his mother. “Just a little while longer...I need to show Aaron and Hernando some things in the lab.”

“Okay,” Isabella agreed. “But don’t linger.”

I looked at Pei Ling with a knowing smile and whispered in her ear that we retire for the evening, too, and thought of my pleasurable and physical bond with Pei Ling. I also realized that as powerful as that was, the strength of our spiritual bond was stronger by many magnitudes.

De Broglie gave us a formal run-through of the lab and dutifully followed Isabella’s orders. Without realizing it at first, we had finished the discussion originally planned for tomorrow and would have a free morning before the feast—a fact that did not go unnoticed by Isabella who suggested a short drive up the road to the ruins at Ollantaytambo.

"Yes," said De Broglie to Pei Ling and me. "I've seen them many times...you will find it a curious place."

"How about you, Hernando?" I asked. He admitted that in all the time he'd been lived in Peru, he'd never been, and Isabella suggested that the four of us enjoy the outing.

The following morning, while mildly interested in the ruins, I was more eager to get started on the project and De Broglie knew it. "You should be able to see the entire area in a couple of hours," said De Broglie. "And by the way, be careful...there are no fences or caution signs alerting you to the obvious."

"Thanks, doc," I said with a smile. "You mean like at the edge of a thousand foot cliff? There's no sign telling us to not walk off it?" De Broglie laughed and said that's exactly what he meant. And we were off to the ruins.

I thought it curious that something so grand was so close. We had driven no more than ten minutes when the great 600-year old hand-hewn rock terraces came into view. Isabella parked the car and led the way up the first set of terraces and to the highest elevation of the ruins on a flat outcropping of rock big enough for a few, but nervously small with the group of guided tourists joining us. "...and at the edge," the guide said to her group "is a drop of more than two thousand feet...be very careful."

The warm, but strong and gusty winds added more tension and I had no interest in going near the edge. I suggested to Hernando, who had donned his trademark hat, to remove it so it didn't blow off. He no sooner acknowledged my suggestion with an appreciative smile than away went his hat with him frantically chasing it through the crowd that stood between us and the mountain's edge. And then there were screams. Horrific screams of shock and I knew what had happened and felt the sick, grinding angst of helplessness and furious anger. My very first thought was that I could shield Pei Ling and Isabella from what had just occurred, as they were speechless with shock and maybe somehow I could deflect the full force of the tragedy.

We were dumbfounded. An hour ago we were sharing a most wonderful morning together that ended suddenly with one bad move. My thoughts turned to De Broglie and how he would bear the news. It almost seemed too much and I entertained telling him that Hernando just disappeared—funny how one can come up with nonsense to avoid the inevitable, I thought. We filled in the details for the authorities and, shaken to the core, somberly made our way back to the compound.

"Who's gonna tell De Broglie?" I asked. On one hand I felt I should break the news, but on the other, I wasn't sure I could take doc's reaction. Isabella volunteered and Pei Ling stayed with me in the car until Isabella got to De Broglie, who was near the front entrance raking leaves. I watched Isabella begin to talk and De Broglie squinting in the sun as his mouth dropped in disbelief. His knees buckled and he nearly fell to the ground. Pei Ling and I ran to him and I put my arms around the old man. The girls left me alone with De Broglie as he unashamedly lay his head on my shoulder and began to sob.

When he finally stopped, he raised his head, wiped his eyes and blew his nose and said, "I wonder if he had time to say 'whoops!'"

We laughed the laugh of tragedy and I commented that it was a hell of a way to go. De Broglie agreed and we walked around for a while before making our way into the house.

Pei Ling and I retired to our quarters and Isabella and De Broglie aimlessly walked their separate ways to nowhere in particular. A couple of hours passed with no one saying anything to anyone, when Isabella sought out De Broglie and found him fiddling in his lab. "I wonder, doctor, if we should still plan on dinner?"

De Broglie took a deep breath and thought for a moment. A hint of a smile came to his face and he looked at Isabella. "You know, I think Hernando would like that...yes, we will have the dinner as planned...in Hernando's honor," he said softly.

Isabella alerted us to De Broglie's splendid idea and the heavy hearts that we had all been bearing noticeably lightened. The bleak afternoon had found some purpose and with it a reason to go on with a small measure of optimism.

Chapter Eight

Exit from a Fine Mess

It was probably the pent up yearning for something positive out of tragedy, or the desire to forget, but after the very best meal any one of us had ever had, the four of us really tied one on, as they say. Even Pei Ling and Isabella got tipsy, though the intake of booze it took for me and De Broglie to achieve a similar state was voluminously more. I just barely recall that, at some point, we all dove in at once to wash the dinner dishes faster than so many dishes had ever been cleaned before, and we somehow found our way to our own beds and rejoined for breakfast. Feeling oddly fresh, I awoke early to pick oranges for juice and found Pei Ling and Isabella concocting French toast and grilling Isabella's home-cured sausage.

"M-m-m…smells good," I said. "Have you seen De Broglie?" The girls were not yet talkative, seeming to need more time to shake off the previous night. "Well, I'm going to go look for him."

I went straightaway to the lab and found the back door propped open to the Urubamba. De Broglie was sitting outside at the river's edge chewing on the dry shaft of a wild oat and watching the water tumble by. "How are you doing?" I asked.

"Come, sit down," he said in a tone broken by the event and too much liquor.

"I liked Hernando...very much," I said. "I wish I'd gotten to know him better."

"And he, you," said De Broglie. "Understand that we all knew each other very well, perhaps more than you think...he is now unbound from the shackles and lies of this life."

"So what, now?" I asked.

De Broglie took the straw from his mouth and bent it in two to form a kind of stylus. He drew a circle in the sand along with some other ad hoc scribbling and looked up at me. "You see this? Yes, it is just a circle...the kind a child would make without knowing why, but I know why...it is the circle of us...our existence in the stretch of time between everlasting to everlasting...each generation with chance after chance after chance."

"Chance for what?" I asked, but which De Broglie did not answer because he knew it must and would come to me.

"Hernando came to the light, you know...a few days before you and Pei Ling arrived," said De Broglie.

"Whew!" I exclaimed with a sense of relief. "But I think he was on to much more...and I was really looking forward to all of us learning and working together...he would have taught me a thing or two, I'm sure of that."

"Yes...well..." said De Broglie kindly tapping my knee with the palm of his hand. "There is no end to learning for us…thank God we have been delivered from ignorance. What do you make of that, Aaron?"

"I don't know," I said exasperated. "…something mostly beyond my understanding…though the writings of the ancients speak of the elect before the world was made and the chosen delivered after…I guess we are the latter?" I asked rhetorically. "What are those other symbols…the ones outside the circle?"

"Ah!" said De Broglie spiritedly. "The principalities and powers in the heavenly places…the Andromedas…the observing realms for which this earth was created to demonstrate the manifold wisdom of the creator."

De Broglie's words connected directly with the Apostle Paul's letter to the Ephesians and I marveled at how everything fit in contrast to the endless contradictions and continuous reshuffling of manmade versions of history and existence. "Well," I said. "You know that the ancient writings never contradict science—they contradict the ever-changing *conclusions* of science."

"Indeed," said De Broglie getting up and brushing his pants to return to the main house. "The project will go on. We will be fine."

"Although," I said getting up to join him. "Everything is easy here in your isolated wonderlab. One of these days, though, I'll be returning to the world outside."

"I understand," said De Broglie rubbing his chin in thought. "But I have some advice—Avoid people when possible for few understand their relationship to the world, pity them most of the time, engage their curiosity when they are serious, love them when they are sincere, but never, ever accommodate them."

"Don't worry about that," I assured De Broglie. "But sometimes...sometimes I will be weak." This was very hard to admit to a man who was like my father, someone whose ambitions and hopes for me I wanted to live up to.

De Broglie sensed my struggle. "When all is said and done..."

I jumped in to finish the sentence. "...more will be said than done...I couldn't help it," I insisted.

De Broglie laughed, entertaining my corny humor. "And for that very reason, this world...this earth...it doesn't need saving. We do."

"Hah, don't I know that," I said.

"However," answered De Broglie. "I still have not figured if you were one of the elect or are one of the chosen. Regardless, I doubt you will be going to hell...you deserve it, mind you, but I suspect you will be joining me and Hernando...and if and when you lose direction, your wife will see you through."

On her way out of the library, Pei Ling and her irrepressible smile met us on our way in. Though no words were spoken, De Broglie and I understood her to be on her way to see Isabella. I stopped and turned to watch her leave, assured by her familiar manner and observed that nearly imperceptible aura that told me that through every lie, every evil word, and every wicked deed of humankind, I would be okay because truth and light were with me.

Random Notes on Items and Places

Introduction

Our story begins at the Amtrak passenger station, 65 Cahill St. in San Jose. At the time of the story, the station featured a gravel parking lot and an assortment of broken, hand-pulled baggage wagons and carts, apparently left in place years earlier where they had been used for the last time.

The restaurant at West San Carlos and 1st Streets was Original Joe's, and remains in business as of this writing.

Book I

Chapter Two

The laundromat was located at E. San Salvador and 2nd Streets. It is now a parking lot.

The song in Aaron's head was "What's Your Name?" by Roland Trone and Claude Johnson (Don & Juan).

The engineering building at SJSU is as described.

Chapter Three

"Langley Virginia fag." The Hollywood stereotype of a Central Intelligence Agency "spook," especially, a covert operations officer.

The Cuban restaurant was the Cuban International, 625 North 6th Street. The building remains as of this writing, but the restaurant is closed.

The "windowless bar" was located at 162 Jackson Street in San Jose. It remains in operation as of this writing. "Miho" is most certainly dead by now.

Chapter Four

The Grey farm was located on Avenue 408 between the Kings River and Road 40 in Kingsburg, California.

Chapter Eight

Ann lived at 453 South 3rd Street in San Jose.

The whiskey was Wild Turkey 101. The beer was Pabst Blue Ribbon. Ro smoked Camel cigarettes.

Chapter Nine

Café Metropolitan was located in the bungalow at 127 E. San Carlos in San Jose. The building remains, but the café has been replaced by a Mexican restaurant as of this writing.

Pei Ling's apartment was the top floor of the Rucker Mansion at 418 South 3rd Street, San Jose.

The gathering of reprobates occurred at a restaurant on South 1st Street between E. San Salvador and E. San Carlos in San Jose.

Chapter Ten

Aaron flew to Hawaii on a Douglas DC-10.

Aaron and De Broglie dined at Azure in The Royal Hawaiian Hotel and Resort, 2259 Kalakaua Avenue, Honolulu.

The bottle of red wine De Broglie shared with Aaron was a 1968 Beaulieu Vineyards Georges de Latour Private Reserve Cabernet Sauvignon.

The telescope and observatory site is Haleakala on the island of Maui.

Boyle's rule is named for the 17th Century scientist who led us from the darkness of alchemy to the light of modern chemistry.

Chapter Twelve

The "Times" in Aaron's dream is the Los Angeles Times where he worked for a time before teaching.

Pei Ling and Aaron met in 1997, which is 4695, the year of the ox, on the Chinese calendar.

Chapter Fourteen

The quotation at the bottom of page 139 is from a speech by Dr. Monty White, raised as an atheist and later convicted in Christ through his studies of geology and chemistry.

Chapter Fifteen

The Las Vegas hotel where Aaron experienced the transformation is the Wynn.

Chapter Sixteen

Pei Ling, Aaron, Ann, and Ro stayed at the St. Regis Hotel at Third and Mission Streets, San Francisco, and dined at Ame, the hotel's fine dining restaurant, which remains in operation as of this writing.

Aaron and Pei Ling stayed at the Fairmont Hotel on Nob Hill on their second night in San Francisco.

The meal at the Chinese restaurant took place in the upstairs dining room of the New King Tin Restaurant at 826 Washington Street, San Francisco. The restaurant is not new, having been in business for more than twenty years at the same location and remains in business as of this writing.

The "Suzy Wong" alley is the view looking down on Waverly Place from the second floor dining room in King Tin Restaurant.

Chapter Seventeen

The basilica is St. Joseph's Cathedral at 80 South Market Street in San Jose.

The "non-descript saimen shop" was Botown Chinese-Vietnamese Seafood Restaurant at 42 E. San Salvador Street in San Jose, in business as of this writing.

Chapter Eighteen

The hotel and restaurant at I-5 and Highway 109 is Harris Ranch.

"The tree" is still out there somewhere.

Chapter Twenty

Aaron and Ro met at the Cinebar at 60 East San Fernando Street, San Jose. It remains in business as of this writing.

Chapter Twenty-One

Aaron met the students at the Cliff House located at 1090 Point Lobos Avenue in San Francisco.

Book II

Peru locations are as described. The De Broglie compound was located on the current grounds of Sol y Luna resort in the Sacred Valley.

Chapter Two

The "inky Cabernet Franc" was a selection from St. Supéry Winery of Rutherford, California.

Chapter Five

The airport barbecue meal took place at Dickey's Barbecue Pit.

Chapter Seven

At the bottom of page 296, Pei Ling quotes from the Gospel of John, one of the twelve original disciples of Jesus.

Chapter Eight

De Broglie's mention of principalities and powers is a reference to other worlds in the universe. At odds with the fantasies and imaginings that pass for modern thinking from contemporaries such as Richard Dawkins and Stephen Hawking, De Broglie's knowledge stems from primary sources—notably, the writings of the Roman, Paul of Tarsus, in about 60 A.D.

Purple Silk in Andromeda: A Cosmic Romance of Life on Earth is formatted with extra space between lines and printed in the Bookman Old Style typeface for easy reading and legibility.

Bookman Old Style is a derivative of Old Style Antique, designed about 1858 by A.C. Phemister for the foundry of Miller & Richard of Edinburgh, Scotland.

www.oldsultanapress.com

www.ingramcontent.com/pod-product-compliance
Lightning Source LLC
Chambersburg PA
CBHW030819310726
48980CB00006B/553/J

* 9 7 8 0 5 7 8 0 5 2 5 3 3 *